"You have a key to m...

"I would have told you when you moved in, Rebecca, but Margaret said you wanted to be left alone. So I left you alone. I certainly didn't expect you to be this upset about it. Margaret thought maybe I should keep it, just in case," Cody admitted.

"I don't think so. I'm perfectly capable of taking care of myself, and I don't need a stranger having access to my home anytime he feels like it."

Cody stiffened, and his low voice was stern with rebuke. "I don't think I'm exactly a stranger, Rebecca. I've known you your whole life."

Fortified by the secrets she guarded and by her own hidden nightmare, Rebecca stared back at him, unbending. And though her heart was filled with regret, there was nothing she could say to defuse the situation.

"Sometimes a lifetime isn't long enough, Cody," she said quietly.

Dear Reader:

Romance readers have been enthusiastic about the Silhouette Special Editions for years. And that's not by accident: Special Editions were the first of their kind and continue to feature realistic stories with heightened romantic tension.

The longer stories, sophisticated style, greater sensual detail and variety that made Special Editions popular are the same elements that will make you want to read book after book.

We hope that you enjoy this Special Edition today, and will enjoy many more.

Please write to us:

Jane Nicholls
Silhouette Books
PO Box 236
Thornton Road
Croydon
Surrey
CR9 3RU

ADA STEWARD
Hot Wind in Eden

Silhouette Special Edition

Originally Published by Silhouette Books
a division of
Harlequin Enterprises Ltd.

First published in Great Britain in 1992
by Silhouette Books, Eton House, 18-24 Paradise Road,
Richmond, Surrey TW9 1SR

© Ada Sumner 1992

Silhouette, Silhouette Special Edition and Colophon are
Trade Marks of Harlequin Enterprises B.V.

ISBN 0 373 58684 1

23-9212

Made and printed in Great Britain

ADA STEWARD

began writing a novel at the tender age of twelve, when romance and romantic fiction were the farthest things from her mind. As a child, she favored the fast-paced action of Westerns, war stories, even science fiction. As she matured, however, she realized that what fascinated her most in life *and* writing were people, and she turned her attention more fully to character. Since she was drawn to travel, the particular flavor and history of a setting also became important. Romantic fiction provided the perfect opportunity to combine the richness of place with the drama of people and possibilities. An Oklahoma resident, Ada Steward parcels most of her time into working, writing, traveling and exercising.

Other Silhouette Books by Ada Steward

Silhouette Special Edition

This Cherished Land
Love's Haunting Refrain
Misty Mornings, Magic Nights
A Walk in Paradise
Galahad's Bride
Even Better Than Before

Dallas

Fort Worth

LOUISIANA

San Angelo

Austin

Eden

San Antonio

Houston

ARKANSAS

OKLAHOMA

NEW MEXICO

MEXICO

Gulf of Mexico

N

Chapter One

Perspiration tickled a narrow path down the back of Rebecca Carder's neck, adding the prickling itch of sweating skin to her already-long list of woes. She was hot, tired, hungry and stranded with an infant at the side of a lightly traveled road, miles from anywhere, on a day when she *really* didn't have time for any of this.

Rebecca slid her hand under the heavy curtain of her long, dark hair and rubbed impatiently at the offending itch on the back of her neck. She couldn't believe this was happening to her, not today. Tuesday was the one day of the week when she left Matthew with a friend and drove into San Angelo for an afternoon tightly packed with errands.

Heaving a sigh, Rebecca struggled to recapture the patience she was normally blessed with, but all she could think of were the minutes ticking away while she sat helpless. She had no idea how long it had been since her pickup had coughed to a halt on the lonely stretch of ranch-to-market road. Baking under the hot August sun, without a watch to guide her, she had lost track of time.

Worst of all was that she wasn't baking alone. Rebecca rested her hand on the infant carrier strapped in beside her on the truck's bench seat. Without much success, she tried not to worry as she looked down at her son, Matthew, who lay still. His eyes were closed while he drew in deep, even breaths of peaceful slumber.

His skin was flushed pink, and the wisps of strawberry blond fuzz that covered his head stuck straight out in damp spikes of rusty red. While Rebecca watched, Matthew's smooth forehead puckered with a frown, and his long, narrow fingers curled into a fist that wobbled into the air, waving aimlessly before coming to rest atop his chubby belly.

As his brow slowly relaxed and he settled once again into restful sleep, the love in Rebecca's heart swelled until there was little room left for breath. She wanted to scoop her son into her arms and hold him until the wild, aching love inside her calmed. Instead, she lifted his tiny hand and kissed the little fingers that curled around her own. Then she gently lowered his hand again and slipped out of the pickup.

Leaving the door open on the driver's side to catch whatever errant breeze might happen by, Rebecca walked to the middle of the two-lane road and lifted her gaze high to where the sun beat down, searingly bright in a cloudless blue sky. With the sun almost directly overhead, she guessed the time to be nearing noon and looked down again across the flat, west Texas landscape.

Yellow spots danced in front of her stinging eyes while Rebecca squinted into the distance, searching for a sign of life through heat waves that rose like steam from the surface of the land and turned far-off views into wavering, miragelike distortions.

Her heartbeat quickened with anticipation as she turned first one way and then the other across the empty stretch of blacktop for some hope of rescue. She found only a long ribbon of pavement, melted at each end into a shimmering pool of heat. There were no houses, no cars, no other people.

Straining her ears, Rebecca listened for any sound but only heard the hollow echo of silence. Nothing, not even the chirp of a bird, broke the stillness. The air was dead calm and sticky hot. Fear inched its tingling fingers across her shoulders and down her back, turning her insides cold and weak with dread. Like the rustle of a mouse in the black of night, she heard the whisper of doubt. She had made a mistake in coming back to Eden.

She shouldn't have listened to the old memories that had drawn her, memories of safety and happiness, of wide-open spaces and a land that had captured her heart during childhood visits to her grandfather's ranch west of Eden, Texas.

After Matthew's birth, the lonely, isolated ranch in the heart of Concho County had seemed the perfect place to hide from a world that had turned unpredictably cruel. At least, it had seemed the perfect place until today, when the very isolation that had lured her became a threat, not just to her, but to the child she had brought here to protect.

Angry with herself and growing more scared by the minute, Rebecca lifted her bowed head and stared hard into the shimmering, still-empty distance, as if she could will a fellow traveler into sight. Her only answer was a hot, dry wind that rustled past, offering little relief from the day that promised only to grow hotter as the sun crested and marched on toward the west.

"Someone will be by," she said aloud. "It hasn't been that long."

But the shaky rasp of her voice did little to build her confidence. Calculating roughly, she decided that close to an hour had passed since she'd first heard that innocent-sounding pop through the open window of the truck. A loud hiss had followed almost immediately. She had first thought a tire had blown, until steam began to billow from under the hood of the truck.

Reliving the moment, she felt fear clutch at her heart all over again as she remembered vainly trying to nurse the pickup to the main highway. In the end, she was barely able to guide the truck onto the shoulder of the road before the protesting engine uttered one last, loud clunk and jerked to a sickening halt.

Remorseful now that her determination had netted nothing but trouble, Rebecca turned to look at the old Ford her grandfather had willed to her along with a ribbon of ranch land, a small cabin and one rental house. She hoped the truck's engine could be fixed because she had long since sold her own car, and the money she had set aside to live on through Matthew's first year wasn't stretching as far as she had hoped it would.

A sharp sputter from inside the cab of the truck cut through Rebecca's thoughts and started her on her way toward the sound. With dazzling speed, the sputter turned to a soft, hiccuping cry, and then to short, fussy barks that brought Rebecca up onto her toes and sent her flying across the tacky surface of the blacktop toward the truck. Matthew's irritated cries were merged into one long, loud wail by the time she slid onto the seat next to him and unfastened the seat belt that held his infant carrier in place.

Crooning words of comfort, Rebecca scooped her baby into her arms and rocked him until his cries hushed and his red, wrinkled face relaxed. Tears clung to his long lashes as Matthew blinked open sad blue eyes and gazed up at his mother with gratitude. Once again Rebecca felt her heart melt with a love like none she had ever known.

To protect him, she would fight lions, move mountains and carve miracles out of disaster. When Matthew was born, she had vowed that his life would be filled with peace, happiness and love, and that so long as there was breath in her body, the violence and turmoil that had been a part of his conception would never touch him.

Closing her eyes, Rebecca brushed her cheek against the soft tickle of his hair. She still had trouble believing that this small wonder, this boundless gift of love, was really hers to hold, to nurture and to protect for a lifetime. Drawing in a breath that carried his scent, she remembered why she had returned to Eden and why she would stay. Here, she and Matthew would be left alone. Here, they would be safe.

Clenched tightly in her arms, Matthew stiffened, turned a deeper shade of red and let out a bellow, reminding his mother that this small wonder, this boundless gift of love, was hot, tired and hungry, and in no mood for cuddling. Duly chastened, Rebecca reached into the cooler on the floor, pulled out a lukewarm bottle and shook off the water that had once been ice.

She looked at the bottle that she had no way to warm, then looked at Matthew's red, contorted face. His mouth was wide open and his wail was at full volume, and her debate with herself was a short one. Popping the bottle into his mouth, she listened as his sobs turned to contented gulps. She consoled herself that cool formula couldn't be much worse than anything else he had been through that morning.

After all, it wasn't so very long ago that babies had crossed Texas in covered wagons and lived. Surely Matthew would survive one morning of air that was too hot and formula that was too cool. Maneuvering herself and her lapful of baby behind the steering wheel and closer to the open door, Rebecca looked up and almost dropped the bottle.

A Concho County Sheriff's Department car was slowing to a halt on the opposite shoulder of the road, facing her truck. Matthew's crying had apparently drowned out the patrol car's approach, and now after an hour of waiting and worrying, Rebecca found herself almost more startled than relieved.

Anxiety pounded in her chest as the car door opened and a black-booted foot descended to the pavement. The officer leaned outward, pivoting his body's weight on the boot heel that crunched into the gravel beneath him. His hat, pulled low over mirrored sunglasses, slowly rose above the car door.

Below the sunglasses, a strong, square jaw appeared, followed by a slowly emerging body, wide shouldered and broad chested, encased in a neatly starched uniform that hugged every well-muscled curve, right down to the bulging biceps that were molded by the tailored uniform's short sleeves.

When the deputy's tall frame was fully extended and solidly planted on both feet, he slammed the door of his patrol car and started across the highway toward Rebecca. With each step he took, the pounding of her heart quickened as she watched, spellbound by his steady, unhurried advance.

Already light-headed from the heat and scorched by a rising breeze that was as hot as the devil's own breath, Rebecca could only console herself that she wasn't in any condition to think rationally. Anyone's pulse would beat faster with a solemn, gun-toting, badge-wearing lawman bearing down on them.

And if this lawman happened to be remarkably good-looking, that had nothing to do with her reaction. Nor did the fact that his build hinted of a man who spent all his spare time in a dingy, hole-in-the-wall gym run by someone called Lefty or Spike. And it was the uniform, not the man or his muscles, that was capable of sending a flutter of fear through even the most innocent of people.

Feeling anything but innocent, Rebecca cut short the wild flight of her imagination and reminded herself that this was the rescue she had been waiting for. No matter what the man looked like, he was a police officer and he was here to help her.

In a vain attempt to relax, Rebecca took a deep breath and let go of Matthew's bottle long enough to run a massaging hand under her hair and over the tensed muscles at the back of her neck. When she raked her hand away, she lifted the loose strands of her hair with it, leaving the nape of her neck exposed to the hot, dry air.

Drawing in one last, deep breath, she seized Matthew's bottle again and let her hair settle back across her shoulders. As the deputy came to a halt on the other side of the open truck door, Rebecca's pounding heart returned and the muscles she had just stretched out tightened once again. Her gaze traveled slowly upward to where mirrored sunglasses glinted from an impressive distance above her, and while her heart settled into a steady drum roll, she reminded herself that this unsmiling giant was one of the good guys.

"Hi," she said a trifle breathlessly, "I sure am glad to see you."

"What seems to be the trouble?"

His voice was the kind of deep, velvety rumble that should have been soothing. But his stock answer was anything but reassuring, and Rebecca felt her hopeful smile tense into something closer to a wince. She'd really been hoping that he would sound friendlier than he looked, a little more like a human being and a little less like Robocop. Maybe in his line of work being scary was an advantage, but she didn't like being intimidated, and with this man's size it was hard not to be.

Rebecca ignored her instincts and gave him a complete account of what had happened, from the engine's first, small pop to its last, loud clunk.

"Hmm," the officer said with the kind of head shake no one ever wants to see from a doctor or a mechanic, "I don't think you should have tried to keep on driving it."

Certain beyond any doubt now that she shouldn't have confided in such detail, Rebecca wanted to crawl into a hole and hide her shame. She had destroyed her grandfather's truck and put her infant son through a miserable hour in the broiling heat, even if Matthew had slept through most of it. Even worse, she had guaranteed her position as this month's poster girl for "Women Who Don't Know the First Thing about Taking Care of Their Automobiles."

While Rebecca squared her shoulders and prepared to explain that she *had* known better but that she had been desperate, the deputy startled her by saying "Why don't you try to start it now?" in a voice that was almost kind.

"Now?"

"Yes. Just see if you can."

Rebecca hesitated. She hated to discourage her rescuer by arguing just when he seemed to be loosening up, but she knew what the engine sounded like and she didn't want to hear it again.

After a minute spent resigning herself and readjusting Matthew, Rebecca dutifully leaned forward and turned the key in the ignition. There was a hum, followed by a ghastly, dry grinding noise, and then a screech before she turned the key off again, unable to listen anymore.

"Doesn't sound too good," he said with a solemn shake of his head. "Not too good at all."

While she watched in amazement, he began to smile for the first time since his arrival. His grin spread until he was almost laughing.

"I guess it's a good thing Margaret sent me out to find you, because that truck—" he cocked an index finger toward the innocent-looking hood of the pickup "—isn't going anywhere under its own steam."

"Excuse me," Rebecca began, failing to find any mirth in the situation. Then she realized what he had said, and her mind switched direction in midthought. "Margaret sent you?"

"You know Margaret," the deputy said with his smile fading only slightly. "She's a real mother hen."

"Yes, she is, isn't she?" Rebecca wasn't surprised that Margaret had called the police. It was just like Margaret to call out the cavalry when Rebecca and Matthew hadn't shown up on time. What was surprising was the sudden change in this man's attitude.

"Just between you and me," he confided, "she thinks this truck's a little too old to be safe. She says if Henry was planning to leave it to you, the least he could have done was to buy a newer one before he passed away."

The deputy's easy manner had Rebecca smiling along with him even as she was thinking how different he seemed from the man who had first greeted her. The more relaxed he became, the less frightening the sheer size of him seemed and the more reassuring she found his presence, but a new worry was forming.

From his manner, she was beginning to wonder if he was someone she might have met before. He seemed to have known her grandfather, and he certainly knew Margaret. But Rebecca couldn't imagine meeting someone who looked like this man and not remembering it. With that face and that build, he wouldn't be easy to forget.

With effort, she tore her thoughts away from the muscular officer and turned her attention back to the problem at hand. Rubbing her hand affectionately over the dashboard of the pickup, she voiced her worst fear. "I hope I haven't ruined it."

"Oh, I'm sure you haven't," he answered lightly. "Old trucks never die, they just get rebuilt engines."

While Rebecca cringed at the words "rebuilt engine" and the thought of what one must cost, the deputy whipped off his sunglasses and tucked the arm of the glasses into his uniform's breast pocket. Lifting his hat, he wiped the sweat from his brow with a deeply tanned forearm and settled the hat back on his head.

"You don't remember me, do you?" He gazed down at her from the shadow of his wide-brimmed hat.

"Should I?" She squinted up through the bright sunlight, trying to get a better look at his face.

"I guess not. There were quite a few years between us."

Rebecca could hear the faint echo of disappointment in his voice. She cast back through her memories for a trace of familiarity in the voice, or in the face, or the— He leaned closer, and with an almost physical impact, she found herself staring into sea blue eyes that sent her tumbling back in time.

"Cody," she said in a stunned whisper that was more of a reflex than a question. Almost immediately she felt foolish. He couldn't possibly be Cody Lockhart. Nothing but the eyes were the same. "I'm sorry. I don't know what I was thinking," she said, apologizing before he could ask her what she was talking about.

Instead, he laughed and held out his hand. "Why, Rebecca, I'm flattered."

Unable to believe that her instinctive guess had been right, Rebecca didn't know what to say next. Stalling, she readjusted Matthew's weight and switched his bottle to her left hand. All the while, her gaze never left Cody's face as she searched for some remnant of the boy she had once known, the slim youth who had been the best friend of her older brother and the secret object of her own pubescent fantasies. Cody, with the turquoise eyes and the incredibly handsome face. Cody, who hadn't even known she was alive.

"Just a lucky guess, I suppose," she said finally, and reached out with her freed hand to greet his. Of all the people on the face of the earth she hadn't wanted to run into, it was a Lockhart. She had known Cody was the tenant in the house she had inherited from her grandfather, but no one had bothered to tell her what Cody did for a living.

Lightly her fingers brushed over his, then continued across his palm and curled around the side of his hand. "Your eyes haven't changed."

"That's about all that hasn't," Cody answered, laughing again. His fingers tightened, locking her hand in an embrace of controlled strength and intimate tenderness. "It's really good to see you, Rebecca. How have you been?"

"Fine. Just fine." She remembered now that his voice had always been able to weaken her knees. She used to think it was because she was young and in love. She didn't know what her excuse was now. "And you?"

She scanned her memories for when she had seen him last. He must have been about twenty, and she, a shy and gawky fourteen, but at the time the six years between them might as well have been a lifetime. The memories drew her in and, for a moment, carried her back to happier, more-innocent days.

Then, as quickly as she had been drawn in, Rebecca retreated. Gently she extricated her hand from his and said, "I seem to remember you as a lanky sort of fellow. Tall and slim. What happened?" Making the best of a bad situation, she tried a teasing smile. "Did you get those muscles playing college football?"

Cody didn't answer. Instead, he silently grew straighter and stiffer until he was again the solemn stranger who had first arrived. "I didn't stay in college very long," he said finally, his voice a monotone. "I guess you could say I got these arms courtesy of the New Orleans' docks."

He slipped his sunglasses back on and glanced toward the glowing yellow furnace directly overhead. "I think we'd better get you and that baby out of here before Margaret gets tired of waiting and comes looking for you herself. Do you want a ride back home, or are you going on to Margaret's?"

Thrown off balance by his sudden transformation, Rebecca was defenseless against the panic that stirred without warning inside her. "What about my truck?" She couldn't just leave the pickup on the side of the road. The truck bed was loaded with the things she was taking into San Angelo.

"I'll call for a tow. It'll be okay." Cody's voice took on the soothing professional tone of a man who was used to calming overwrought people.

Rebecca drew in a deep breath and forced herself to relax before she made a complete fool of herself in front of this gorgeous man who was once the secret love of her young life. "I'm sorry," she said quietly. "I'm hot, and I'm tired, and I'm worried, and this is a terrible day for this to happen. On Tuesdays, I leave Matthew with Margaret while I go into San Angelo for the day." She turned halfway around and pointed to the boxes in the bed of the pickup. "Those are full of quilts and crafts that I supply to shops in San Angelo."

"Maybe you can go tomorrow," he suggested gently.

"No. I have to go on Tuesdays. The rest of the week I work. I don't have the time or the money to deal with—" she waved her hand toward the engine "—this." Her voice almost cracked. She forced herself to stop, take another deep breath and slow down again. "I'm sorry," she apologized once more in a near whisper. "I know it's not your problem. But I'm afraid to leave all of this here, and there's no need to go on to Margaret's if I'm not going into San Angelo."

"Don't worry." Cody's voice was soothing as he removed his sunglasses once again and tucked them into his pocket. He held out his hand to help her, coaxing her toward him. "Everything will be okay. Right now we just need to get you and that little boy out of this heat. Then you'll feel better."

Still able to recognize the voice of reason when she heard it, Rebecca nodded. "All right, but we have to take all of this with us."

"That's fine. I'll take care of it. You just come over to my car, and I'll turn on the air conditioner so you can cool off some."

She released her pent-up breath in a sigh that took with it all the strength she had left. "Okay."

Cody stepped closer and slipped one hand under Rebecca's elbow and one hand under Matthew. "Have you got a good hold on him?"

"We're fine, I think." She inched closer to the edge of the seat.

"No offense, but you're as white as a sheet."

"I'm fair skinned."

"Oh. Well, I'm glad that's all it is." He secured his grip on her arm. "For a minute there, I had the mistaken impression that your legs might buckle as soon as you stepped out of the truck."

"I'm fine," Rebecca insisted. She set one foot on the ground to brace herself while she tightened both arms around Matthew and stepped out with the other foot. As soon as she straightened, her head began to swim and her legs all but crumpled under her.

Cody put one arm around her waist and pulled her against him at the same time he slipped his other arm under Matthew and held him steady. When Rebecca's head stopped swimming, she found herself cradled against Cody's rock-hard chest and staring up into eyes the same clear, deep turquoise blue as the Caribbean waters.

"Thank you," she said, and immediately tried to detach herself from his disconcerting grasp. "I'll be all right now."

"You're still white as a sheet."

"I'm fine." She tugged weakly against his steadying embrace.

"Well, you're definitely Henry Carders' granddaughter. There's no question about that," Cody grumbled. He reluctantly released her, but stayed close while she took her first, uncertain step toward the patrol car.

"What's that supposed to mean?" Rebecca's head was still swimming, and her legs were as wobbly as a newborn foal's. She clung to Matthew as if her life depended on it, but she wasn't a little girl anymore, and Cody Lockhart wasn't going to talk to her the way he did when she was twelve—not if she had anything to say about it.

"That means you're about as stubborn as a Missouri mule, just like your granddad was. You can at least let me help you with that baby before you drop him."

Rebecca opened her mouth to argue, but she realized it would be foolish, and she wasn't a fool, even if she *did* act like one at times. "I was running late this morning, so I skipped breakfast," she said in a voice that sounded as unsteady as she felt. "I guess it *might* be a good idea if you held him."

With Rebecca's help, the baby was transferred safely to Cody's left arm, where Matthew's diapered bottom balanced on one, muscular bicep while his tiny body was tucked snugly between a brawny forearm and chest. Matthew's small, damp head rested against the crisply starched left shoulder of Cody's uniform.

When the baby was secured, Cody slipped his right arm around Rebecca's waist, and they continued their slow progress across the road. If she had had a choice, Rebecca would have rejected his help, but at the moment her legs could have been made of jelly for all the strength they had.

"I'm really not the type to faint," she said, more to reassure herself than Cody.

"Margaret will have lunch ready. You'll be fine once you eat."

Running her tongue over her dry lips, Rebecca tilted back her head and smiled her gratitude. "Bad timing." She intended to say that, of all the days for her truck to break down, it had to be in a hundred-degree heat wave on the morning she skipped breakfast, but she was startled into silence by the alarming wheeze in her voice.

Instead, she trudged on and was about to congratulate herself on having made it across the two lanes of blacktop when, without warning, Cody stopped, turned her around and leaned her against the front fender of his patrol car.

"Just stand there a minute." He kept his eyes on her while he backed away, still clutching Matthew in his left arm. "I'm going to get the air conditioner started."

Feeling more like a rag doll than a woman, Rebecca clamped a lid on her simmering temper and reminded herself that Cody was only trying to help.

"I think I can manage to do that," she said with an attempt at biting sarcasm that, thanks to her wheeze, sounded pathetically sincere.

Mortified by her own weakness and helpless to do anything about it, Rebecca watched him give her a final, encouraging smile before he opened the driver's door and reached inside to turn on the air conditioner. In little more time than it took her to blink and draw in a few shallow breaths, he was back.

Cody's hand slid around her waist and pulled her into the curve of his arm once again. More wobbly-kneed than ever, Rebecca leaned against the strength he offered as he guided her around the front of the car. With each step, she became more aware of the hard muscles of Cody's chest pressed against her shoulder. With each breath came the smoldering scent of his cologne commingled with his own body heat and the warm, baby smells of Matthew. With each second, Rebecca's suspicion grew that Cody, and not just hunger and heat, was to blame for her sudden, uncharacteristic weakness.

When they finally reached the car door on the passenger side, Rebecca was grateful to be able to separate herself from him. Ignoring the rush of superheated air that blasted past her from inside the patrol car, she collapsed onto the seat and was rewarded by the cooling tendrils of air pushed toward her by a softly humming air conditioner. Rebecca closed her eyes, drew in a deep breath, and strength flowed into her. The spiraling black spots that had been spinning faster and faster, slowed and began to recede. She was in heaven until the car door shut and she realized she was alone in the front seat.

Shoving the door open again, Rebecca bounded upright and shouted, "Hey, you. I want my baby!"

At the front of the car, Cody stopped and turned around. His frown suggested the heat might be getting to him, as well. "I'm going back after the infant carrier," he whispered. "Matthew's going to have to ride in the backseat, strapped in, and if we keep passing him back and forth, he's going to wake up before we can get out of here."

Rebecca scowled, wishing she could argue. But as much as she wanted to hold Matthew, she knew that for his own safety, she couldn't, and that he was more likely to wake up if he exchanged arms many more times. Her rebellion turned to resignation as she looked from her baby to the virtual stranger who held him. "Be careful."

Cody nodded and smiled. "I've done this before. You just close your eyes and get some rest."

Rebecca craned her neck to stare over the top of the county car toward her wounded truck and the cargo that was so important to her survival. "I need all those boxes," she said in a halfhearted attempt to get in the last word.

Cody nodded again, still smiling. "I know. You'll get them. Now get back in the car."

Reluctantly Rebecca got back in the car without another word, and in spite of her intention to watch every move Cody made, she closed her eyes, let her head drop back against the seat and drifted peacefully away on a cushion of cool air.

"Rebecca?" A feather-light touch brushed her arm. "Rebecca, we're here."

"What?" Disoriented, Rebecca tried to lift her head, but it felt like a block of granite, and her neck screamed with pain at the effort. Groaning, she squeezed her eyes shut and stayed where she was.

"Are you stiff?"

Before she could answer, a strong hand slipped under her hair and cupped the back of her neck. Strange fingers gently massaged the cramped tendons along the side of her neck for the half minute it took Rebecca to spring bolt upright and stare wildly in the direction of the offending hand.

"What are you doing?" she demanded.

Cody's startled face reminded her of where she was and who the overly friendly fingers belonged to. He held his hands up, palms toward her, in a universal gesture of surrender.

"Sorry," he said. "Didn't mean to upset you."

The fear that jolted her awake was receding, but adrenaline still surged through her. Rebecca's heart pounded, her mouth was dry, and tension coiled like ropes down the muscles of her back. She definitely wasn't sleepy any longer.

"You just scared me a little," she explained. "I wasn't awake yet."

"Oh. Sorry. I'm one of those instantly awake people."

"I'm not."

"I'll remember that."

From the gleam in Cody's eyes, Rebecca thought maybe she should ask exactly what he meant by that, but a sputter from the backseat warned her that Matthew was about to erupt. She turned to find out where "here" was, and saw Margaret standing on the front porch of her house.

"We'd better go in," Rebecca said. "Matthew probably needs a diaper change, and he doesn't sound like he's going to be too happy about it."

No sooner were the words spoken than the hiccuping cries from the backseat escalated to a relentless wail.

"He's got a good set of lungs," Cody said over the racket. "For such a little guy."

Rebecca didn't even try to answer. She just got out, opened the back door and began to unstrap Matthew. She lifted the carrier with the screaming infant still inside and eeled her way backward out of the car, rear end first, until she bumped squarely into the solid thigh of Deputy Cody Lockhart, who had walked up behind her.

If she'd backed into a branding iron, Rebecca couldn't have tucked, straightened and pivoted faster. But with her backside now safe, she found herself shoulder to chest with Cody, who hadn't budged an inch, and staring once again into his ocean blue eyes, which looked for all the world as if they were laughing at her.

"Excuse me," she said pointedly, hoping he would take the hint and move.

"No apology necessary."

No doubt about it. He was enjoying himself, which didn't impress Rebecca as being very wise, considering the adrenaline that still pumped through her with every breath. "The diaper bag," she snapped. "You didn't forget it, did you?"

"No. It's right behind you."

The laughter finally left Cody's eyes as he glanced down into Matthew's red face, which was drawn into a lumpy mask of rage, and whose healthy lungs were now blasting Cody from close range.

"If you'll get it," Rebecca said sweetly, "I'll take Matthew on inside."

Cody wasted no time getting out of the way, and Rebecca walked toward the porch with a small, satisfied smile curving her lips.

Margaret Potter came forward to greet her with open arms. "Honey, are you all right? What happened? I died a thousand deaths until Cody called to say you were on your way."

"Oh, Margaret." Truly relieved, Rebecca stepped into the motherly embrace. "I'm fine. Just a little hungry."

"Well, I've got lunch ready. You just come on in here and sit down." Opening the screen door, Margaret led Rebecca inside. "Lord, what's wrong with Matthew? I don't know when I've ever heard him holler like that."

In the cool, shadowed interior of the house, Rebecca leaned her head down and kissed her son's hot, puckered brow. "He's been such an angel all morning, Margaret. I think he's just tired of being good. And I know just how he feels," she finished softly.

"Honey, why don't you go sit down and let me take him? Where's his diaper bag?"

"Right here," Cody said. The screen door banged closed behind him as he entered the living room of the farmhouse.

"Good." Margaret scooped up Matthew and took the diaper bag from Cody. "Why don't you take Rebecca on into the kitchen and dish out what's on the stove?" With a toss of her head toward the kitchen, the older woman turned and started in the opposite direction. "I'll take this little one back to the bedroom and change him."

"Yes, ma'am," Cody said. For a moment he smiled in the direction of Margaret's retreating figure. Then he held out his arm to Rebecca. "Shall we?"

"Oh, you really don't have to. I can take care of myself. I've already caused you enough trouble, and I know you need to get back to work." As Rebecca talked, she backed around Cody toward the kitchen, eager to be away from him and the confusing mixture of emotions he aroused in her.

"Not at all. Cops need to eat, too."

"What?" Dismayed by his answer, she took another step without looking behind her and felt her heel hang on the leg of an end table. Already in motion, Rebecca tilted backward helplessly while her voice went up an octave and her flailing hands grabbed nothing but air.

An instant later, those same hands found muscle and flesh as Cody reached out to gather her in. Her heart pounding, Rebecca wrapped her arms around his broad shoulders and clung with all her might.

"You okay?" Cody's warm, deep voice asked in her ear.

"Oh, yes," she gasped. "Sure. Fine."

His hands held her gently but firmly within the solid wall of his embrace. When her heartbeat began to slow and her breath no longer came in gulps, Rebecca realized that her cheek rested against Cody's chest, and the scent of him was beginning to do the same unacceptable things to her that it had done earlier.

She lifted her head quickly, and her eyes became level with a damp spot on the shoulder of his uniform. "Oh, my goodness." She tilted her head back and stared up into his solemn face. "Did Matthew spit up on you?"

Cody's quick smile was followed by a soft chuckle. "A little."

Embarrassed that her child had ruined such an impeccable shirt, Rebecca frowned and caught her lower lip between her teeth. "He's just started doing that. I don't know why."

Cody shrugged. "Babies do that sort of thing. It's a risk you take." Then his smile faded and his eyes grew solemn again. "Does it upset you that I'm staying for lunch?"

"No," Rebecca said too quickly. "No, not at all. Not really."

"Not really? But maybe it does, just a little?"

She couldn't think of a thing to say that wouldn't be insulting or incriminating and would still explain how she felt.

"It has been a little strange, hasn't it?" Cody asked. "Us running into each other again like this after all these years?"

"Just a little," Rebecca agreed in a way that made it sound more like a lot than a little.

"But you know, we still have to figure out how you're getting into San Angelo."

"Oh, my goodness." His gentle questions had almost lulled her into relaxation. Now, remembering what lay ahead, Rebecca stiffened and pulled away from the close body contact Cody's embrace had maintained. She had to think, and she couldn't do that with his heart beating next to hers.

"It's okay," Cody said. His hands still held her around the waist. "I think I've got a solution."

"What?" Something about his pleased expression made her instantly defensive.

"Let's talk about it over lunch."

"I'd rather talk about it now."

"You need to eat first."

"I can't eat if I'm worried," Rebecca insisted.

Looking determined, Cody shook his head. "Call it a lawman's instinct, but something tells me that you really should eat first. Trust me."

"Trust you?" She wavered. If only his last name were anything but Lockhart.

He nodded. "Trust me."

Too tired and hungry to argue further, Rebecca turned and started toward the kitchen. Cody walked with her. His hand remained just below the curve of her waist, and his arm brushed against her back with each step. His cologne wedded with his body heat and continued to tease her with tendrils of scent that were uniquely his.

Whether she could or should trust him was beyond Rebecca's ability to answer, but there was one thing she knew for certain. Cody was a hard man to ignore.

Chapter Two

At the first red light in San Angelo, Rebecca checked the dashboard clock of Cody's pickup and winced. Not only was she an hour and a half behind her usual Tuesday schedule, but until that moment she had briefly managed to forget whose truck she was driving.

Margaret had offered her station wagon to Rebecca for the afternoon, but Cody wouldn't hear of it. He had said that it wouldn't be safe for Margaret and Matthew to be at the farm without transportation and that he wouldn't be needing his own vehicle until after he got off work.

If Rebecca hadn't been so worn down already from the morning, she might have been able to think of a reasonable excuse to turn down his offer and leave Margaret stranded without a car. But after lunch Cody drove Rebecca to where his truck was parked, transferred her belongings, gave her detailed instructions on how to drive his precious pickup and said that he would try to have her truck waiting at his place when she got back that evening.

Every time Rebecca thought of him, she wanted to gnash her teeth in frustration. Why, of all the deputies in Concho County, had Margaret called Cody when Rebecca and Matthew were late? Between the rescue and the loan of his truck, she had become indebted to him twice in the space of one day, and the Lockhart family was the last in the world Rebecca wanted to be indebted to in any way.

Now she had an entire afternoon to dread seeing him again—when she'd return his truck, thank him kindly and tell him that while she appreciated his concern, she wasn't in the market for renewing old friendships right now and just wanted to be left alone.

Here's your hat, and here's your coat, and don't let the screen door hit you on your way out. Rebecca groaned at the thought. She hated doing it. She liked Cody. A lot. But she just couldn't take the risk.

Creeping through the afternoon traffic, she watched the clock tick away still more precious time while her frustration grew, but with the way her day was going, she couldn't afford to hurry. One ruined truck a day was all she could handle. If she put even a scratch on Cody's pickup, she didn't know what she would do.

When Rebecca finally arrived without incident at her first stop, she turned off the ignition and draped both arms over the steering wheel while she breathed in slowly and deeply to steady her nerves. Inwardly calmer, she climbed out on shaky legs and unloaded the biggest box from the back of the truck.

The top of the carton bumped her chin as she started toward the door of the baby boutique. Her fingertips clung to the bottom edge of the box, heavy with a bounty of matching crib quilts and pillows, hanging appliquéd and quilted diaper bags, matching rocking chair pads, wall hangings and countless other accessories for a baby's room.

Staggering under the load, Rebecca backed through the door of the boutique and called out, "Linda! Help!"

"Oh, Rebecca, I'm so glad to see you. I was afraid something had happened." The store's owner hurried to help Rebecca carry the box into the back room.

Once there, Linda began to unpack the carton immediately, talking while she worked. "Great!" She held up a crib quilt with a polka-dot pink elephant in the center. Rising above its head were multicolored balloons, their strings grasped in the elephant's tightly curled trunk. "Mrs. Washington's been calling every day. She'll be thrilled."

Linda reached deeper into the box and next brought out a matching pillow, hanging diaper bag and crib bumpers. Coos of joy accompanied each new find, until Linda finally shut up long enough to take a breath and Rebecca opened her mouth to say that she was in a terrible hurry. But before she could begin, Linda recovered and rushed on.

"And Mrs. Parker wants a set just like it, only with a bear instead of an elephant. And she wants him sky blue, of all things, because the baby's going to be a boy. Her first grandson, and the shower's in three weeks. She'll pay extra if you can have them done by then. And if you can't have them all done, at least have the quilt, and she'll still pay extra." Linda finally paused and looked to Rebecca for an answer.

"That shouldn't be any problem," Rebecca told her, lying through her teeth. It seemed that with each new order she had less and less time for anything but work. And even with the orders pouring in, she could still barely make ends meet. Now, with the truck...

For a moment, a dark cloud of despair draped over Rebecca, shutting out hope and leaving her too tired to fight the inevitable. Then, as quickly as it came, Rebecca shook off the oppressive mood. She didn't have the luxury of failure. For Matthew's sake, she had no choice but to make things work out. And she had to make them work out here and now, because she had nowhere else to go.

"Are there any other orders?" she asked. A lingering fatigue was the only outward sign of the turmoil brewing inside her.

"A few. Just let me get this stuff inventoried, and I'll give you the list I made up. I can't tell you how thrilled everyone's been since I've started carrying your quilts. If this keeps up, I swear we're going to have to clone you."

Linda's voice dropped to an awed hush, and she looked up from her work long enough to stare at Rebecca with round, wondering eyes. "Why, I got a call all the way from El Paso last week, from a woman wanting a catalog, of all things. Can you beat that? I told her I'd send her some snapshots and a list of prices, and if she saw anything she liked, she could either buy from stock or special order and pick her own colors."

Linda's busy hands paused, and she reached out to squeeze Rebecca's arm with affection. "You're putting my little shop on the map, Rebecca. Why, we may have to form a partnership and start printing catalogs if this keeps up."

Buoyed by her friend's exuberance, Rebecca smiled. "That's a wonderful idea, Linda. If only it wouldn't cost an arm and a leg."

Linda waved away Rebecca's worry, then went back to her task. "If it comes to that, we'll find a way," she said. When Linda looked up again, her gaze went past Rebecca's shoulder to the truck that was parked outside. "Is that what you're driving? Where'd you get that fancy thing? Where's old faithful?"

"Old faithful bit the big one this morning," Rebecca said, ignoring the other questions.

Linda clucked her tongue in sympathy. "Is it bad?"

"It's not good, but they're supposed to have it running again by the time I get home tonight."

"So, whose is that?" Again she nodded to Cody's big, sparkling, fully tricked-out truck.

"It's a loaner. From a friend of my grandfather's."

"From an Edsel to a Cadillac, huh?" With that, Linda went back to work, reached a tally on the merchandise and wrote out a check for the amount she owed Rebecca. "You going to have anything else ready next week?" she asked when she handed Rebecca the check and the list of special orders.

"Some. Probably not as much." With the check in her hand, Rebecca's sense of urgency returned. Her Tuesday afternoons were always busy. Today she simply wasn't going to be able to do everything. "I have a few big pieces I need to finish for the gallery and for Ilene's." She picked up her empty box and took a backward step toward the exit.

Linda nodded. "Just so you have Mrs. Parker's stuff done in three weeks. She's the only one who's going to be pushing me for anything."

"See you next week, then." Rebecca turned and walked quickly away.

"Keep your chin up," Linda called out as Rebecca pushed open the door. "Everything'll be okay."

Rebecca paused in the doorway and smiled back at the woman who had become such a good friend. "Thanks, Linda. Thanks a lot."

If Blanche DuBois had always been dependent upon the kindness of strangers, then Rebecca had always been blessed by the generosity of friends. With that thought nagging at her, she climbed into the luxurious pickup that Cody had insisted on lending her and drove away, feeling like even more of a first-class heel for what she intended to do the next time she saw him. But some things couldn't be helped, and this was one of them.

Consoling herself with that thought, Rebecca resolved to at least be nice to Cody when she saw him this evening. She owed him a deep debt of gratitude, and it wasn't his fault that all men seemed to trigger anger and resentment in her these days. She would do her best to hold her temper—and her tongue—and remember that Cody had never been anything but good to her.

Nor had a lot of other people. Each Tuesday, purely out of friendship, Margaret kept Matthew so that Rebecca could have one afternoon free to run errands, errands that took her to Linda's baby boutique, to Ilene's bed-and-bath shop and to Simon's art gallery. Three, who were once strangers, had believed in Rebecca enough to give her an outlet for her work.

In doing so, they had become friends who enabled her to put food on the table and clothes on Matthew's back. Without all of them, her new start at life would have been a farce, and she didn't know how she would ever repay so many people for so much kindness.

Almost skidding to a halt in front of Ilene's, Rebecca bounded out of the pickup, retrieved the remaining two boxes from the back and entered the shop practically at a run.

Ilene, who was older and calmer than Linda, looked up and smiled. "Running late?"

"Very," Rebecca said, not slowing until she reached the storeroom and set the boxes down on a worktable in the center of the crowded room.

"I have your check all made out."

"Great." Rebecca reentered the front room of the sweetly scented, feminine and frilly bed-and-bath shop. "I have an inventory list here for what I just dropped off."

"Your check's next to the cash register. You can leave the inventory list there." Ilene stopped rearranging towels for a moment, pivoted on one very high heel and asked, "Did you bring the wedding ring quilt?" An expectant light danced in her eyes.

Rebecca laughed. "Yes. It's back there. But you can't look at it until I'm gone."

"Drat." Ilene stamped her foot, but she was smiling. "Is it beautiful?"

"It's apricot and white and trimmed in lace."

Ilene sighed. "It'll sell in a minute. You'd better start working on a new one right away."

Rebecca laughed again, relaxed by Ilene's lighthearted teasing and the air of serenity that permeated the little shop. "You're such a slave driver. Are you running low on anything else?"

"Just gewgaws and doodads. There's a list on that pad there."

"Gewgaws and doodads, huh?" Rebecca repeated as she tore the top page from the pad. "Can I use your phone?"

"Sure. Help yourself."

Ilene returned to her aesthetic arrangement of the shelves while Rebecca dialed Simon's art gallery to tell him she wouldn't be making a delivery this week.

"Simon?" she asked when the ringing stopped. "This is Rebecca. I don't have anything for you today, but I'll try to have the wall hanging done by next week. I don't suppose anything sold. No? Oh, well, maybe next week."

She hung up and tried not to feel too dejected. The original pieces that she did for Simon's gallery were different from what she did for Linda or Ilene. The wall hangings she placed on consignment with Simon usually took longer to produce and longer to sell, but the checks, when they came, were larger, as well. If her income from Linda and Ilene was the meat and potatoes of Rebecca's diet, then the income from Simon was the dessert, and dessert didn't come with every meal.

"You okay, hon?" Ilene asked quietly.

Rebecca straightened her shoulders, looked up and smiled. "I'm fine. Just a little tired. Thanks for the use of the phone."

"Any time. Now maybe you'd better get on out of here so I can go back there and unpack that box."

Smiling again, Rebecca headed for the door. "A wall doesn't need to fall on *me*. I'll see you next week."

Outside again, she started the truck's engine and drove off with more speed than Henry's old pickup would ever have allowed. At the first stoplight, she allowed herself her first peek at the two checks that represented her week's earnings, and as always, the amount was enough to make her breathe a huge sigh of relief.

Once again, she had worried for nothing. Even with truck repairs, the balance on her savings account should be more than adequate by the time winter's uncertain weather forced her to put more time between her trips to San Angelo. When the light changed, Rebecca drove on with a lighter heart while her thoughts raced ahead to focus on the day's next challenge.

With each minute that passed, her foot grew heavier on the accelerator and her impatience mounted until she finally slowed in front of a blue-and-gray cottage set back from the street. A rush of anxiety replaced her impatience as she guided the truck down a narrow driveway that circled behind the house and opened into a small parking lot that was once a backyard.

Rebecca parked under the shade of a tree and hurried inside what was now a private clinic, through the kitchen and into what was still used as a dining room. From here, she could see the reception desk in the next room where a young woman, college aged and blond, looked up from her telephone conversation and paused long enough to put her hand over the mouthpiece and whisper, "They've already started. You can just go on in."

Rebecca nodded and walked as quietly as possible from the dining room down a narrow hallway to what would once have been a front bedroom. She turned the knob silently and slipped inside the door, then stood there as all eyes turned toward her.

A tall, slender woman, dressed in a simple gray suit, leaned forward in her chair and motioned for Rebecca to come closer. "Hello, Rebecca. We were hoping you'd show up. Come on over and sit down. Joanne was just telling us about her weekend. Go on, Joanne.''

While Joanne, who was about Rebecca's age, went on with her story, Rebecca took the only empty chair left in the circle of women. Donna, who was nearing sixty, smiled in welcome when her gaze met Rebecca's, and Rebecca smiled back. She had only been in the group since moving back to Texas several months earlier, but already this group had become a little like family, all victims of rape, a sisterhood in pain who were fighting back against the damage that had been done to them.

Though she tried to listen to Joanne, Rebecca couldn't keep her thoughts from wandering. Too much had happened since the sun had risen. In the space of a few hours, Rebecca's world had been turned upside down again, not as badly as it had been a year earlier, but enough to leave her tilted and confused.

''Rebecca?''

A soft voice broke into Rebecca's thoughts and drew her gaze to the slender woman in gray, whose hands lay folded in her lap on top of a notepad.

''I'm sorry, Dr. Connor, did you say something?'' Rebecca asked, embarrassed by her wandering mind. They were all there to help each other, to share, to support, to respond, not to be lost in their own thoughts and add nothing to the group.

''You seem distracted today. Did something happen? Is there something you'd like to talk about?''

''I—I don't know. There are a lot of things happening in my life right now, and they're all making me wonder if anything I've done since Matthew was born has been the right thing.''

Until the words were out, Rebecca hadn't realized how worried she'd been. All day she'd tried to convince herself the problem was Cody, but it wasn't. She'd been worried, even scared, for weeks, long before Cody had appeared.

"Are you talking about your decision to move back to Eden?" the doctor asked in her soft, uncondemning voice that probed gently at the tenderest spots.

"That," Rebecca said, nodding in agreement. "And my decision to stay home with Matthew and make my living quilting. There are times when it seems so unrealistic. I mean, my truck broke down this morning, and if it costs very much to fix it, it's going to wipe out what's left of my nest egg. Of course, Matthew's only three months old, and our expenses are low right now. What I really find myself worrying about is later, when he's started school. I don't want to be struggling then the way I am now."

Dr. Connor smiled sympathetically. "That's a problem even two-income families deal with every day, and it isn't an easy one to solve because sometimes money isn't even the real problem. Going back to the beginning, Rebecca, why *did* you choose to move to Eden after Matthew was born?"

Rebecca tried to focus her thoughts and ignore the nagging little voice that kept telling her she should have told them about Cody, that Cody was the real problem bothering her today. She closed her eyes and forced her mind past the chaos to the heart of her that never lied, no matter how painful the truth.

"I think, in a way," she began slowly, "I didn't want to face the world. My grandfather's ranch outside of Eden was the most isolated place I could think of, and it was mine. At least, the houses were, along with the acres they sat on. With a tenant already in the main house..." Again Cody pressed to the forefront of her mind, and again she pushed him away.

"I'd have a small rental income," she went on, scrambling to regain her train of thought. "And if I lived in the cabin where my grandfather had lived, all I'd need money for would be food and utilities, and I thought I could easily sell enough quilts to cover that."

"It sounds like a very reasonable plan," the doctor agreed.

There were general murmurs of assent around the room, along with a few *yes, but*s that Rebecca chose to ignore for the moment. She had lain awake enough nights wrestling with the *yes, but*s that kept coming back to haunt her.

"That's what *I* thought," she continued. "At least this way I can be with Matthew, instead of leaving him with a baby-sitter all day while I'm gone."

"Aren't things working out?" Dr. Connor probed gently. "Is money a real problem?"

"Only because I can't seem to stop worrying about it," Rebecca said with a perplexed shake of her head. "When I was a teacher, I had a paycheck that I could depend on. I had a retirement plan, a nice apartment, a new car. I wasn't rich, but I was comfortable and I had security."

"Ah," the doctor said with a smile of enlightenment, "so, for the freedom of your new independence, you're paying the price of insecurity. And are there more unpleasant surprises that you've stumbled across?"

"Oh, yes." Rebecca's answer came with a short, bitter laugh at the joke she had played on herself. Remembering the lonely, frightening trip to the doctor the first time Matthew had gotten really sick, she said, "When you have the responsibility of another life, especially one as vulnerable as a child's, isolation isn't always such a wonderful thing. Besides, the world's too small a place these days to hide out anywhere for long."

"Is that what happened today?" the doctor asked softly, demonstrating her uncanny ability to find and lay bare even the best-hidden can of worms. "Did your world suddenly become too small, Rebecca?"

With a defeated sigh, Rebecca hung her head. It was time to stop beating around the bush, trying to convince herself that everything would be all right. She came to this group to share honestly and to get help for the things she couldn't face alone.

"When my truck broke down this morning," she said, almost whispering, "the man who stopped to help me is a cousin of the one who raped me."

From the gasps that went around the circle, she knew that Joanne's story must have been much tamer. Rebecca was sure that a reaction like this one would have been enough to capture her earlier wandering thoughts. She could feel everyone in the group putting themselves in her place, just as she did when they each talked.

"He doesn't know, does he?" one of the women asked. Her voice reflected the horror of being publicly exposed.

"No, he doesn't know." She looked at the woman and identified her as one from the group who was married and, like Rebecca, had chosen to tell almost no one what had happened to her. Unlike Rebecca, shame was a strong factor in this woman's need for secrecy.

"No one knows except for my sister and the police who took the call," Rebecca said calmly. They had all heard the story before, but with six people in the group, it was sometimes hard to remember everything that was said. "Except for them and the two counseling groups I've been in, no one else even knows it happened."

"Rebecca."

At the new voice, Rebecca turned and identified Donna, the older woman who had been raped and robbed at gunpoint by a masked assailant in the middle of the night.

Donna leaned forward and made eye contact. "To refresh my memory," she said, "you were attacked by a childhood friend, am I correct? While you were living in another town."

"Yes," Rebecca answered. She knew that Donna, who was admirably straightforward and not at all shy, had never hidden what had happened to her and had completed two years of counseling. Rebecca had formed the strong suspicion that Donna stayed in the group more for the companionship and for what she could offer the others than for her own psychological needs.

"And the reason you didn't prosecute is that your family and his are close, is that right? And you didn't want to, what, tear the families apart?"

"I just didn't see what it would gain," Rebecca said, dredging up old memories and emotions that were still frighteningly close to the surface. "My sister tried to hide it, but I could see what it did to her that night. My family is very old-fashioned, and I have three headstrong, protective brothers. Jessy is my twin, and I reached out to her without even thinking. At the time, anyone else who knew would just be someone else who was needlessly hurt."

"But what about you, Rebecca? What about what you were going through?" Donna argued. "Was it good for *you* to keep all of that inside so that others wouldn't be upset?" She frowned and shifted her well-padded weight in her chair, warming up to an issue that she obviously felt strongly about. "I know a lot of women do that in this situation, and I don't like it. I don't think it's good, and I don't think it should be done. We're women, not saints, damn it."

"Well, some of us have our reasons," another woman put in defensively.

Rebecca spoke up before the debate got out of hand. "I think that if the police had been able to find him the next day, I would have pressed charges. But when I found out that he was gone and that I would probably never see him again, I just wanted to put it behind me and forget that it ever happened."

"Except that it doesn't happen that way," Joanne said quietly, and all eyes turned to her. "It doesn't just go away because you want it to."

"I know," Rebecca answered. From her personal experience, she knew that silence didn't heal, at least not quickly.

Joanne was a living testament to that. Her attack had occurred ten years earlier, and she had only sought counseling a year ago, after two failed marriages and a near nervous breakdown.

"I have one more question," Donna said, holding up a hand, "and then I'm through. Rebecca, we all understand that it's not really the rape you're worried about, it's people discovering about the pregnancy. So my question is, how well do you know this cousin? And what are you going to do if he starts getting curious about that baby of yours? Are you willing to spend the rest of your life running, to keep this all a secret?"

"I don't know." Rebecca shook her head, too tired to deal with the question, too tired to even think about it. "I just don't know."

With that, all the fight went out of her. She'd worried enough and talked enough. Now all she wanted was to go home to escape from the world for a while longer in her isolated little hideaway, with only her son and her work to keep her company.

Maybe someday she'd be strong enough to stop running away when the questions became too frightening, but not today. Today she still needed to hide.

Through the distance of her thoughts, Rebecca could hear Dr. Connor turning the group in another direction. "Okay," the woman's soft voice said, "who else has something they want to say? How about you, Flo? You've been pretty quiet today. What's happened with you in the last week?"

When the session was over, Rebecca found that her thoughts didn't turn off so easily and her memories wouldn't go away merely because she wanted them to. In bits and pieces, the images returned again and again as Rebecca accelerated and left San Angelo behind. Alone on the long highway to home, with her nerves frayed and her emotions raw, she wondered if she would ever put that one night behind her or if she would drag it with her for the rest of her life.

Tuesday was always her day of greatest hope and deepest despair. It was the day when she rebuilt herself, hoping each time that this was the day the puzzle pieces of her life would finally fall into place and she could leave behind the legacy of fear, distrust and anger that J.D. had left her.

Tuesday was the day when her mind told her heart that all men weren't like J.D., and her heart replied that the pain was too great and the betrayal was still too recent. "Ah, J.D.," Rebecca whispered with a sadness that had no end, "I'll never understand it."

The image of Jimmie Dale Lockhart as a little boy rose up to taunt her. Sweet and tart, devil and angel, he had been a tribulation even then to everyone but Rebecca. To her, he had been friend, brother and soul mate. Fun, flashy and reckless, he had led her into childhood escapades that would have impressed Mark Twain, and if trouble resulted, Jimmie Dale was Rebecca's defender, protecting her from all danger or blame.

It was that Jimmie Dale and the special place he would always hold in her heart that she remembered when J.D. had arrived on Rebecca's Austin doorstep and asked her to dinner for old times' sake. It was that little boy that she had tried to find in the bitter, angry young man who drank too much and laughed too loudly as he told her that he was leaving Eden for good.

Rebecca had watched his rumpled, easy smile slip sideways to reveal the pain he was trying to hide, despite his assurances that the job waiting for him in Alaska was the answer to his dreams. The laughing charm that was once such a part of him had grown tattered and stained with misuse, but remembering all that J.D. had meant to her, Rebecca had wanted to help him.

Certain that he felt the same way about her, she had invited him back to her apartment to talk in private, and once there, he'd admitted that he was only leaving Eden because he had no choice. Almost in tears, J.D. had told her that he'd had a few too many one night and picked a fight with a friend of the town judge. In court he'd been given the choice between six months in jail and leaving town. Seeing how upset he was, Rebecca had put her hand on his to comfort him and was taken by surprise when J.D. had grabbed the back of her hair and kissed her.

Embarrassment had turned to anger and then fear when she'd tried to pull away, only to have him tighten his hold. When she had cried out and struggled to get free, he had knocked her down and held a pillow over her face.

Disbelief was the last emotion Rebecca could remember feeling before she'd passed out. She couldn't believe this was happening. J.D. wouldn't do this to her. When she had come to again, she was alone.

Then and now, the whole night seemed like a bad dream, disjointed, without logic or continuity. She didn't remember using the phone, but she must have because Jessy, Rebecca's twin sister and the one person she could trust above all others, had arrived within minutes.

Later, two officers had arrived. The younger one had asked his questions gently, with sympathy in his voice, while the older one stood by, watching with ancient suspicion in his eyes. Later still, a medical examination had dashed the hope Rebecca had clung to that J.D. had come to his senses once she had passed out.

Between San Angelo and Margaret's, there was enough time to relive that night, to try to make some sense out of it, to try to kill the ghost of the past and move on to the future. There wasn't enough time to give her back all that she had lost—the easy laughter, the simple trust that had once been so much a part of her. There wasn't enough time to make her whole again.

Rebecca picked Matthew up from Margaret's and couldn't thank her enough for everything she'd done for them. She was truly grateful.

The sun was low in the west when Rebecca turned off the ranch-to-market road and onto the single-lane farm road that led to the house Cody rented, first from Rebecca's grandfather and now from Rebecca herself. Past the turn-off to Cody's, the road crossed a low-water bridge toward the little cabin where Henry Carder had spent his last days and where Rebecca now lived.

The ruts that usually jostled her old pickup were hardly noticeable with the newer suspension in Cody's truck. Matthew sat happily beside her, staring out the window behind the seat and burbling to himself. The air conditioner hummed softly, making the atmosphere inside the cab more like a crisp autumn morning than a sultry summer evening.

Music from one of Cody's many tapes seeped gently into the air from four separate speakers. Surprisingly the tapes were mainly love songs, from country and western to jazz, but almost all slow, a little sad and very romantic. Once again Rebecca tried to imagine the tall, muscular Cody driving around tapping his finger to the lonely sounds of Billie Holiday. And once again she came to the realization that she really didn't know Cody at all, and never really had.

Even though he had been the best friend of Rebecca's older brother, Houston, Cody had always been a loner. With his quiet manner and ready smile, he had been easy to like, and when the laughter in his eyes had faded to sadness, he had been easy to love, at least for a girl of thirteen who had wanted to be the one to make him laugh again.

Lost in thought, Rebecca almost drove past the turnoff to the big white house where her grandfather and grandmother had once lived and reared their family. Braking sharply, she turned onto the gravel road and drove a short distance to the driveway, where she stopped next to the house.

As she pulled the key from the ignition, she felt a brief, traitorous pang of regret at having to relinquish the comfort she had come to enjoy in spite of herself. Running her palm over the padded steering wheel, she bid a silent fare-well to the luxurious pickup. Then she pushed open the door and let out a shriek when she saw Cody standing there.

Putting her hand over her racing heart, she gasped, "Where did you come from?"

Cody pointed to a vegetable garden at the side of the driveway. "Over there."

"You nearly gave me a heart attack."

"Sorry. I thought you'd seen me." A slow, teasing smile spread over his face. "But I guess you were too busy fon-dling my truck."

Anger, quick and hot, flushed through Rebecca, an overabundance of emotion she had become used to. Taking a deep breath, she reminded herself that, in spite of the strain it would put on her, she had to be nice. She owed Cody a debt of gratitude, and she couldn't just spit in his eye and be gone the way she wanted.

"Thank you very much for the use of your pickup," she said through jaws stiff with tension. Despite the pep talk she had given herself, her unreasonable anger wasn't abating. "I don't know what I'd have done without it." None too gent-ly, she jammed the fist that held his keys into his open palm. "If I could have my truck now, I'd like to be going."

"Wouldn't you like to stay for some iced tea?"

"No." Her anger seeped away, and her chest tightened with the tears she had held in through the long drive from San Angelo. Almost home now, she was reaching the limits of her endurance. "I just want to get my truck and go."

"The tea's fresh."

Rebecca frowned as she looked into his eyes, and suspi-cion rose to the surface of her shifting emotions. Realizing that she hadn't seen her pickup yet, she shifted her focus to the landscape behind Cody and saw a vegetable garden tall enough to hide a man. On the other side of the driveway was a one-story white house and a neatly manicured lawn. At the end of the drive itself, the doors to a detached garage stood open, revealing a shadowed, empty interior.

"Where *is* my truck?" she asked sharply.

"Why don't we go inside, and I'll explain there?" Cody said gently.

"Oh, no!" Rebecca's heart plummeted, knowing that if he couldn't tell her outside, the news must be awful. Without her pickup, she was lost, helpless. She should never have sold her car. No matter how much she needed the money, she needed a reliable vehicle more.

"It's okay. It's not that bad."

Cody's voice was a soothing balm, and as easily as he had aroused her temper, he now drew her trust.

"It's not?"

A coaxing grin lifted the corners of his mouth. "No. It'll be fine. Why don't you let me carry Matthew inside, and you can bring in whatever else you need?"

Rebecca released a heavy breath of resignation and turned to unbuckle Matthew, whose cobalt blue eyes widened with pleasure as she lifted him out of the truck.

Cody took Matthew from Rebecca and handed back to her the ignition keys that she had practically stabbed him with minutes earlier. "Why don't you leave these in the truck? Just be sure you don't lock it."

While Cody started toward the house with Matthew, Rebecca gathered up her purse and the diaper bag from the floorboard. When she sat up, she bumped her arm against the infant carrier and realized how truly frazzled she was to have lifted Matthew out of the carrier and left it there. She was about to unfasten it and bring it along when she stopped herself. The more uncomfortable the situation was inside the house, the sooner Cody would stop thinking of excuses and take her home.

Putting the keys in the ignition, Rebecca carefully left the truck unlocked and went into the house. Once inside, she was mystified to find that Cody and Matthew were nowhere in sight. She went through the dining room and into the kitchen only to find it empty, as well.

"Cody?" Rebecca turned around and retraced her steps, raising her voice as she went. "Cody?"

Her answer was the sound of squeaking wheels and the sight of Cody pushing a baby bed ahead of him up the hallway from the back of the house. "Recognize this?" he called out over the sound of the wheels.

"Should I?"

"Well, I'm just guessing, but I found it in the attic, so I'd say you and your brothers have probably spent some time in it. Maybe even your father and his brothers."

Something about the domestic sight of Cody, with his broad, T-shirt-clad shoulders and bulging biceps pushing a noisy crib and a cooing baby up the narrow hallway, struck Rebecca as funny. "Just my brothers and me?" she asked, smiling broadly. "What about Jessy?"

Cody shook his head and pushed the crib and Matthew on past Rebecca and into the dining room. "It looks in too good a shape to have withstood Jessy. They had to have done something else with her."

With the trip over, Matthew lay quietly for a moment, staring up at the ceiling. Then, without preamble, he thumped both heels down hard on the bed and emitted a grumpy huff.

"Uh-oh," Rebecca said. "Where's your microwave?"

"Don't have one."

Momentarily stumped at the thought of a bachelor living without a microwave, she pulled herself together quickly and asked, "Well, have you got a pan I can heat a bottle in?"

"No problem." Cody walked into the kitchen and retrieved a saucepan from the cabinet. Then he filled it with water and put it on the stove to heat.

Rebecca put a bottle in the pan and went back into the dining room to check Matthew's diaper. It was then she noticed that while the bed might be old, not a speck of dust clung to it, and the mattress pad and sheets were new, so new that the sheets were still creased where they had been folded in the package.

She found it hard to believe that Cody would have gone to so much trouble for a baby who would only be there for a few minutes, and yet...

"Cody?" she said, not quite sure what she was planning to ask. She turned and found him standing in the doorway of the kitchen with Matthew's bottle in his hand.

"I think this is ready." Cody held out his wrist for Rebecca to see the splatter of formula where he had tested the bottle's temperature.

"You seem to know quite a lot about babies." She didn't know why she found the idea suspicious, but nevertheless, she did, and it must have showed.

"I hope that doesn't count against me," Cody said with a soft smile that left the edge to his voice unblunted.

Rebecca stiffened defensively. "I'm not keeping score."

"Aren't you?" Cody left the doorway and walked toward her, his eyes fixed on her. "If I make dinner, will you stay?"

Relieved by his rapid change of subject and tone, Rebecca had to remind herself that she was supposed to be avoiding him. "I really shouldn't."

He handed her the bottle. "We have things to talk about, and it would save you from having to cook when you get home. I promise it won't take long."

Rebecca racked her brain for an excuse to refuse again, but her brain wouldn't cooperate. He was dangerous, but she was having trouble remembering why. "I guess it will be all right."

Cody smiled his approval. "Good girl. You won't regret it."

The wrist of the hand that held the bottle went suddenly limp as she returned his gaze. His after-hours uniform was work-worn jeans and a faded turquoise T-shirt the same shade as his eyes. When Cody finally broke off his stare and walked back into the kitchen, Rebecca's eyes remained fixed on him.

She watched the play of his muscles under his T-shirt as he moved and the flexing of his thighs under the softly faded denim of his jeans. And even though he wore sneakers, she could see that he had the loose, sensuous walk of a cowboy.

Cody opened the door of the refrigerator and looked in. "How about sliced tomatoes, fried okra and some grilled chicken?" He leaned his forearm against the top of the refrigerator and twisted halfway around to look at her. "I haven't been shopping in a while, so the selection is pretty limited."

Caught by surprise, Rebecca tore her gaze away and scooped up Matthew. Looking down, she fed the bottle into his ready mouth while she cradled him close. "That sounds just fine."

"Well, now I'm confused," Cody said in a teasing drawl that was unmistakable. "It's been my observation that you say things are just fine regardless of how you really feel. So now I have to ask myself, is it really fine? Or does this mean that she's so hungry she'd eat anything if I'd just shut up and cook it?"

Rebecca chuckled softly and slowly drew her smiling eyes from her baby to Cody. "When you're right, you're right," she said with a shrug. "And I really am hungry. So, don't you think you should be getting that charcoal started?"

"I started it a while ago." He smiled back at her. "It should be just about right by now."

Her volatile emotions started another downward swing. "You mean you were going to have grilled chicken whether I stayed for dinner or not?"

"I was pretty sure you were going to be staying."

"How could you be so sure?" A cold, hard, protective fist clamped around her heart.

"Because I figured you wouldn't be going home until I took you."

"Oh, damn." Her combative mood died in a burst of anxiety that took her appetite with it. She had forgotten about her truck since she had entered the house. Now she felt helpless and hopeless all over again.

Cody took a step toward her and stopped, his face a mask of sympathy that had no outlet. "Rebecca, it'll be all right. I promise. Everything's going to be okay. Look, there's a rocker in here." He motioned to the corner of the kitchen. "Why don't you come in and sit down while I put the chicken on the grill? We can talk while I fry the okra."

"Okay." Rebecca snuggled Matthew against her for comfort. The day had been a long one, and all she wanted now was to get it over with. In the past year she had had her life shattered and her hopes and dreams destroyed. Then she had been given Matthew and a new reason for living.

Feeling weak and shaky from the ups and downs of the day, Rebecca settled into the rocking chair and told herself she was just tired. After a good night's sleep, things would seem better. They always had before.

"How are you feeling?" Cody asked quietly as he came back in from the backyard.

Rebecca looked up and watched him adjust the flame on the gas range, set a skillet over the burner and cover the bottom of the skillet with oil. "Better," she said without much conviction.

Cody reached into the refrigerator and pulled out fresh okra and tomatoes. He walked to a freestanding butcher's block, spread out the vegetables and began slicing the okra into a bowl of cornmeal.

From where she sat, Rebecca watched him. The old butcher's block was slightly hollowed on the top from long years of use. The longer she stared at it, the more familiar it looked.

"Was that grandmother's?" she finally asked, not believing that it could really be.

He nodded, walked to the stove and dropped the battered okra into the hot grease. "When Henry rented me this place, he left it partially furnished." Cody shook the skillet, spreading out the okra as he talked. "He never said, but I got the feeling that after your grandmother died, some things had too many memories to take with him to the cabin, but they also had too many memories to get rid of. I always thought that Henry left them here so he could come and visit them any time he wanted to."

"Things like the baby bed?"

Cody nodded and returned to the butcher's block to slice the tomatoes and spread them on a platter. "Small things, mainly. You know Henry. It was the small things that really meant something to him."

It was Rebecca's turn to nod as a mist of tears stung her eyes. Sitting here in her grandmother's kitchen, listening to Cody talk about her grandfather, brought back some of the best memories of her childhood. Memories of standing on a chair and kneading dough left to rise on the butcher's block. Memories of sitting beside her grandmother and taking her first, unskilled stitches on a quilt. Memories of standing in a sunbaked garden with her grandfather, holding the basket while he gathered the vegetables for the evening meal.

"I didn't mean to make you cry," Cody said softly.

"I'm not really crying," Rebecca rasped through a throat that was achingly tight with nostalgia. "I just forget sometimes how much I loved them and how much they taught me."

"I know Henry would be very happy that you've come back here. I don't know how, but I think he always knew you would."

Puzzled, Rebecca looked up at Cody through eyes that still swam with tears. "Why do you say that?"

"Well." He walked to the stove and stirred the okra. "One of the last conversations I had with Henry was out on that screened-in porch at the back of the cabin. It was then that he told me he was leaving this house and the cabin to you, and that he was setting up an account at the bank for me to send the rent payment to. By the way, I've been meaning to stop by and ask you if that was working out okay. Now that you're living here, I could always pay you in person."

"Oh, no. It's fine just the way it is," she answered, quick to end any thought of regular monthly contact. "It saves me the trouble of sending it on to the bank."

Cody smiled, and for a second, Rebecca had the uncomfortable feeling that he could see right through her.

"Anyway," he continued, "Henry asked me to do him a favor that night. He asked me to look out for you if you ever came back here. And I told him that I'd watch over you like you were my own child. Henry was like a second dad to me, Rebecca, and I take the promise I made to him very seriously."

Rebecca didn't know whether to feel flattered or frightened. She had been doing everything in her power to avoid Cody for the past two months, and now she found out that her grandfather had recruited him as her guardian angel. "Watch over me how?"

Cody shrugged. "Oh, little things, like saving you from sunstroke on the side of the road. Neighborly things like lending you my pickup." He held up a finger. "Excuse me for a minute. I have to go check on the chicken."

He left in a hurry, and while he was gone, Rebecca carried a sleeping Matthew back to the crib in the dining room. Then she returned to the kitchen and checked on the okra just in time to save it from burning.

All the while, memories pulled at her, memories that welcomed her home and reminded her of how truly Eden was her home. Rebecca was still in college when her grandmother, Becca, had died. Six months later, Henry had moved back into the little cabin that had been his childhood home and the first home where he and his young bride had lived. Their first two children had been born while they'd lived in that cabin, and one of these was Rebecca's father, Hank.

By their third child, Henry could afford to build the bigger, more modern home down the road from the little cabin, the home where they had raised their children and coddled their grandchildren, the home that had grown too large and lonely for Henry to live in without Becca.

A blast of warm air came in the back door when Cody entered the kitchen. He stopped and smiled when he saw Rebecca standing at the stove, dishing up the okra. "Thanks. It can be a little embarrassing when you invite someone to stay for dinner and then burn it." He walked behind her to the refrigerator and peered in.

Stifling a gasp, Rebecca braced herself against the stove and waited for her pounding heart to slow. She had thought she was used to Cody's size until he passed within inches of her, and the sheer height and breadth of him left her with a fresh bout of jitters and palpitations that had nothing to do with fear.

"I've got iced tea or milk," Cody said, looking at her over the refrigerator door. "Which do you want?"

"Iced tea's fine." This situation was almost as bad as when she had been a girl and turned into a stammering fool every time he came near. But she wasn't a girl anymore, and she didn't have a crush on Cody anymore, and she had to get a grip before she embarrassed herself beyond redemption.

Cody stepped away from the refrigerator, pitcher in hand. "It's already sweetened," he warned.

Rebecca held the bowl of fried okra in front of her like a shield. "Sugar's good."

"If you'll put the okra and tomatoes on the table, I'll bring the chicken in from the grill and we can eat."

"Great." She started toward the dining room, searching her mind for anything that would get her schoolgirl fantasies under control. When she found what she was looking for, it almost knocked the wind out of her.

"Cody," she said, whirling back toward him, "you never told me about my truck? Where is it?"

He paused in the process of filling two glasses with tea. "It's being worked on. It'll be ready in about a week."

"Oh, my God." Once again her knees quivered with dread and her stomach clenched into a tight knot that revolted at the thought of food.

"Rebecca." Her name was a soothing caress, and Cody's gentle smile was filled with understanding. "Even if I could turn my back on a woman and a defenseless baby, I couldn't turn my back on my promise to Henry. So stop worrying. Everything will be okay."

"But how? It's going to cost a fortune."

"No, it's not. And if you haven't got the money to pay for the repairs, you can pay for them when you do. You're Henry Carder's granddaughter, and in Concho County you're among friends."

Rebecca didn't make a sound, but a huge tear of gratitude rolled from her eye and down her cheek. "Thank you," she mouthed silently.

"Now, go sit down." With a smile, Cody turned and walked out the back door.

Rebecca leaned against the dining-room doorway and watched him. She didn't even want to think about how she felt except to admit that Henry certainly knew how to pick guardian angels. Once she felt strong enough to move, she carried the two platters to the dining table and looked around for something else to do, but there wasn't anything left.

Little waves of emotion continued to well up inside of her, threatening outbursts of tears or worse and bringing with them an extremely strong urge to kiss someone. Knowing that under no circumstances would it be Cody that she kissed, Rebecca walked to the crib and leaned over the rail.

For a minute she just watched Matthew sleeping. The gentle rise and fall of his chest and rounded tummy, the soft sounds of his breathing, answered the loving need in her. She brushed her fingers over his soft cheek and lifted his small, pink hand to press a kiss against his wrist.

"How about the cook?" Cody asked quietly from behind her. "Don't I get one of those, too?"

Chapter Three

Cody had expected a reaction, but not quite the one he got when Rebecca gasped and whirled to face him. Her look of shock held elements of fear, and he would have regretted his teasing remark, except for the fact that he wasn't entirely teasing.

His memories of Rebecca were of a quiet, skinny, pig-tailed little girl of eight or nine who drew out his protective, playful side but who was largely to be ignored. When Margaret had been patched through to his patrol car with the message that Rebecca was overdue and possibly broken down somewhere on the road between the cabin and Margaret's, Cody had gone looking for the little girl he remembered. What he had found was a woman.

In a smooth recovery, Rebecca said, "I don't think so."

She looked cool and in control, but when she straightened, Cody could tell she was ready to run if he made a wrong move. He hadn't meant to frighten her, but it was expecting too much for any man to look at her and not notice that somewhere between puberty and motherhood, Rebecca had grown up in all the right ways.

"I guess we'd better eat, then." He smiled, keeping his manner light in the hopes of putting them both at ease once again.

If only he hadn't known her when she was so young. Maybe then he wouldn't feel like such a dirty old man every time he looked at her and felt the burgeoning lust in his heart.

"What exactly is wrong with the truck?" Rebecca asked when they sat down to eat.

Cody took two healthy sized pieces of chicken and passed the platter to Rebecca. She was almost wincing as she waited for his answer, and he thought that he had never seen a woman who needed hugging more than Rebecca did at that moment, nor had he ever seen a woman more likely to either bolt or slug him if he tried it.

"Well," he began, trying to ease into the news gently, "a hose blew, and that caused the engine to overheat. It's not as bad as it could have been, but..."

"Cody," Rebecca interrupted sharply enough to cause him to look up in surprise. "Just tell me what's wrong with the truck."

"It's going to need some new parts, and some of them have to be ordered," he said, deciding to keep it simple and vague.

"How long is that going to take?"

He could see tears forming again in her big, brown eyes. "Not too long," he said gently. "Like I said earlier, not much over a week." He was no mind reader, but it didn't take one to know that there was a lot more troubling her than the truck.

"How much is it going to cost?"

"Not nearly as much as you think it's going to. Now, why don't you stop worrying and eat your chicken before it gets cold? It's got a secret marinade on it and everything. My own recipe, and I won't share it with a soul. But you might be able to wheedle it out of me if you'll give me a smile."

For a moment, Rebecca just stared at him, her eyes glittering with tears she refused to shed. Then slowly she smiled, a small, tremulous smile that grew stronger, wider and brighter as he watched, and from the swelling of triumph in his heart, Cody knew that it was a lot more than just lust that was nagging at *him*.

A little girl whose family was entwined with his through generations of friendships had faded from his life many years ago without causing a flicker of regret. Now she had returned to his life as a lush, beautiful woman with a baby in her arms and whispers of scandal in her wake, and he found himself drawn to her like steel to a magnet. He didn't even know why, not really.

It wasn't just that he had promised Henry to look out for her. It wasn't just that her brother Houston had once been Cody's best friend, or that his cousin J.D. had been Rebecca's playmate almost from birth. Old bonds were a beginning, but only that, just a beginning.

Somehow he was sure that if he had never met Rebecca Carder before today, he would still be sitting across the table from her, watching for every emotion that crossed her face, listening for every nuance of her voice and wondering what had brought her to the middle of nowhere, alone and with a child. He would still find himself wanting to help her, to make her laugh and chase that look of sadness from her eyes for good.

"Cody, the chicken really *is* terrific, but do you suppose they'll have my truck ready by next week? I can do without it until then, but I'll really need it to go into San Angelo on Tuesday."

As excellent as the dinner was, and as much as she appreciated Cody's attempts to cheer her up, Rebecca found that her mind kept circling back to the catch-22 problem of her truck. She really wouldn't be fine without it. She would be totally isolated without it, far from the nearest doctor or grocery store. Even Cody's house was more than four miles from her cabin, and he was the only neighbor anywhere near.

Worse still was that when she did get the pickup back, the repair bill was going to cost her everything she had saved up. After that, she and Matthew would be living week to week when she was just starting to get her feet under her again. If anything else went wrong any time soon, she didn't know what she would do.

"What's the matter?" Cody asked gently. "Didn't you like my truck?"

"Yes, Cody, I liked your truck. It's a wonderful truck, but—"

"Use *my* pickup until you get yours back."

"Well, I really appreciate that. I suppose if mine isn't back by next Tuesday, I'll have to borrow somebody's to get into San Angelo. It's very nice of you to offer, but I hate to keep putting you out like that."

More than that, she couldn't keep increasing her debt to him. Until today, she had done a very good job of avoiding the entire Lockhart clan since her return to Eden. And the fact that she was enjoying Cody's company made it even more important that she stay as far away from him as possible in the future.

"I didn't mean next Tuesday," Cody said. "I meant this week."

"What?"

"If not for your own sake, then for Matthew's. Keep my truck, at least while I'm at work. I just wouldn't feel right knowing you're alone way out here without transportation."

"Oh, no."

Recognizing the same line of reasoning Cody had used to press her into borrowing his truck earlier in the day, Rebecca shook her head emphatically. She wasn't giving in to him twice in one day. She couldn't. Absolutely not. There was no way she was going to agree, and she couldn't allow him to talk her into it.

She had made one unshakable rule for herself when she moved to Eden, and that was to stay away from the Lockharts. Today was an unavoidable exception, but that was it. No more.

"Rebecca, be reasonable."

"I am being reasonable. I can't take your truck for a whole week."

"You wouldn't be keeping it. We'd share it. While I'm off duty, I'll keep it, and while I'm on duty, you'll keep it. I'll just have someone pick me up and drop me off at your cabin each day."

"I can't. I just can't."

"Well, the only other option is for me to stop by and check on you three or four times a day to make sure you and Matthew are all right."

Damn him. Defeated, she said, "I'll take the truck."

"I thought you would. How's the okra?"

"Really good." With all the wrangling that had gone on between them, she hadn't tasted a bite of what she had eaten.

Cody smiled that knowing little smile of his, and Rebecca wanted to throw something at him. If she wanted someone to read her mind, she had a twin who could do it without gloating.

Laying her napkin beside her plate, she pushed her chair away from the table. "I guess I'd better be getting home. There's still a lot to do before the night's over."

"I imagine you are pretty tired." Cody rose with her. "You've had quite a day."

She was about to agree when, without warning, a mammoth yawn overtook her, ending in a sigh and a stretch that left her yearning for a bed and the comforting cloak of darkness.

Cody laughed. "From the size of that yawn, I'd say if I don't get you home soon, I might have to be finding a bed for you."

Rebecca looked into Cody's smiling eyes and started to apologize when a second, even bigger yawn followed the first. "Good grief," she gasped with eyes that were watering and a nose that had her sniffling. She didn't know whether to be amused or embarrassed.

Cody walked over to her and took her hand, slipping his fingers through hers in an act that was both casual and cozy. Then he led her to the crib where Matthew slept, and whispered, "Why don't you carry him on out to the truck while I gather up your things?"

Nodding her agreement, Rebecca slipped her hand from Cody's and in the brief time it took her to reach down and lift Matthew, she was dismayed to find that her hand felt empty without the touch of Cody's.

Too tired to dwell on the thought, she promised herself that it was nothing to worry about. She wasn't about to let her guard down around a man, any man. As tempting as the idea might be at the moment, she'd already been betrayed once by old memories and old loyalties, and if her judgment had been that bad once, she couldn't take the chance of it happening again. Not now. Not ever.

Not even with Cody.

Cody parked between two trees at the side of the cabin and turned off the pickup's engine. Twisting around in the seat to face Rebecca, he asked softly, "Are you okay? You haven't said a word since we left my house."

"I'm fine. Just tired."

"I wish I could believe that." He smiled slightly. "But since 'fine' almost invariably means the opposite, I have to wonder if I've done something to upset you. Because if I did, I sincerely apologize."

Rebecca opened the door of the pickup and prepared to run. Tears after a Tuesday session weren't uncommon, and the ones she had been holding back during the ride home were about to come crashing down on her and anyone else who was near.

"I just need to get inside." She fumbled at the seat belt that held Matthew and the infant carrier prisoner. "A little nap and I'll be as good as new."

"Can I help you with that?"

"No." Her eyes swam with unshed tears that turned the buckle on the seat belt to a silver smear amid blurs of yellow, red and blue. "If you'll just put the other things on the porch, I'll carry everything inside after I get Matthew in."

"If you say so."

Cody didn't sound convinced, but he gathered up the diaper bag and cooler without further argument, and Rebecca gratefully kept her head down and her face averted until he had gone. Then she swiped a furtive hand across her eyes, smearing her tears but clearing her vision enough to finally see what she was doing.

Unbuckling the seat belt, she lifted Matthew, infant carrier and all, and stepped from the comfortable interior of the pickup into an evening that was as still and hot and almost as bright as the afternoon had been. Involuntarily Rebecca groaned.

"Every day just seems to get a little hotter, doesn't it?" Cody asked from the porch. His task done, he started back toward her. "It wouldn't be so bad if it'd cool off a little in the evenings, or at least rain." He held out his hand. "If you'll give me your keys, I'll unlock the door for you and carry this stuff on inside. I don't want to sound like a worrier, but you're beginning to look a little peaked again."

Rebecca opened her mouth to say that she could do it herself, then realized that it wasn't worth the argument. "They're in the front pocket of the diaper bag."

She would let him open the door. She would let him carry her things inside. She would even let him check the closets for boogeymen if he wanted, but after that Cody was leaving, whether he wanted to or not. And then, alone at last, she would give Matthew his nightly bath and carry him out to the rocker on the front porch where she would give him his bottle while they rocked and watched a dying sun set the western sky aflame.

She needed to be alone. She needed the small rituals. She needed to hold Matthew in her arms and know that whatever else went wrong in her life, she still had the one wonderful miracle of her son. Having him near her gave her the strength to get through the night and a reason to get up in the morning.

"Whew!" Cody stepped back from the open door of the cabin and fanned himself.

Rebecca looked up and chuckled automatically while the traitorous thought went through her mind that maybe what she really needed was not to be alone so much. Maybe what she really needed was to start living life again instead of hiding from it.

"And I thought it was hot *outside,*" he gasped.

Joining Cody on the porch, Rebecca said, "It cools off pretty fast once I get the air conditioner turned on."

Cody held up his hand to stop her from coming any closer. "You stay out here. I'll go in and do it."

Rebecca shook her head and laughed. "You know, if my truck hadn't broken down..."

"We'd come out here someday and find your dehydrated body stretched out on the floor, reaching toward the air conditioner you never got a chance to turn on. And that reminds me of another thing. You've got to start wearing a hat when you're outside, young lady."

"Don't fuss at me," she warned, only half in jest. "I'm too tired and I might start crying."

Cody's finger traced a path across her cheekbone. "It looks to me like maybe you already *have* been," he said softly.

Rebecca looked up at him, frozen by an abrupt and wholly irrational urge to rest her weary head on his strong, broad chest and offer up her troubles into his capable and sympathetic hands. For one crazy instant, she found herself wanting to confide in him, and the realization scared her badly.

"Really, I'm fine," she said, shaking her head and taking a step away from him. "And you're right about the hat. I realized at the time that I probably wouldn't have gotten so weak so fast if I had been wearing one. I will in the future. Are you still going to turn on the air conditioner?"

He stared down at her for a heartbeat, his eyes narrowing while he pondered some private thought. Then he nodded. "Sure. Why don't you sit down out here until the house has had a minute to cool?"

With that, he turned and went into the cabin while Rebecca frowned after him. She appreciated his concern, but she was getting a little tired of being told what to do. Still frowning, she sank into the rocker and wrapped her arms around Matthew and the carrier, pulling them close to her body as she began to rock.

Within seconds, a huge yawn rose up from nowhere, ending in a sigh that reached all the way to her toes and left her groggy with relaxation.

"You know," Cody said softly from the doorway, "every time you do that, I expect to see you fall over asleep, the way you used to when you were little. One or two big yawns, and the next thing I knew, Houston would be picking you up and carrying you home asleep in his arms. You know, I haven't even asked you about Houston. I haven't seen him in years."

Wide-awake, Rebecca smiled tightly. She didn't want to exchange family news. "He's doing fine. Someday when I'm not so tired, I'll tell you all about him."

"That sounds good. Maybe I can return the favor. I guess it's been a while since you've seen J.D."

Propelled by panic, she rose from the rocker and brushed past Cody into the cabin. With every nightmare she'd had for the past year howling behind her, Rebecca took a deep breath to steady her trembling and said, "I really do have to get Matthew ready for bed now. I don't want to make you feel unwelcome, but it's been a very long day."

Without turning, she set Matthew's carrier on a table, lifted him out and took him to his bed, where he would be safe. Until her hands stopped shaking, she was afraid to hold him for fear of dropping him. She clutched the side of the baby bed for support and stared down toward her son, unable to see him clearly through the tears that spilled silently down her cheeks.

"Good night, Cody," she said in a voice that was only slightly husky. "Thank you for everything."

She could feel Cody's hesitation, but the only outward sign he gave was the short pause before he said, "I'll bring the truck back in the morning."

Rebecca nodded, then realized he couldn't see her inside the darkened cabin. "That'll be good. Matthew gets me up early."

"If you need anything, call me."

She nodded again, never turning. "Good night, Cody."

After that, she didn't move until she heard the sound of the truck starting and driving away, and then she moved only because Matthew was awake, tired and fussy. Lifting him from the bed, Rebecca brushed her cheek against the rose-petal softness of his forehead, and as always, she drew strength from the feel of him in her arms.

Carrying Matthew, she crossed the room, turned on the switch for the overhead light and closed and bolted the front door. With the gloom of twilight dispelled, she studied the cozy room where she spent most of her waking hours. On one side was a rocker, a wingback chair and a plaid couch, all left over from Henry's occupancy. Behind the couch was Matthew's baby bed and a chest of drawers. Next to the crib was a steep staircase that led to the loft above the bedroom.

On the other side of the main room was the kitchen, which consisted of a refrigerator, a sink with a window above it, a stove and cabinets, all in a row along one wall.

In the center of the room was an old, pine harvest table and four mismatched chairs. On the partial wall that separated the living area from the bedroom was a fireplace that was the main source of heat for the cabin.

Arranging Matthew against her shoulder, Rebecca walked toward the sink and began to set up for his bath. There was just enough of the day left that if she worked very hard, she might be relaxed enough to sleep by the time she finally went to bed. First she would give Matthew his bath and fix his bedtime bottle, and then they would go out to the porch and watch the sunset together.

And after the red-and-gold sky faded to lavender, and night crept out of the shadows to steal across the land, she would put Matthew to bed and treat herself to a long, luxurious bath in the old-fashioned clawfoot tub that was one of the cabin's major assets.

Supporting Matthew with one hand and gently scrubbing him with the other, Rebecca promised herself that after a good night's sleep, the day's events would evaporate like a bad dream. When she awakened tomorrow, her life would return to normal, or at least as normal as her life would ever be again.

And it might have worked, except that Matthew was tired and irritable and couldn't sleep for more than a few hours without waking to tell his mother one more time that while he had been sweet and quiet all day long, he now had a huge reservoir of pent-up frustration to deal with, and if he couldn't sleep, no one was going to sleep.

At 3:30 a.m., Rebecca staggered out of bed for the fourth time. Her body ached with the need for sleep, and her eyes refused to open beyond slits. She felt her way across the open space between the bedroom and the living room. Her right hand found the loft staircase railing and let it guide her. With her left hand, she felt her way along the back of the couch until she came to the baby bed.

Rebecca lifted Matthew into her arms and carried him to the rocker. While she rocked and he fussed, she cast around inside her tired brain for how long it had been since he had eaten. The clock had read two-fifteen when she had last crawled gratefully back into bed. Two-fifteen to three-thirty, that was— Oh well, it wasn't very long, anyway. He couldn't possibly be hungry.

Rebecca stood and paced, patting Matthew's back with one hand while she explored for a wet diaper with the other. Dry as a bone. Maybe he was just as miserably tired and achy as she was. Maybe his stomach hurt. She twinged with guilt at the memory of the unwarmed bottle earlier in the day.

Whatever the problem, Matthew was expressing himself the only way he had, and the least she could do was to put her own comfort aside, since whatever was bothering him wasn't something he had brought on himself. Hoping fresh air might help, Rebecca laid Matthew in a cradle she kept near the front door and started the cradle rocking. Then she felt around until she located the bench that should be against the wall and reached under it to retrieve the cowboy boots that were stashed there.

Sitting on the bench, she shoved, pulled, twisted and stomped her way into the boots that came up nearly to her knees. Then she retrieved Matthew and carried him outside into the welcoming embrace of the hot, still night. The light of a full moon bathed the landscape in a pearl gray glow.

Shadows were slashes of charcoal painted flat against the ground.

With Matthew on her shoulder, Rebecca left the porch and took bouncing steps toward the east side of the cabin to where a walled garden, open only to the south, sheltered her grandmother's cherished antique roses. Planted over sixty years ago and still growing, most of them paraded their glory only in the spring, but a few cast blossoms sparingly in even the hottest months.

Standing a few yards from the porch, at the open end of the garden, Rebecca faced the stone wall that extended from the back of the cabin a good distance outward before it made a ninety-degree turn and came toward her, parallel to the outside wall of the kitchen. On the back wall of the garden, where the sturdy vines of the ramblers climbed the yellow rock wall, a single rose glowed ghostly white in the moonlight. In full bloom, its thick cluster of petals revealed a brave and haunting beauty.

Rebecca imagined she could smell the sweet, heavy scent of the creamy blossom. Its perfume was a familiar part of her memories, carried from childhood and cherished as some of the best her life had to offer. Memories of kneeling beside her grandmother, spade in hand, while a whisper of air carried the attar of roses through the garden.

Memories of full-moon nights that set loose the magic of childhood. Memories of laughter, shrill with excitement. Memories of J.D., wild even as a child, teetering at the outer edge of control, reaching out at the last moment for safety, reaching out for her.

Damn. Rebecca wiped away the tear that trickled down her cheek and sniffed back the grief that always seemed to surprise her whenever she remembered the Jimmie Dale of old—the sweet, willful little boy who was her best friend and constant companion during those long summer visits with her grandparents. She loved that little boy, and God help her, she still missed him deeply whenever she thought of those golden days of summer so long ago.

She sniffed again and swiped at another tear. Why did it always have to be in the middle of the night that she remembered what J.D. had once been? It wasn't fair. During the day, she hated and feared him. During the night, she cried for him, and it just wasn't fair.

Holding Matthew closer, breathing in the sweet, baby scent of him, she turned and paced across the sun-scorched front yard, past the porch and down the dirt road that ended under the trees beside the cabin. It was three miles to the low-water bridge. Surely by the time she reached the bridge, she would have burned off this sadness that, from experience, she knew would turn to fear and then to anger before finally leaving her exhausted but at peace.

She rubbed her cheek against Matthew's head and prayed that by the time he was old enough to notice such things she would have conquered the emotional storms that raged inside her. Already a year of therapy had helped. The innocent, unconditional love of her son had helped. Time had helped.

But some of the things that would help the most, she couldn't do, because for Matthew's sake no one else could know, at least until he was mature enough to deal with the truth. To protect him, she had to keep the secret of his conception, and as long as she kept that secret, the acid burn of rage and humiliation would continue to eat away at her.

Nor could she ever allow herself the healing act of confrontation, but that was a sacrifice she would willingly make. If she lived the rest of her life without seeing J.D. again, she would be more than happy. If he hadn't told her himself that he was persona non grata in Concho County, and if the police hadn't confirmed that he was indeed in Alaska, she wouldn't be here now, living in the backyard of his family and in the midst of so many memories that strangely left her more sad than hurt.

She could live in hiding. She could bear the scarlet stain of being an unwed mother in a small town. She could endure the inevitable whispers of speculation and disapproval. But if the world fell apart and the sun went nova, J.D. must never find out Matthew was his son.

The night's magical glow began to fade, and the shadows' crisp edges had blurred by the time Rebecca turned toward home. She was tired beyond belief, but more at peace with herself than she had been in weeks. Matthew slept quietly on her shoulder as the eastern sky grew paler.

Along the horizon, streaks of lavender were brightening to hot pink by the time Rebecca finally reached the cabin. She gently lowered Matthew into his crib and then sank face-first into the pillowy softness of her own bed. She was asleep before she had time to blink. When the sound of Matthew's cries and the pounding at the door finally penetrated her ears, Rebecca raised her head and groaned.

When the crying and pounding continued, she knew she was going to have to get up even if she had to crawl. With a mighty heave, she tilted herself upright and slid backward off the side of the bed until the toes of her boots thunked against the floor. Surprised, Rebecca staggered upright and blinked until she could focus on the knee-high cowboy boots she had fallen asleep wearing.

"Wow," she whispered, "I *must* have been tired."

"Rebecca!" Cody shouted.

Something in his voice told her he had called to her more than once. She glanced toward the crib and saw a foot sticking out from under the pad that was designed to prevent such things.

"I'm coming! Hold on!" she shouted back to man and infant alike. When she reached Matthew's bed, he was twisted in his sheet, arms flailing madly, with one leg through the bars of the crib, trapped, while the other leg kicked angrily at the pad that was supposed to protect him from such indignities.

"Hold on, little fella," Rebecca crooned as she set to work freeing him. He looked so angry, frustrated and impatient that she couldn't help laughing. "You certainly have the temper to go with the hair, sweetheart." She lifted him into the air and laughed again. One tiny fist swung just past her nose.

Still laughing aloud, Rebecca held Matthew lower and went to open the door. When she did, she found Cody in his uniform, his hat in his hand, standing practically against the door. Gasping, she stepped back.

Since she had seen him last, she had once again forgotten how large he was. Standing six foot three at least, he had shoulders so wide and arms so muscled that by the time he filled the door frame, there was no room left for anything else. And once again she didn't know whether to feel comforted or threatened by his size.

"Sorry," she managed to say. "I was sleeping."

For a minute he said nothing. He just stared at her, looking her up and down and up again slowly. A smile that made him seem entirely too pleased with himself spread across his face. Finally he asked, "In that?"

Embarrassment flushed through Rebecca when she remembered the cowboy boots. She glanced down quickly to confirm her fears, wondering all the while if she could think of an explanation that wouldn't sound ridiculous. It was then that she realized the true extent of the damage.

The black-and-white, hand-tooled leather, pointed-toed cowboy boots that ended about three inches below her knees were the least of her problems. Above that was bare leg until her sleep shirt began at midthigh, and even that wasn't so bad compared to the thinness of the sleep shirt's white cotton fabric and the fact that she was wearing very little under it—too damned little, in fact.

Without preamble, Rebecca stepped back, slammed the door shut and bolted it.

"Hey!"

Cody's irate shout was barely muffled by the heavy door.

"Go away." She took another step back and looked down at Matthew, quiet now that he was in her arms. She would have to put him down to change clothes, and she dreaded the noise he would make when she laid him down again.

"What?" Cody's voice was ripe with disbelief, and he didn't sound like a man prepared to obey meekly.

Frowning, Rebecca concentrated on the dilemma of Matthew. "Go a-way," she said again, emphasizing each syllable as she walked slowly toward her bedroom, then turned and retraced her steps.

"Rebecca!" The door rattled with the impact of Cody's pounding fist. "I can't go away. I'm leaving my truck with you, and my ride to the station isn't here yet. Look, I'm sorry I laughed. Damn it, I hate talking to a—" he stumbled on the last word when Rebecca threw the bolt and swung open the door again "—door," he finished, careful to let his eyes go no lower than her face.

"Here." She thrust Matthew toward him. "Why don't you rock him while I change clothes?"

"Okay." Cody smiled as he gathered Matthew into his arms and took a step toward the open door just as Rebecca closed it in his face and bolted it shut once more. "Hey!"

"Use the rocker on the porch," Rebecca called sweetly.

She twirled on her heel and started once more toward the back of the cabin with a smile spreading slowly across her face. She really didn't know why she enjoyed bedeviling Cody so. It couldn't be that he was J.D.'s cousin, because the two men didn't look or act anything alike.

And yet Cody did arouse a rebellion in her, and frequently. It could have been a reaction to his size or, possibly, to his more-than-adequate supply of self-confidence. Or maybe she simply resented him because he was a man. So very much a man.

Chapter Four

"There!" Rebecca swept open the door with a flourish and waited for a reaction.

Dressed in a drop-waisted jumper with a T-shirt underneath, she had worked hard to achieve a reasonable attractiveness while remaining as close to sexually neuter as possible. The jumper was pink, and the T-shirt was a floral print. A white-ruffled underskirt peeked out below the hem of the jumper, adding a touch of femininity and a double dash of modesty.

The outfit wasn't exactly maternity wear, but it was close. Since Matthew's birth, she had adopted a style of attire that could best be described as camouflage. After a year of therapy, nine months of which was spent hiding behind her pregnancy, Rebecca still wasn't comfortable with herself as a woman. Every day she told herself she needed just a little more time, and every day she saw her hopes for the future moving just a little further away.

She grew even more ill at ease with the long silence that greeted her return. Hesitantly she refocused her gaze from the tan grass of the front yard to Cody's recumbent form, tilted far back in the rocker. His eyes were closed, and, with a sleeping Matthew angled across his chest, Cody showed no signs of imminent movement.

Free to study the incongruous tableau without detection, Rebecca's own soft laughter caught her by surprise, and the stirring in her heart that followed was even more of a surprise. Asleep, with one large hand protectively covering Matthew's small back, the man on her front porch was a world away from the stern stranger who had stopped to help her yesterday. And he was equally far away from the young man with the sea blue eyes who had once held her heart in his hand. This man was everything she should be afraid of, and yet . . .

As if he could hear her thinking, Cody slowly dragged open his eyes, just enough to gaze up at Rebecca from under heavy lids. "I don't suppose you made a pot of coffee while you were in there, did you?" he asked in a voice gravelly with sleep.

"Yes." She made no attempt to hide the soft smile that still adorned her face. "As a matter of fact, I did. Have you had breakfast yet?"

"Nope."

"Do you have time?"

Cody lifted his head from the back of the rocker and leveled suspicious eyes on her. "Do I have to eat out here?"

Torn between amusement and chagrin, Rebecca pressed the tips of her fingers to her lips to halt her broadening grin. "Oops." She had to admit that she hadn't given Cody much reason to expect hospitality. "I'm really sorry," she said, truly repentant when she remembered belatedly that Cody was only here to do her a favor. "Please, come in."

Cody rose from the rocker, taking care not to jostle the sleeping baby in his arms, and crossed the few steps to the doorway. "What should I do with Little Bit here?"

Rebecca pointed to the cradle just inside the door. "If you'll put him in there and give it a little push, I don't think he'll wake up. If he does, his bottle's in the microwave, ready to heat."

She turned away and went to the refrigerator. In a further act of contrition, she pulled out the thick slabs of ham she had been saving for Sunday dinner. "Do ham and eggs sound... Yikes!" she cried, and jumped back from her unexpected contact with Cody's very solid body, which was much closer than she had thought it was.

Shaken, Rebecca sagged against the counter. The package of ham dangled from her hand as she drew in deep, calming breaths and stared at him, still only a few inches away from her.

"I didn't mean to scare you," Cody said, offering a smile of apology.

"What are you?" she gasped, hugging the counter for support. "Part Indian?"

He laughed. "You know, when you get riled, you sound a lot like Jessy."

"Thank you."

His face still wreathed in a grin, Cody leaned his hip against the counter and looked down at her. "That reminds me of something that used to puzzle me, way back when. I could never figure out how a rowdy kid like J.D. picked a quiet little thing like you for a friend instead of that hellcat sister of yours."

Cody shrugged and eased away from the counter. "Maybe he just saw a part of you that most of us overlooked. Now, if you were about to offer me ham and eggs, I accept. In fact, if you've got an extra skillet, I'll do the ham while you do the eggs."

Relieved to have the stroll down memory lane over, Rebecca handed the ham to him and pointed to the stove. She waited until Cody moved away before she let out the breath she had been holding and reached under the counter to retrieve two skillets. "How do you like your eggs?"

"However you like yours. I'm easy."

"Oh, really." She handed him a skillet. "I hadn't noticed."

"That's because you insist on arguing with me about *everything,*" Cody explained, and then moved to the stove to arrange the ham in the frying pan.

Rebecca turned to the refrigerator and began to count out the eggs. "Well, if you weren't so bossy," she mumbled as she counted, "I wouldn't have to spend so much time arguing about what I'm going to do with my life."

Over the soft sizzle of ham, Cody said quietly, "Sorry. I'll try not to be so pushy in the future."

Rebecca straightened and closed the refrigerator door. "Do scrambled eggs sound okay to you?"

She clamped her jaws shut around the urge to apologize and held on tight until the desire passed. She was sorry if she had hurt his feelings, but there was nothing she could do about it.

"They're my favorite," he said. "Do you have any brown sugar?"

Rebecca reached into the cabinet and pulled out a small bag of brown sugar. Cody's fingers brushed hers and lingered for only an instant when he took the bag from her. But an instant was long enough for an electrified jolt to tingle through Rebecca's arm, reminding her of why she felt the need to run for her life whenever she was around Cody.

Nothing he said or did was to blame. The problem was Rebecca herself, the way he made her feel, the way he made her forget the danger. And if she couldn't make herself run from him, her only other course was to keep pushing him away until he finally gave up and left her alone for good.

Silence settled over the kitchen, broken only by the sizzle of cooking ham and the whipping of eggs in a bowl. Cody pushed the ham slices around the skillet while Rebecca seasoned the beaten eggs and joined him at the stove. The corners of his mouth tipped in a companionable greeting, and he moved over to give her room.

After more silence while Rebecca tended her eggs with diligence, Cody asked, "Did you two have a rough night?"

Her first impulse was to give him another nudge out the door, but she couldn't do it. In spite of her fears and the flutterings of hostility and other, far worse things that he aroused in her, Cody was simply too nice a man for her to be purposefully mean to him. Besides, even with all the ups and downs of her bruised emotions, she was beginning to enjoy his company.

"Matthew was too restless to sleep for more than an hour at a time," she answered finally. "I didn't get to bed to stay until after dawn."

"No wonder you didn't answer when I knocked." He checked the underside of the ham and turned off the flame. "I hope my pounding didn't scare you. I was getting worried, and I guess my training kicked in."

Rebecca reached into the cupboard for two plates to scoop the egg onto. "I thought for a minute you were going to break the door down before I could get to it," she said with a laugh as she handed the plates to Cody.

"It was getting close," he admitted. "If you want to pour the coffee, I'll take these to the table."

"What do you mean it was close?" Rebecca watched him over her shoulder as she filled two mugs with coffee. "Close to what? Close to you breaking down my door?" The longer she talked, the higher the pitch of her voice went.

"Rebecca," Cody said reasonably, "the baby was crying, and I wasn't getting any answer from you."

"For that, you'd break down my door?" she practically shouted.

"If I thought you or Matthew were in danger, yes. Hell, yes." His voice was strong enough that he didn't have to shout to make his point. "Henry gave me a key so I could keep an eye on the place, but I didn't bring it with me. And if I really thought something had happened to you, I'll be damned if I'd take the time to go back home for a key."

Rebecca set down the coffeepot with a thunk. "You have a key to my house?" Something in what he said lit a warm glow deep inside her, but she wasn't about to listen to that part of her right now.

"Yes, and the only time I've ever used it was the night I came in here and carried Henry to the hospital, so sick he didn't know where he was."

She ignored Cody's indignant frown and tipped her chin skyward in defiance of the glow that was getting warmer. "The whole time I've been living here, you've had a key?"

"I would have told you when you moved in, but Margaret said you wanted to be left alone. So I left you alone. I certainly didn't expect you to be this upset about it. Margaret thought maybe I should keep it, just in case."

"I don't think so. I'm perfectly capable of taking care of myself, and I don't need a stranger having access to my home any time he feels like it."

Cody stiffened, and his low voice was stern with rebuke. "I don't think I'm exactly a stranger, Rebecca. I've known you your whole life."

Fortified by the secrets she guarded and by her own hidden nightmare, Rebecca stared back at him, unbending. And though her heart was filled with regret, there was nothing she could say to defuse the situation. She had known J.D. her whole life, too, and she had risked everything on her belief that he would never hurt her.

"Sometimes a lifetime isn't long enough, Cody," she said quietly, knowing that he couldn't understand. She had hurt him without wanting to, and there was nothing she could do to make either one of them feel better.

"I'll bring you the key in the morning."

"Thank you. I would appreciate that." She held up his mug in an attempt at reconciliation. "Do you take milk in your coffee?"

His jaw was clenched tight, and his face was a mask that revealed nothing. "I don't think I'm very hungry anymore. My ride should be here soon. I think I'll wait outside for him."

Sick at heart, Rebecca watched him walk to the door. In the open doorway, he paused and her spirits lifted as he turned to face her.

"I left the pickup keys in the ignition in case you need it for anything," was all he said.

Rebecca nodded. "Thank you." He closed the door behind him, and she stood there, feeling like a worm. Cody didn't deserve the things she'd just said to him. He didn't deserve to suffer for the things J.D. had done, but trust was one of the things she had lost that day, and it was one of the many things she had begun to wonder if she would ever find again.

Sadness burned inside her chest, a wild, aching grief that never totally eased. Walking carefully to the table, Rebecca scraped all of the untouched eggs into one plate and piled all of the ham in the other. Her hands shook as she carried the plate with the ham to the kitchen, wrapped it in plastic wrap and returned it to the refrigerator.

Then she took her coffee to the table and began to eat the eggs, not bothering to taste them, just fueling her body for the onslaught of a new day. And try as she might to fight them, the memories came rushing toward her.

Jimmie Dale, the lovable, unreliable scamp who had brightened her summers and her life as a child. J.D. at fourteen, content to skate through life on charm and good looks. J.D. at eighteen, Rebecca's last summer before college, when his handsome face and easy laughter weren't enough to hide the troubled youth inside and Rebecca was secretly relieved she would be spending her next four summers somewhere else.

She wanted so badly to hate J.D., purely and without confusion or compassion. She wanted to remember only that in one act of drunken violence, he had rocked her life—stripping her of her peace of mind and her trust in men, and leaving her with a legacy of fear and anger. But she could never think of him without remembering that while J.D. may have taken her innocence, in its place, he had given her the miracle of Matthew. And for that, Rebecca could never be sorry.

Wiping away the tears that were never more than a memory away, Rebecca stood and cleared the table. On the way to the sink, she squared her shoulders and took a deep breath. There was a lot to be done before next Tuesday, and she was wasting precious time rehashing old sorrows.

When Cody came by after work to retrieve his pickup, she would try to find a way to apologize. Her problems weren't his fault, and she couldn't keep lashing out at him just because he was a man and his last name was Lockhart. He would only be around for a week. Then she would have her truck back, and there would be no reason to see him again.

Things could go back to the way they were. She would be alone, and Matthew would be safe. And no one would ever know.

Rebecca walked backward until she bumped into the railing of the loft, all the while studying the pieced work on the quilt frame that was tilted toward her. She had spent the morning working on fabric-covered baskets and ruffled pillows that were part of the inventory Ilene had requested for her shop. Quickly done and highly profitable, they were the sort of frilly accessory items that kept Rebecca's income flowing steadily and not totally dependent upon the larger, more time-consuming quilts, some of which took months to complete.

When Rebecca stopped for lunch, she took long enough to sketch out an idea for a wall hanging that had nagged at her throughout the morning, and in the early afternoon, she began the crib quilt she had promised Linda to have done in three weeks.

Late in the afternoon, the urge to work on the new wall hanging returned stronger than ever. Roughing the idea in on a sketch pad was a start, but nothing more. Seeing cut cloth arranged in a pattern of colors and shapes and basted onto a piece of backing four feet high and six feet wide was a real beginning, and with any luck, she could be finished in time to take the piece to Simon's gallery next Tuesday.

Lost in thought, with the air conditioner blasting away loudly downstairs, Rebecca almost missed the sound of a car driving away.

"Damn!" She had waited all day for a chance to apologize to Cody, and now he was driving off without saying a word.

Rebecca whirled around and rushed to the loft staircase that hugged the side wall of the cabin. Thinking that if she hurried she might still have a chance to stop him, she raced down the steep, rough-hewn stairs, dodging around the crib and across the living room to throw open the front door.

Momentum carried her out the door and onto the porch, where Cody stepped quickly away from the porch post he had been leaning against and caught her by the arms, pulling her to a halt. For a long moment they stood like that, facing each other. His hands grasped her just below the shoulders, while Rebecca gasped for breath, her chest rising and falling inches from his, and neither of them made a move to draw away.

Then, as if sense returned to both of them at once, Cody dropped his hands from her arms, and Rebecca took a small step backward. With no acknowledgment of their encounter on his face, he stared down at her. A stem of straw brown grass perched in the corner of his mouth twirled lazily with the unseen movement of his tongue.

"Is there something chasing you?" he asked.

Her gaze transfixed on Cody's lips and the stem's sensuous dance at the edge of his smile, Rebecca was dismayed to discover that she had enjoyed their brief contact much too much.

"I thought I heard a car." She lifted her hand in the direction of the settling dust on the road.

"My ride." Cody studied her as he slowly withdrew the grass from his mouth and tossed the stem away with a flip of his fingers.

"I thought you were leaving."

His eyes locked on hers, he nodded. "I was debating it."

"Without saying anything?"

"After this morning, I thought maybe you'd prefer it that way."

Rebecca caught her lower lip between her teeth and frowned. This was the moment she had waited for. This was the time for her big apology, but the words she had practiced all day suddenly vanished, leaving her mind blank and her tongue tied. She drew a deep breath and expelled it.

"I've been giving some thought to our disagreement this morning, and, well, is there something bothering you, Rebecca?" Cody asked softly.

Her head snapped up. "Wh-what?"

He looked down at her, lost in thought, taking the time to feel his way through the words. "You probably weren't old enough to realize what my life was like with Reever and Dora after my parents died."

"Yes, I was," Rebecca answered with old anger flaring inside her. "Dora was awful."

One side of Cody's face crinkled in a smile filled with more sadness than joy. "I guess you were paying more attention than I thought," he said quietly. "Anyway, your grandmother and grandfather, and Margaret, too, made a lot of difference to me back then. They got me through some very painful years. They made a difference in a way that Reever alone could never have done."

He sighed, lifted his hand and then dropped it to his side again. "What I'm trying to say is that I know what it means to have a friend when you really need one. If you have some kind of trouble, Rebecca, if you need a friend—"

Suddenly terrified, Rebecca took a step back, and Cody followed her, reaching out but not touching her.

"I just want you to think of me as someone *you* can turn to if you ever need a friend. I know how important that can be."

"What makes you think I might need a friend?" Her voice was breathless, ruining any chance she had of laughing off his suggestion.

His shrug was casual. He retreated to the porch post, giving her room. "Nothing specific. You could call it lawman's intuition if you want. The things you don't say. Your body language. They all tell me that you're afraid of something. I just wanted to make the offer, it's up to you if you want to take me up on it."

Casting about for some graceful way out of this, Rebecca shook her head and breathed out her tension in a long sigh. "You know, this really reminds me of the time Jessy took a psych course just for the fun of it."

Cody laughed suddenly and held up his hands in self-defense. "No, wait. I'll stop. Don't compare me to Jessy. Please."

The hard pounding of Rebecca's heart slowed, and she crossed her arms below her breasts in a gesture of nonchalance. "Well, I realize that she had only the best intentions, too, but I thought she was going to drive me nuts the way she analyzed every little twitch I made."

Cody cocked his head to the side and riveted her cinnamon brown eyes with his turquoise blue ones. "So, there's really nothing bothering you? There's nothing wrong?"

"Well, of course there's something wrong. There's always *something* wrong."

Rebecca pulled her gaze away from his and concentrated on the clusters of pink surprise lilies outlined against the white picket fence that was just for show across the front of the yard. The fence went nowhere, and separated nothing from nothing, but it was pretty, and her grandmother had felt that that was reason enough for being.

"I'm broke," she continued. "I blew up Granddad's truck. The weather's too hot, and the summer's too long. I've got a baby who depends on me for everything, and I'm not always sure I'm strong enough." She paused to blink back the threat of tears, then lifted her chin and turned her gaze back to Cody's with challenge in her eyes. "But that's life, isn't it? We do what we have to do, and we pray for the strength to make it work."

Cody looked at her in silence while he raked his fingers through the crisp brown waves of his hair. "Was that really so hard?" he said finally.

Inexplicably a laugh bubbled up from nowhere, startling Rebecca when it slipped out. She covered her mouth with her fingertips, but was too late to stop the laughter that had already escaped.

"Did I do that?" Cody asked, looking very pleased with himself.

"You must have. But I don't know how."

"Neither do I, but I think I like it."

Considerably more relaxed than she had been, Rebecca said, "Look, I owe you an apology from this morning. I overreacted. And if you could please forgive my bad manners, I'd like it if we could forget that it ever happened."

The warmth of a smile crept first into Cody's eyes, then stole across his face as he looked down at her. "That's a very nice apology, and a very good suggestion. I think that's what we'll do."

"If you'd like to stay for dinner, I have some ham already cooked."

"I think I'd like that very much. You know, I never got any breakfast this morning, and my lunch wasn't very big."

"Would you like to come inside?"

"Yes, indeed." He pushed away from the porch post he had retreated to and followed Rebecca into the cabin. Inside, he stopped and looked around. "Where's Matthew?"

"In the loft." She gave her head a toss in the loft's direction and continued on to the kitchen.

"Asleep?" Cody asked.

"He was awake and playing in his playpen when I came downstairs. I've got a salad chopped. You want some?" She pulled a plastic container from the refrigerator and held it up.

"Sounds good."

"What kind of dressing?"

"I'm not picky."

Rebecca put the salad on the counter and stared at him in exasperation. "Are you picky about anything?"

"Not if it's food." He grinned at her from the bottom of the staircase. "Do you mind if I go up?"

"Go right ahead." She waved her arm for him to proceed. "You seem to have made quite a hit with Matthew."

"The feeling's mutual. I felt a real bonding between the two of us yesterday. Right around the time he shared his meal with my uniform."

Rebecca answered with a burst of laughter that she managed to smother almost instantly. "I really am sorry about that," she said with sincerity.

"No problem," he answered from the top of the staircase. "I keep a spare in my locker. Well, hello there, fella." Cody's voice rose half an octave once he reached the loft. "What are you doing up here all by yourself?"

Turning back to the refrigerator with a broad smile on her face, Rebecca pulled out the plate of ham, a bowl of potato salad and another of freshly snapped green beans she had cooked at noon. That, along with a loaf of Margaret's homemade bread, should be enough to fill even a man the size of Cody.

"Mom, I think we've got a problem here," Cody said as he descended the stairs with Matthew in his arms.

Rebecca looked over her shoulder while she dumped the beans into a pan and turned on a low fire under them. "Diaper?"

Cody nodded.

"Wet?" she asked.

"Worse."

"Oh, my."

"That's what I said."

She left the kitchen and went to meet Cody at the foot of the staircase. "I do hope this uniform escaped unsullied."

"Clean as a whistle." He deposited Matthew in her arms. "But I *was* impressed to discover that you use cloth diapers."

"Well, to be totally honest, I'm glad it helps the ecology, but I really do it because it's cheaper and because the cabin came with a washer and dryer."

"Just an old-fashioned girl." He stood a safe distance from the changing table.

"Grandmother's influence, I guess."

"If Henry's looking down, I know he's smiling. He always said that of all his kids and grandkids, you were the one who belonged here."

Noting that the light tone of Cody's voice had turned serious, Rebecca paused in her diapering to look up. "Did he really?"

"Yeah." Cody's smile was gentle and teasing. "He said you were a throwback."

"A what?" she asked, laughing.

"A throwback. He said you were born a couple of generations too late, that you had the strength and simplicity of a pioneer woman. He was afraid there weren't any men around today who would really appreciate a woman like you.''

"He said all that?" She didn't know what to think.

"Pretty much."

"Well, I guess it's a compliment."

"He said you were your grandmother all over again."

"Okay," Rebecca said, trying to ignore the tears in her eyes as she wrestled Matthew back into his diaper, "it's a compliment."

"Definitely."

"Ouch!" She jerked her hand back and stuck her bleeding finger in her mouth, then just as quickly reached back down to keep Matthew from wiggling himself into the point of the diaper pin.

"Did you stick yourself?"

"Yes!" she snapped, finally getting the pin through the diaper and fastened. With the battle won, she gazed up at Cody with apologetic eyes. "I didn't mean to snap at you."

"I guess there *are* certain advantages to disposable diapers."

"That depends." She laughed at the memory of her oldest brother, Jack, trying to change a diaper on his first baby. "I once watched Jack pull the tabs off of three diapers before he finally gave up and taped one closed with electrical tape."

Cody smiled. "Jack and Jessy always reminded me a lot of each other."

"They did?" She could see the similarities. They were both the fun-loving, free-spirit types. Of course, Jack had settled down considerably since he had married Susan.

"Yeah. And I always thought you and Houston were a lot alike."

"Really?" She was flattered by the comparison. Houston had always been her hero, her knight in shining armor. She adored him.

"Of course, I could be wrong."

"Really?" Rebecca repeated for effect, grinning as she slipped the plastic pants on over the diaper. Then she handed Matthew back to Cody and hurried to turn off the green beans before they cooked dry.

Cody wandered along behind her and peered over her shoulder into the pan. All he said was, "Hmm."

"I thought you weren't picky." She turned her head to glare at him.

"I didn't say a word."

"Good."

He backed away, holding Matthew in front of him. "Anything I can do to help speed this feast along?"

"I just have to heat the ham in the microwave, and everything will be ready. You might see if Matthew will be content on his pallet while we eat."

"You think there's much of a chance?" he asked, turning toward the living room.

She put the ham into the microwave. "There'd be a better chance if you'd go get his cuddle rabbit out of the playpen. And a couple of his rattles."

"Will I recognize this cuddle-rabbit thing when I see it?"

She cut her eyes toward him and smiled with the memory of days when she had had no knowledge of cuddle-rabbit things. "I think so," she said softly. "It's green and has long ears."

Cody nodded and, armed with that knowledge, climbed the stairs to the loft with Matthew on his shoulder. Rebecca heated the platter of ham, put the beans and potato salad in china bowls that she would never have used if she had been alone and set the table.

"Cody?" She looked up and saw him standing at the railing of the loft with his back to her while he studied something that was hidden from view, deeper in the loft. Peeking over the back of Cody's shoulder was Matthew's tiny face, eyes closed and sleeping peacefully.

Cody twisted to look down at her. He held up her sketch pad in his right hand and used it to point toward the back of the loft. "That's this, isn't it?"

She frowned up at him, confused. Then she realized what he was talking about. The sketch on the pad was the design for the wall hanging, the same design she had begun to piece out on the quilt frame that he was apparently pointing to. "I'm surprised you could recognize it at this stage."

He held up the sketch pad again. "It's going to be a quilt?"

"A wall hanging, actually. About the size of a lap blanket."

"Are those the colors?" He waved the pad in the direction of the quilt frame again.

"The basic ones, I think. What you see up there is how I work out the color scheme and the composition before I begin the actual quilting."

"Do you do that for everything?"

Rebecca shook her head and rubbed the back of her neck. The muscles in her shoulders were beginning to tighten from tilting her head back to stare up at Cody. "Only for the original designs. The other quilts already have patterns. You know, since Matthew's asleep now, you might just bring him down and put him in his bed."

Cody moved away from the railing to put the sketch pad back on the worktable where he had found it. Then he descended the stairs, holding Matthew steady with both hands. "I didn't mean to pry. I hope you don't mind."

His tone held the offer of an apology and helped to soothe the nervous tension that was building in Rebecca. Her original designs were very private creations, and until they were finished, she never shared them with anyone. "Was I that obvious?"

"Not really. I just realized midway through my questioning that you might not have meant for anyone to see that." He laid Matthew gently in the bed and pulled a sheet over him, then tiptoed across the room to the dining table. "I really didn't mean to poke around up there. I just noticed the sketch, and I was impressed because I didn't know you were an artist. And then I saw the quilt you were beginning and realized it was the same as the sketch."

"And the rest is history. They really do train you people in observation and deduction, don't they?" No longer so sensitive to the invasion now that it was over, Rebecca sat at the table and waited for Cody to join her.

"Then again, some of us were just born nosy," he said, taking his place across from her. "Did you make this bread?"

"It's Margaret's. She says she's going to teach me some day, but I don't think I'll ever be able to match hers."

"Well, she taught Dora, and I assure you, Dora's bread can't hold a candle to Margaret's. But then it's always been my opinion that my dear aunt could turn honey sour if you left her alone with it long enough."

Rebecca flinched at the mention of Dora Lockhart, J.D.'s mother and Cody's aunt, and one of the most self-centered, self-righteous women it had ever been Rebecca's misfortune to know. Dora had spoiled J.D. rotten, and had treated Cody with heartless disdain when he was orphaned at ten and came to live with his Uncle Reever and family.

"Sorry," Cody said when he noticed Rebecca's long, distracted silence. "I didn't mean to bring the conversation to such an abrupt halt. You never did like Dora, did you?"

"No, I didn't." Whatever J.D. had become, Rebecca was certain that Dora's kind of poisonous, smothering love had had a lot to do with it.

"She never liked you much, either," he said thoughtfully, presenting the information as if it were a compliment. "Even when you were just a little girl, she was jealous of you. Plain, mean jealous, because J.D. thought you were the sun and the moon, and that just about killed her. You ever hear from him anymore?"

"Who?" Rebecca's heart lurched down into her stomach and then jerked back up to thump wildly against the inside of her rib cage. "J.D.?"

"Yeah. I just thought he might have gotten in touch with you. He's been gone for a while now."

"Why would he have gotten in touch with me?" She fought to keep the telltale breathless wheeze of panic from her voice.

Cody shrugged. "Just a feeling I had. He always thought so much of you."

"You and your feelings." In the brief instant that Cody looked away, Rebecca gave in to the shudder that crept up her back.

"You haven't heard from him, then?" He turned back, studying her as if he could read between the lines.

"No, I haven't," Rebecca said firmly and with feeling. "I'm sorry, Cody, but the only J.D. I ever cared about didn't make it out of high school. He got lost somewhere along the way. There's a stranger out there now, walking around in his body and using his name, but he's not anyone I know or want to know. I'm a grown woman now, with a little boy to take care of, and I just don't have the time to worry about the lost soul of J.D. Lockhart."

Cody sat back in his chair and gazed at her with an expression somewhere between amazement and amusement. "That's a damned fine speech. Mind if I use it sometime?"

Rebecca felt a smile struggling through the turbulence in her heart. "Well, leave out the part about being a grown woman and having a little boy. Other than that, you're welcome to it."

With a throaty chuckle, Cody passed her the platter of ham. "This is a very nice-looking dinner."

"Thank you."

"Aren't you just a little bit curious?" he asked quietly.

"About what?" She dished up a helping of potato salad and handed the bowl across the small table to Cody.

"About J.D. About what he's doing. Where he is. Don't you ever wonder?"

Sick at heart, Rebecca put down her fork and looked at Cody, knowing she was going to ask. Fear and nausea boiled in her throat at the possibility that J.D. had left Alaska and was on his way home. She didn't want to hear anything Cody had to say, but she had to know.

"Okay," she said in a near whisper. "Tell me."

Chapter Five

"**Y**ou really *don't* want to talk about him, do you?" Cody laid down his fork, as well, and rested his forearms on the edge of the table. "I know how you feel. That's pretty much how I came to feel about J.D. And you're right about the rest of it, too. He didn't turn out to be worth very much."

Rebecca sensed a sadness in Cody that closely matched her own, reminding her of how hard he had once tried to be a big brother to J.D. She remembered, too, the way J.D. had looked up to and resented Cody in almost equal measure.

"Do you ever hear from him?" Her initial revulsion was fading, and without it to cloud her instincts, she realized that Cody wasn't trying to find out what she knew. He was simply wanting to talk about something that bothered him.

He answered her question with a noise somewhere between a laugh and a grunt. "No way. Not me."

"So where is J.D. these days?" Again Rebecca's stomach clenched while she waited for his answer. Like someone

watching an accident, sickened by what she sees and unable
to look away, she leaned forward to hear.

"Alaska, working in the oil fields. I never thought he'd
stick it out, but he's been there about a year now. Of course,
for the first six months he really didn't have much choice."

"Didn't have a choice?" She had never been sure that the
story J.D. had told her was true. With J.D., the truth was
never very important if a better story could be improvised.

"Well, it just seemed like the older he got, the wilder he
got. He drank too much, fought too much. What he called
harmless pranks, the law called destruction of property. And
I don't know if it was coincidence or on purpose, but he always seemed to pull his worst stunts on my shift."

Cody speared a piece of ham with his fork and laughed.
"This is a bad subject to try to eat to, isn't it?"

"You really cared about him, didn't you?" She took a
drink of tea, hoping to wash the lump of regret from her
throat. She could tell that, like her, Cody still remembered
Jimmie Dale, the little imp who had been so easy to love.

"Oh, maybe, once upon a time, I still hoped we could all
be a family. But for too many years now, it's been J.D. and
Dora on one side and me on the other, with poor old Reever
caught in the middle." Cody paused to spread margarine on
a piece of Margaret's homemade bread. "It's even worse
now. Dora blames me totally for J.D. being sent away."

Rebecca took a bite of green beans and was pleased to
discover that she hadn't ruined them after all. As she listened to Cody's story, she tried to forget who they were
talking about. She didn't want to consider the probability
that what had happened in Eden had turned J.D. into a time
bomb waiting to explode and sent him straight to her.

"How was J.D. sent away, and why would Dora blame
you?" Rebecca asked when Cody didn't go on immediately.

"For the last couple of years, it had gotten almost embarrassing the way J.D. arranged his hell-raising so I'd have

to be the one to arrest him. It got so bad, I even considered moving away just to see if that would stop him.''

''Oh, no.'' Her first thought was of a selfish little boy who needed a good paddling to straighten him out, but she quickly remembered that J.D. was no little boy, and the twisted motives that drove him went far beyond mere self-ishness.

Cody nodded. ''I know. I realized that I wasn't the prob-lem, and if I left, it wouldn't solve a thing. Meanwhile, I think the judge had reached the same conclusion because the next time J.D. got hauled in, he got a choice of six months in jail or six months as far out of Concho County as he could get. So J.D. packed his bags and went off to make his fortune in Alaska, and Dora has tried to make my life hell ever since.''

''I'm really sorry,'' Rebecca said with feeling. ''I sup-pose you were the arresting officer that time, too.''

''You've got it.'' Cody took a second helping of ham. ''You know, I had expected to feel guilty when J.D. left, but instead, I've never been so glad to see somebody go in my life. I have been kind of worried about your reaction, though.''

''My reaction? To what?''

''Well, you and J.D. were so close. I was a little afraid that you might feel the same way Dora does when you found out why J.D. left town. I was worried that you might blame me.''

''Oh, Cody.'' Rebecca recoiled in genuine horror. ''Don't ever compare me to Dora.''

''Sorry,'' he said, laughing. ''I felt a lot better after your comment about the lost soul of J.D. Lockhart, but just to be sure, I wanted you to know the whole story.''

She smiled softly, touched that he had cared enough about her feelings to bare his soul. ''Are you telling me that this whole story was a confession for my benefit?''

''More or less.''

"Then, if I say I've heard all I want to hear about J.D., can we move on to something else?"

"Without a moment's hesitation." He lifted a forkful of green beans and chewed appreciatively. "These aren't bad." He sounded as surprised as Rebecca had been. "How about the wall hanging in the loft? What are you going to do with it when it's finished?"

His question elicited a shy burst of pride in Rebecca and chased away the tangle of bad feelings that had hung over her since J.D.'s name entered their conversation. "It's going to an art gallery in San Angelo."

"An art gallery?" Cody's brows lifted in surprise. "Really?" He put down his fork and leaned forward, waiting with impressed interest for her to continue.

"Really. There's a gallery there that takes some of the original picture appliqués that I do. The idea for this one came from Grandmother's walled garden, and from stories I've heard of roses found still blooming in the gardens of ruined castles. They're such delicate flowers to have such endurance."

Cody's hand reached easily across the table to cover hers. "Like someone else I could mention." His fingertips lightly stroked the back of her hand.

Wide-eyed, heart pounding, Rebecca looked into the deep blue-green of his eyes and froze. Her mouth opened and closed while she tried to form words, but coherent thought was beyond her.

"Rebecca?" Cody's hand tightened on hers. "That was supposed to be a compliment."

Heat radiated through her in waves, heat from embarrassment, from confusion, from pleasure, and she wasn't prepared to feel any of it. She needed more time. There was still too much bottled up inside of her. But with Cody, whether she wanted to be or not, Rebecca found herself remembering more and more what it was like to be a woman responding to the presence of a man.

When she could think clearly again, she tactfully withdrew her hand from his and said, "Thank you. That was very nice of you. I guess I've just forgotten how to take a compliment."

"Then let me try again. The ham is excellent." He held up a piece, speared at the end of a fork, and placed it in his mouth with relish.

The pendulum of her emotions still swinging wildly, Rebecca answered him with a laugh. "Well, you cooked it. It's what we didn't eat at breakfast."

Cody paused in his chewing to form the word *oh* with his mouth. Swallowing the ham, he raked in a forkful of potato salad, chewed diligently and washed it down with tea.

"Now, this is great potato salad," he said, scooping up another forkful. "You did make this, didn't you?"

"Yes." She laughed again. "I did, and thank you very much."

He smiled at her and set her emotions to swinging again. "You're quite welcome." Then he unexpectedly turned his head toward the crib and pointed with his fork. "Uh-oh. We're busted."

When Rebecca looked, she saw Matthew's fists gripping the bars of the baby bed, tugging. Her mind leapt ahead to the coming months when he would be sitting and then crawling and then walking, with his busy hands grasping for anything within reach. "Oh, dear. I'd better go get him." She laid her napkin on the table and pushed back her chair.

"So that's how young mothers stay so slim," Cody said as she hurried to the crib. "You never get to finish a meal."

"I'm thinking of writing a dieter's handbook." She lifted Matthew out, holding him up while she cooed to him and he cooed back. She cradled him in her hands and zoomed him over the couch, then came back for a second, slower pass to scoop up a chew toy and a noisemaker before she brought him in for a landing on the pallet. Rolling Matthew onto his stomach, she put a toy within reach of each hand and slowly backed away.

"Very slick," Cody said as Rebecca took her place at the table.

A short distance away, Matthew cheerfully gummed one edge of the colorful, chewable cloth block while he inched his way toward the plastic clacker.

"He'll be happy for a little while before he realizes that he's hungry or wet or bored. He's still pretty amazed by the fact he's getting some mobility." She smiled as she turned back to her plate and took another bite of ham.

"You're pretty happy here, aren't you?"

She looked around the room at the four walls that contained her world, her home, her baby, her livelihood, and she liked what she saw. The cabin was compact and cozy. It made her feel comfortable and protected. And just outside the door was a porch with a swing for contemplating, a walled rose garden for strolling and a lot of wide-open space between her and the rest of the world. One road in and one road out. She might as well be at the end of the earth, and that was the way she liked it.

"Yes," she said finally, "I do. I like it a lot. I can sleep at night here."

"Where were you living before? Dallas?"

"Austin. And I stayed with Houston and his wife in Savannah for a while."

"What's her name? Houston asked me to be his best man, but I couldn't get away, and now I can't even remember his wife's name." Cody tore a piece of bread in half and put the other half back in the bread basket. "Laura? Is that it?"

Finishing the last bite of potato salad on her plate, Rebecca nodded. "I hope you get to meet her someday. She's pretty terrific. In fact, if I ever want to go back, Laura has a job waiting for me in her shop."

Cody's brow crinkled in a frown. "Do you think you might go back?"

"No. They were wonderful to me, but it felt too much like charity. After I had Matthew, I needed to be on my own. At least for a while."

"Then you may not be here for good?" His frown grew. "Where would you go? Back to Austin?"

"It would be as good as any," she said with a shrug. "Jessy still lives there, and I could always go back to teaching school. But until Matthew's older, I want to be home with him, and this is where I can do that."

With a satisfied smile, Cody pushed away his empty plate and shoved his chair back from the table. Sliding lower in the seat, he stretched out his long legs. "What do you usually do in the evenings here?"

"Work."

"At what?"

"My quilting. If the evening's not too hot, I'll sit on the porch with Matthew and do hand-stitching until it gets dark. If not, I work inside."

"And then what?"

"We go to bed. Matthew's an early riser."

Not satisfied, Cody shook his head. "What do you do for fun?" he explained.

"Fun?"

"You know, entertainment. Movies. Dinner. Miniature golf. Bowling. How long has it been since you've been on a picnic?"

"I don't know." Rebecca thought back, and the only picture that came to mind was from childhood. "Years, maybe? Why?" She had gotten too relaxed. Now a feeling of unease began to creep back in.

"How about Saturday? We could take a picnic lunch down to the Concho River."

"What?" She sat straighter in her chair, trapped behind the table.

"You and me. Fun and food. We could bring our suits and go swimming. Maybe we'd get lucky and find one of those Concho River pearls. Have you ever seen one of those?''

"No."

"You haven't? They're freshwater pearls from mussels, and they come in shades of pink and lavender, and some are almost purple."

"No," Rebecca said again, more strongly, and pushed her chair away from the table. "I've seen those. I meant, no, I don't want to go. I have too much to do."

Not taking her noes for an answer, Cody leaned across the table and pinned her with his blue dagger eyes. "It would do you some good to get out, Rebecca. You can't work all the time. It's not healthy."

"I know that, and I really appreciate your asking, but I just can't spare the time right now. Not with truck repairs to pay for and all the orders I have to fill. And a wall hanging I want to have done by next Tuesday."

"Okay." He held up his hands in surrender. "I give up for now." He pushed his chair back farther and rose to his feet. Looking down at Rebecca from his considerable height, he said, "But I'll be back. I'm going to ask you again, and I'm going to keep on asking you until you say yes."

Rebecca returned his gaze from beneath sheltering lashes and answered quietly, "Maybe someday I will."

"Good enough." Cody nodded his approval. "I'm going in early tomorrow, so I'll just leave my pickup in the same place with the keys in it. I'll let you know when I come to pick it up tomorrow night."

"I'll see you tomorrow, then." Resisting the urge to walk with him to the door, she remained where she was and watched him leave.

In the doorway, Cody paused to look back at her one more time. "Good night, Becky Sue," he said softly and, without waiting for a reply, closed the door behind him.

Rebecca sat without moving, her eyes tightly shut against the sudden sting of tears at hearing the pet name her grandfather had given her for when no one else was around. She could still remember the day Cody had first affectionately called her Becky Sue.

She had been a bashful thirteen and proud to be working side by side with her grandfather and Cody to bring down a tree split by lightning. At the end of the long day, a mature, nineteen-year-old Cody—shirtless and with streaks of dirt adding a rugged look to his bronzed, sweat-glistening skin—had smiled down at her as he scruffed her pigtailed hair, congratulated her on a good day's work and called her Becky Sue.

Her heart had danced a jig in her chest, her knees had turned to water and she was never, in all the years to come, more in love than she was at that moment.

Now, with one soulful gaze from his turquoise eyes and one whispered endearment from long ago, Cody had opened doors long closed and sent her spiraling back into emotions long forgotten. Tired of fighting her own needs and frightened by vulnerabilities she never realized she had, Rebecca slumped over the table, laid her head on her arm and let her tears flow with an indulgence she seldom allowed herself.

When Matthew's sympathetic cries eventually joined hers, Rebecca pulled herself together, wiped her tear-stained cheeks with a table napkin and went back to the business of being a mother and wage earner.

She still didn't know what she was going to do about Cody and the chaotic effect his mere presence was having on her simple life-style. In another week her truck would be fixed, and he wouldn't need to be around every day. But she wasn't sure the solution was going to be that simple, not anymore. She wasn't even sure she wanted it to be. After tonight, she wasn't nearly so sure about anything.

Rebecca stood at the entrance of the garden and looked around the oasis of green in a land of sun-scorched beige.

Heat sizzled in the air, undaunted by a slow southern breeze and the gradual setting of the sun.

Curling, dark chocolate wisps escaped the combs that held her hair high on her head. Tendrils blew across her eyes. Strands drifted down onto her neck and pasted themselves to her sweat-moistened skin. Rebecca lifted her head and breathed deeply of the perfumed air, letting the light and the heat and the quiet peace of her surroundings seek out the cold, dark corners of her soul and ease the pain that was always with her.

Here, unthreatened and unwatched, she was herself, as she had always been, and she was happy. Here, alone, she didn't have to endure the speculation in the eyes of others, the unspoken questions, the curiosity, the disappointment, the polite avoidance of the obvious. Here, Matthew was her child, pure and simple, without labels.

"Stop feeling sorry for yourself, Rebecca," she said sternly. "You shouldn't care what other people think. You know who you are, and that's all that matters."

Squaring her shoulders, she advanced into the garden and followed the gravel path to a gray stone bench against the east wall. Behind the bench was a row of climbing roses that only bloomed in the spring. The same month Matthew was born in Savannah, the walled garden would have been at its peak. By waiting until he was old enough to travel in June, she had missed the roses' true glory by a month. In the autumn, a few of the bushes would bloom heavily again, but in the hottest months of the summer, only a few scattered roses graced the garden.

To Rebecca, they were all the more precious for their rarity, and it was this quality that she wanted to recreate in the wall hanging. Since Matthew was sound asleep and she could have some time to herself, she was going to sharpen her artistic skills. Taking a seat on the bench, she pulled her sketch pad and colored pencils from a canvas tote bag and turned to study the wall at the back.

Fieldstones, from cat's-eye yellow to rusty amber, formed the ten-foot-high north wall where rambler roses, climbers and tender noisettes scrambled for supremacy. It was the single blooms of two intertwined noisettes, one a delicate, drooping yellow, the other a deep, full-petaled violet, that caught Rebecca's eyes.

Working quickly, she sketched in the colors. Irregular patches of sulphur, bronze and nutmeg outlined with mottled gray mortar for the wall. Leaves of forest and apple green with new growth of wine red. An old, gray stone bench at the base of the wall, and two roses close together, two-thirds of the way up the wall, one pure yellow, the other a lush violet.

Head bent, concentrating, Rebecca heard the sounds of a car arriving, a car door slamming and the crunching of gravel as the car drove away again, but she ignored the sounds as she worked on the contrasting colors of the flowers. Alternately studying the wall at the back of the garden and the sketch pad on her lap, she added a golden highlight here and lavender shadow there, until the focal points of the picture were perfect.

Only then did she straighten her stiff back, stretch her cramped neck and turn her head toward the front of the house. And when she did, the vision awaiting her brought an instant hoot of laughter.

Casually leaning against the corner of the house was a blue-jean-and-T-shirt-clad Cody. Propped upright in the crook of his arm was Matthew, wearing an orange-and-teal playsuit that Rebecca had never seen before. On his head was a matching striped cap and below that he wore a tiny pair of neon orange sunglasses with the aplomb of a baby who was born for stardom.

"What have you done?" Rebecca set her sketch pad aside and stood, still laughing.

"Well, Matthew thought that his wardrobe could stand a little livening up. So I told him I'd see what I could do. He's pretty pleased with it. What do you think?"

"Those aren't real, are they?"

"Sure are. UV protection and everything. They're very practical for Texas summers. Every three-month-old should have at least one pair."

At a loss for words, Rebecca just shook her head. She had to admit that Matthew looked as cute as the dickens, and sunglasses weren't really a bad idea, even for a baby. But she couldn't seem to conquer her urge to laugh every time she looked at him.

"He's going to pull them off and try to eat them any minute now," she said, still skeptical as she arrived to stand in front of Cody and her newly hip son.

"That's okay. I bought him an extra pair."

"You're kidding!"

"In a pink so hot you'll break out in a sweat just looking at it. And wait'll you see the outfit that goes with *that* pair of sunglasses."

"You're serious." Uncertain of how to react to Cody's largesse, she stared at him as if he had just confessed to a felony.

"Rebecca," Cody said softly, "it's not going to hurt anything. He's too young to be spoiled, and it's been a long time since I've had a kid to do things for."

Rebecca shook her head and shrugged her shoulders. "No harm, no foul, I guess," she said, giving up on a fight that wasn't worth the effort it would take to win. "But this is it. No more. I'm already in your debt more than I want to be."

"What about the ball glove I put in layaway?"

"Cody!"

"Just kidding. Have you eaten yet?"

More than a little dazed and confused by the ups, downs and arounds their conversation had already taken, she hated to admit that she had been waiting for him before starting supper. "No. I had thought about grilling some hamburgers, but I wasn't sure how many to put on."

Cody's instant smile was brilliant to behold. "You were waiting for me."

"Call it intuition," she said, hoping to shrug it off. "I had a feeling you'd be by around dinnertime, and I thought you might be hungry. By the way, where's your uniform?"

"I changed before I left the station. But I'm not letting you switch subjects that easily." He shook his head, still smiling. "I think you were waiting for me, and I don't think you were going to eat until I got here."

Caught in the act, Rebecca made a halfhearted attempt to return his smile, partially because he seemed so pleased with the thought and partially because there was nothing else for her to do. But her smile hid a bitter sadness at the knowledge that Cody was right, and it was useless for her to deny it.

In a few days time he had become so important that she was waiting for his arrival in the evenings and postponing meals until she could share them with him. She was even dressing for him. The yellow, oversize T-top and the floral-print leggings that she wore under it were gifts from Jessy that had gone untouched until today.

Instead of the simple ponytail she usually wore when she was working, her hair was an artful tumble of curls held by combs, and for the first time since Houston's spring wedding, she was wearing mascara and lip gloss. But the simple act of wanting to look good for a man, something that should have been so simple and so right, left her feeling as sullied as if she were selling herself on a street corner.

Turning before Cody could see the tears that burned behind her eyes, Rebecca walked back into the garden, heading blindly for the bench where her pad and colored pencils were. When she reached the bench, she sat with her shoulders twisted away from the cabin where Cody still stood, holding Matthew. Blinking away the tears, she cursed her own stupid vanity as she gathered up the pencils and replaced them in their box.

She should never have accepted the loan of his truck. She should never have let him hang around. She should have realized that anyone who looked as good as Cody did was going to become a temptation, especially someone who had been the single most serious heartthrob of her life. She should have known. She should have stopped it before it got this far.

Unconsciously smearing her tears with the back of her hand, she reached for her tote bag and stuffed the sketch pad and pencils inside. Cody was a nice guy, and he didn't deserve to be drawn into problems that had no solution. The best thing she could do for him was to send him on his way, truck and all, and never see him again if she could help it. Just because her life was ruined, there was no reason to ruin anyone else's.

"Rebecca."

"Ahh!" Startled, Rebecca cried out and nearly dropped the box of pencils when she jerked violently in reaction.

Cody went down onto one knee in front of her, taking her hand in his. "I'm sorry. I didn't mean to scare you."

Rebecca pulled her hand away and held it to her pounding heart while she caught her breath. The man was like a ghost the way he kept appearing without warning.

Ignoring her agitation, Cody stroked his thumb across her cheek, smoothing away the glistening tracks of her tears. "Are you still going to tell me there's nothing wrong?"

She looked squarely at him, and for the first time noticed that his arms were empty. "Where's Matthew?" Irrational panic entered the swirling melee of her emotions, and she surged to her feet, intent on pushing past Cody and going in search of her child.

"I put him in his playpen," Cody said, taking her by the arms and forcing her back onto the bench. "I took off the sunglasses, but left the cap. He won't hurt himself if he wants to chew on it.''

"But..." She tried to stand again.

"Matthew's fine. You're not." Cody held her with one arm while he swept the canvas tote onto the ground and took its place on the bench beside her. "Come on, Rebecca, talk to me. I'm worried about you. Margaret's worried about you. You can deny it until you're blue in the face, but something's wrong."

"I told you what's wrong."

"You gave me some cock-and-bull story about your finances, and I was polite enough to let it drop for the moment, but good grief, Rebecca, give me a break."

"What I told you was the truth."

He shook his head. "Part of the truth. But not all of the truth, and not the most important part."

Instantly cold, Rebecca turned to face him with her jaw set and her eyes flashing icy determination. "Let go of me."

"I hit a nerve, didn't I?"

Ice melting in a flash fire of anger, she jerked her arm from his grasp. "I said, let go of me." She didn't wait for his reaction before she bounded to her feet and started from the garden.

Cody caught up with her in an instant. His strong hands closed around her upper arms, and he pulled her back against his chest, ignoring her struggle to be free. "Stand still and listen to me, damn it."

She couldn't get away and she knew it. He was far too strong. But, strangely, she wasn't afraid of him, either. His grasp and his words were gentle in spite of his serious intent. He made her want to turn to him. He made her want to trust. If only she could forget the horror that clouded her mind every time she tried to reach out.

"Please, let go," she whispered, giving up the fight. "Please."

"Can we talk—without fighting?"

Dropping her head back against the hard muscles of Cody's chest, she sighed with futility. "You want what I can't give." Even if she wanted to, she couldn't allow herself to forget that he was J.D.'s cousin, J.D.'s blood. The only family Cody had left was J.D.'s family.

As much as Cody might claim to dislike Dora, she was the closest thing to a mother that he had. And J.D.'s father, Reever, was a good man who truly loved Cody like a son. Whatever Dora's shortcomings had been, no one could fault Reever in the role of father to his brother's son, and no one could question the devotion that still existed between Reever and Cody.

Even if she was tempted, in a moment of weakness or insanity, to unburden her troubled soul to Cody, she could never allow herself to come between him and his family, and that was exactly what the truth would do.

"You're a stubborn woman, Rebecca Carder," Cody said as he released her and stepped back. "You win."

Standing alone, with the hollowness of empty victory ringing through her, Rebecca missed the solid mass of Cody's body against her back. Without his strong hands around her shoulders, her arms hung limp and useless at her sides. She didn't know how to go back to the way things were before, back to when she didn't care.

"You forgot your things," Cody said quietly, and pressed the canvas bag he had retrieved into her hands. More softly still, he whispered, "Wait." Moving to the side of her, he touched her arm lightly as he blocked her way with the edge of his body.

Rebecca lifted her face to him, wondering in silence if he had felt the lack of her as keenly as she had felt the absence of him. She waited for him to speak while she asked herself what she would do if he kissed her. She wondered so strongly how his lips would feel on hers that she could scarcely think of anything else.

Cody's intense gaze moved from her eyes to her lips and back, again and again, restlessly seeking an answer words couldn't give him. With his body still as a statue, his lips parted, and Rebecca held her breath, waiting.

For an instant, he moved toward her. Then he stopped, closed his eyes and drew in a deep, ragged breath. When he opened his eyes again, the moment was gone.

"I don't want you to be angry with me," he said.

Caught in a vacuum between relief and disappointment, Rebecca shook her head in automatic reaction. "I'm not." She wasn't sure he could ever do anything again that would make her angry with him.

The smile he gave her was slightly off center and a little sad. "Are you still going to feed me?"

"Sure." She was coming out of the trance she had been in. The tension in her chest released, and reality sharpened the edges of the day. "You start the fire, and I'll make the hamburger patties."

"Rebecca, I..."

She waited, eager to return to where they had been only a moment earlier, but he didn't go on. "Yes?"

He shook his head. "Nothing. Let's go in."

Chapter Six

Darkness edged nearer while a silent wind blew from the northwest, pushing aside the hot, still layer of air that blanketed the earth. For a few brief moments, the heat of the day was almost a comfort.

Filled with a rare sense of well-being, Rebecca sighed and stretched. "I'm stuffed," she said, resting her head on the back of the glider where she and Cody sat.

"Likewise," Cody agreed from a comfortably slumped position at the other end of the glider. He ran a massaging hand over his flat stomach. "Why is it the simplest meals always seem to be the best?"

"I don't know, but it's true, isn't it? Maybe they bring back childhood memories."

Cody slumped lower, tilting his head back to rest on the glider the way Rebecca's was. "That could be it," he said solemnly. "I can remember a time when hamburgers, fries and Kool-Aid flavored drink was a feast."

Rebecca stared at the ceiling of the screened porch where they sat. Rough beams extended from the back of the cabin, supporting a corrugated tin roof over the porch. "Boy, kids are cheap dates, aren't they?" She cut her eyes to the side, regarding Cody with a teasing half smile. "What happens to us when we grow up?"

He rolled his head to the side and matched her light-hearted tone. "I think I'm still a fairly cheap date."

She chuckled, remembering that she had just fed him hamburgers, salad and tea, with canned peaches for dessert. "Well, yes, actually you are. And I appreciate it."

He ducked his head modestly. "Any little thing I can do, ma'am."

Rebecca looked at him, laughing easily, and was struck anew that while it seemed she had known him forever, this Cody was a very different man from the boy she had known. So great were the changes that if it weren't for the unusual color of his eyes, she would never have recognized him.

She had refused to answer his questions about her, and yet she longed to ask him the same questions. Something more than time alone had changed him, and though it went against every self-protective instinct she had, Rebecca wanted to know what had happened to Cody in the almost ten years he had been away.

"Are you aware that you're staring?" He asked the question softly as he returned her steady gaze with his head still resting on the back of the glider.

"I'm sorry." Rebecca blinked and shifted into a less reclining position.

"What were you thinking?" He followed her with his eyes, but didn't move.

She hesitated, listening to the quiet voice inside her that warned her not to ask. "Nothing, really. Just how different we both are from when we were younger."

Cody grinned and shook his head. "You're not that different. You've grown up. And done a very good job of it.

But you were always quiet and sweet and sort of innocent. And you were always the perfect little mother, looking out for anybody who seemed to need it, especially J.D. and Jessy. All I have to do is close my eyes, and you're in pigtails again.''

A little shaken by his assessment of her, Rebecca drew back ever so slightly. ''Really?'' she asked in a voice that made it more of a challenge than a question.

''Really. Does that upset you? It shouldn't. You were a pretty terrific little girl, and I'd say that as a woman, you've lived up to your full potential. That's something not many of us have been able to do.''

Once again she saw the sorrow in him that seemed to go much deeper than the sadness he had carried inside as a youth, and once again she sensed closely guarded secrets and a burden of disappointment that was at times hard for him to bear.

''Cody,'' she said before she could stop to think, ''you're not the only one who notices things.''

A frown slowly drew his dark brows low over his eyes. ''What do you mean?''

Rebecca took a deep breath and plunged ahead. ''The sheriff's deputy who stopped to help me the other day is light years away from the twenty-year-old boy I last saw leaving here for his sophomore year of college.''

Cody lifted his head from the back of the glider and sat straighter, no longer looking at her. ''What did you hear?''

''Nothing.''

''Nothing?'' He glanced at her. ''Nobody ever said anything? Not even Henry?''

She shook her head. ''No. That next summer, when you didn't come back, I was too timid to ask anyone about you, except for J.D., and he wouldn't tell me anything.''

''Really? You asked about me?'' He sounded genuinely pleased and more than a little surprised. ''I thought you barely knew I was alive.''

Emboldened by the gathering darkness, Rebecca answered honestly. "Not exactly," she said softly. "I think it was more the other way around."

"You were a little girl."

"I was fourteen the last time I saw you, Cody. I was fifteen the first summer you didn't come home."

"That's..." He stopped and was silent for a moment. When he spoke again, his words were quiet. "I guess that's not really so young anymore. At least, it doesn't seem young when you're fifteen, does it?"

"No," she said with a sigh, remembering the frustration of those long-ago days. "Not at the time, it doesn't. You're old enough to dream but not old enough to do anything about it."

"Not that it means anything now, but it's possible that J.D. didn't know where I was. It'd be just like Dora not to tell him."

Rebecca practically had to bite her tongue to keep from asking what Dora hadn't told, but she could sense the discomfort building inside Cody. Whatever had happened, he obviously wasn't accustomed to talking about it. She knew how he felt.

Sympathetic ripples of disquiet crawled through her, leaving her shoulders knotted tight with tension and her stomach queasy with dread. Unable to take the waiting any longer, she sprang to her feet. "I have a pitcher of lemonade in the refrigerator," she said, starting toward the back door. "Do you want some?"

"Sounds good," Cody agreed quickly. "Do you need any help?"

She held up her hand to keep him where he was. "That's okay. I can get it. I need to check on Matthew anyway."

With that, she slipped through the doorway and disappeared into the cabin, leaving Cody alone on the porch. He took a deep breath, laced his fingers together and stretched his arms in front of him until he could feel the pull across the back of his shoulders.

"Damn." Pushing himself up from the glider, he paced to the end of the porch and back, skirting the furniture that had seemed so heavy and solid when he had sat on this same porch during an evening with Henry.

The once-dark wood was now painted pale blue, and brightly flowered cushions softened both the look and feel of the glider. In the matching chairs, the pillowy cushions were ruffled, turning the cabin that had once been a primitive, manly retreat into something cozy, comfortable and feminine, much like Rebecca herself.

At the end of the porch, Cody stopped his pacing and, with the glider to his back, faced the western sky. One bold slash of hot pink remained among the mauve and lavender streaks that melted into the horizon. There had been a time when he wouldn't have noticed.

Not so long ago, his life had consisted of daylight and darkness, without the subtleties of dawn and dusk to separate them. He had lived with no past and no future. He had worked hard all day and gone to bed exhausted at night. And he had pretended not to notice the huge, empty hole inside of him, the hole that had been there since the day his parents had died and left him alone and frightened and too young to protect himself.

Staring at the sunset but no longer seeing it, Cody ran his hand over the porch post that had been there years before the screen was added. He found it strange to think that after years of holding his feelings inside, he wanted to tell Rebecca everything. Since the day he had found her stranded at the side of the road, he had wanted to bare his soul to the touch of her tender hands.

With her chocolate hair and her cinnamon eyes, she had gone straight to his heart and filled the hole inside him that had been empty for such a long, long time. When he watched her with Matthew, Cody ached with the longing to be a part of such love. When he saw the pain inside her that Rebecca couldn't hide, he wanted to hold her until the demons that haunted her were gone for good. He wanted to share himself with her, his secrets, his hopes, his sorrow. He wanted to be a part of her life, and he was afraid she would never let him be.

"Help," Rebecca said, pushing the screen door open with a tray that contained two ice-filled glasses and a pitcher of lemonade. "I'll give you your choice. Catch the screen so it doesn't slam, or take the tray and put it on the coffee table."

Holding the screen open with her shoulder, she waited while Cody came around the glider and took the tray from her. With her hands free, she closed the screen door and turned on a small lamp on a table against the cabin wall. The lamp cast a soft glow that allowed them to see each other without destroying the intimacy that was a special gift of twilight.

"Did I take too long?" Rebecca turned to him with a smile, and hoped she would find him more relaxed than she had left him. She knew she wasn't being fair, asking him to confide in her when she had refused to do the same. If he had decided not to say anything more, she wouldn't ask again.

Cody returned her encouraging smile with a gentle one of his own and shook his head. "No. I had studied the landscape about as long as I wanted to."

Rebecca laughed and came around the coffee table to take her place beside him again on the glider. She was relieved to see that he was calmer and much less like the caged tiger she had left a few minutes earlier. Her feelings of guilt began to ease.

"How was Matthew?" Cody asked. He lifted the glasses of lemonade he had poured and handed Rebecca's to her.

"Sleeping like a baby." She smiled at Cody over the top of her glass, then lifted it in a salute, and together they took a long drink.

"So where were we?" he asked after the refreshing and time-consuming pause.

"I believe you were about to spill your guts," she said. "Reluctantly."

"Oh, yes." He set his glass down and leaned forward, elbows on knees, fingers laced together in front of him, brows knitted in concentration. "Not so much reluctantly as awkwardly. Confessions are not usually very comfortable."

Rebecca stared at her glass, giving him privacy. "Cody," she said quietly, "you really don't have to tell me anything, if you don't want to." She wanted to tell him that she understood, that she had secrets of her own that she couldn't, or wouldn't, talk about, but he already knew that.

He shook his head. "It's really not that big a deal. You already know I went to Houston on a football scholarship. That paid for college, but I still had to work summers to earn money for clothes and anything extra I needed. Reever couldn't help out, and Dora wouldn't have let him if he could have. I'd never been on my own before, and at the end of my sophomore year I met a girl."

Rebecca was shocked by the sudden acid burn of jealousy inside her. She would have been fifteen at the time, too young to get serious about anybody. Certainly too young to interest a twenty-one-year-old.

"She was from New Orleans, and she talked me into getting a job there for the summer. Within a month, we were living together," Cody said with a heavy sigh. "And by the time I should have been leaving to go back to school, she was pregnant."

In spite of her best intentions to control her reactions, Rebecca gasped. "I'm sorry," she said quietly. "I shouldn't have done that."

"It's okay. That was pretty much my reaction, too."

"Did you love her?" She held her breath, waiting for his answer.

He shook his head no. "I tried. For a while, I really tried. She was barely nineteen, and she didn't want an abortion."

"And so?" She had expected to feel relieved that he hadn't loved the girl, but instead she felt sorrow. Now she held her breath again, waiting for another answer and knowing that for the Cody she had once worshiped from afar, there would have only been one answer.

"We got married, and I never went back to college. Eventually I got a job on the docks. It was hard work, but the money was steady, and we had a lot of bills to pay off. Brenda didn't have any hospitalization. She hadn't thought of that when she decided to get pregnant."

"You mean she did it on purpose?"

"Yep. She didn't like college, and she didn't like living at home, so she decided to try marriage. I guess I looked like a good candidate. Of course, she didn't tell me any of this until a couple of years later, when she decided she didn't like me anymore, either."

The bitter, hollow sound of Cody's voice said more than his words ever could about the lasting effect of those few years. Rebecca wanted to reach out to him, just to remind him that he wasn't alone, that every woman wasn't as blindly selfish as his young bride had been.

"And the baby?" Rebecca almost whispered.

"A little girl. She was two and a half the last time I saw her. Brenda and I had fought the night before. She was running up bills we didn't have the money to pay. I told her she had to stop or she was going to bankrupt us. She told me what a disappointment I was and what a mistake she had made in getting pregnant so I'd marry her."

With a sad half smile, Cody shook his head. "She said things that made Dora sound like a saint, and I just stood there. I couldn't believe what I was hearing. I gave up my future for that little witch. I married her, knowing I didn't love her. I worked like a slave to make a good home for her and our baby, and I was a disappointment to her."

He shook his head again, reliving his disbelief, while Rebecca cringed inside, imagining the horror he must have felt at that moment. Rape had many forms, and she wasn't sure that she wouldn't choose her own, if given the choice, to the one Cody had endured.

"I slept on the couch that night, and the next morning it was like the night before had never happened. Brenda fixed breakfast and I played with the baby, kissed them both goodbye and went off to work. When I got home that night, the house was stripped bare. My clothes were still hanging in the closet, but everything else was gone. My wife, my daughter, the furniture, the pots and pans, right down to the dishes. Brenda didn't even leave a note, just a pile of debts it took me three years to pay off, and I never saw my little girl again. They're out there somewhere, but I don't know where. I'm just thankful that Brenda was at least a good mother, even if she wasn't a good wife. I just pray that she's taking care of—"

Cody's voice dissolved into choked half words and then faded to silence as he turned his face toward the cabin wall and away from Rebecca. His shoulders quivered with the effort it took for him not to cry. Never had Rebecca longed to hold her own baby more. Her arms ached with the need to embrace Cody while her heart offered up prayers of gratitude that she still had her own child to hold. Cody had nothing but memories, memories she had encouraged him to relive.

Remorse, compassion and shared pain gave Rebecca the strength to stand and walk to where Cody sat isolated in his own private hell. Without stopping to wonder whether she was right or wrong, wise or foolish, Rebecca reached her arms around his broad shoulders and cradled his head against her bosom as she brushed her cheek over the soft waves of his hair.

"I'm so sorry," she whispered. "I shouldn't have asked. I never would have caused you such pain if I had known. You've been through so much. I wish there was something I could do to apologize for all womankind. I'm so sorry."

"Oh, God, Rebecca." Cody's hands tightened around her waist, clinging to her, while he buried his face in the deep valley between her breasts.

His whole body shook against her, and she only held him tighter. Her hands moved over the muscles of his back as she marveled at the awesome strength that held her so gently and yet so fiercely. Rebecca tried to imagine a woman so foolish that she could have had Cody for a lifetime and yet tossed him away.

"Cody," she whispered as her lips brushed his hair and a fire of longing swept through her. How different both their lives might have been if six short years hadn't separated them.

"Rebecca." His answering breath was hot against the skin of her breasts.

Her lips ached to touch his. After so many years of empty dreams, she was in his arms. After so many nights of imagining how his mouth would feel against hers, his kiss was only inches away. The drumbeat of her heart was like a primal rhythm, driving out her objections and leaving only the blind seduction of passion, wild, dark and untamed.

When Cody lifted his head from her breasts and stared into her eyes, she saw the same passion reflected in his gaze and she was lost.

"Rebecca," he whispered again. His arms gathered her closer still, guiding her into the open V of his legs, pulling her gently onto his lap.

The muscled arms and broad chest that had frightened her so only days earlier, now made her feel safe, protected and cherished as Cody slowly lowered his head toward her. Rebecca's heartbeat skipped to double time when Cody's lips brushed hers with a feathery touch. The warmth of his breath washed softly over her, warming her skin with its touch, mingling with her own breath as his lips returned to hover, almost touching.

"You're not like any woman I've ever known, Rebecca," he murmured. His mouth moved against hers as he spoke, touching and retreating. "Sometimes when I'm with you, I think it's all a dream, that I'll wake up and you'll be gone. Every morning when I drive up, I'm afraid I'll find the cabin empty and the dream over."

His lips pressed hers tenderly. "Show me you're not a dream, Rebecca," he whispered, his mouth still hard against hers as he spoke. "Show me that you're flesh and blood and not just the figment of a lonely heart."

"Cody." His name was a sigh. Weak with a longing like she had never known and never believed she would be able to feel, Rebecca clung to him. Her hand clutched the thin cotton that covered his back. Another fistful of material was wadded in the hand at his shoulder. She trembled in his arms, storm tossed by awakening desire and the resurgence of emotions that had been buried in the pit of her soul, she had thought, forever.

Tenderly, as if he were still afraid of waking from a dream, Cody moved his lips against hers, deepening his kiss by slow degrees. Savoring each taste and exploring each nuance of touch, he poured his body and soul into the union of flesh on flesh. As the quaking of Rebecca's body grew stronger, he pulled her closer, tightening his hold on her and warming her with the fires that raged in him.

Deep in the heart of her, icy spikes of fear fought for life against the wildfire burning out of control within Rebecca. She was alive again. After a year of being dead inside, she was alive and aflame with desire for a man she had given up all hope of ever having. Tremors shivered up from the pit of her stomach. She wanted to laugh and cry and scream— scream with joy, with life, with...

"Oh, my God, no," she cried out. "No." Without warning, it all came back, rushing toward her with the speed and force of a mammoth avalanche. In the blink of an eye, embryonic fear burgeoned into terror.

The arms that had comforted her suddenly smothered her, and the panicked scream inside her mind became real—a long, shrill cry of terror and pain as Rebecca's hands shoved against the overwhelming strength of Cody's embrace.

Dumbfounded, Cody only held her tighter in an instinctive act of comfort until he realized that her struggle was for real and he let her go. His heart shredded with pain as he watched her scramble away from him, practically clawing her way over the top of the coffee table and dragging a chair behind her, keeping it between them while she used it for support.

Halfway across the porch, she finally stopped. Her terror-glazed eyes were bewildered as she clutched the back of the chair, leaning against it while she gasped in lungfuls of air and gazed at him across the distance.

Cody stayed where he was, afraid to move. He wanted desperately to go to her to take her in his arms again until whatever demons chased her were gone forever, but he saw the fear in her eyes and he knew it was directed at him.

Every instinct had told him to be cautious, told him she was fragile, but her response had tricked him. For a moment, she had wanted him as badly as he wanted her. For one passionate instant, she had been his without restraint, and he had forgotten to be careful.

"What did I do?" he whispered, not knowing he was going to speak until he heard his words aloud.

Nothing, Rebecca answered silently. Pain was clamped around her middle like a smothering vise. She could barely breathe. She had stopped running only because her legs wouldn't carry her any farther, and without the chair to lean on, she was afraid she wouldn't be able to stand at all.

"I'm sorry," he whispered again.

His eyes begged for a response, any word that would explain what had happened, and Rebecca longed to give him what he wanted, but she was afraid to. So long as she kept her jaws clamped tightly together, the scream was only in her head. If she opened her mouth to speak, she was afraid that the wild, terrible scream would come rolling out again, bringing the black pit of her soul into the light of day and leaving her with no way to ever explain the secret pain that trapped her in her lonely world.

"Rebecca." Cody stood, his hand reaching out to her while his voice pleaded with her.

Rebecca's reaction was a shrill, wavering "no-o-o" as she released her grip on the chair and took a giant step backward toward the rear entrance of the cabin.

"Please." He took two steps toward her, both arms extended.

His voice was tender, his arms inviting. He only wanted to hold her. Rebecca flattened herself against the cabin wall. The rough bark of the logs scraped her hands, and her trembling legs threatened to collapse entirely. He could be her salvation. All she had to do was reach out to him. All she had to do was to let him help her. All she had to do was trust one man, the man whose strong arms reached out to her now, Cody. All she had to do...

Cody saw the change in her eyes. He saw that she was waiting for him. Relief swept through him, turning to a joy that was almost painful. "Rebecca," he said softly, and took another step toward her with his arms outstretched, ready to gather her in.

The low moan that answered him turned the pounding of his heart to a thud. He staggered to a halt and listened helplessly while the moan rose and chills swept up his spine and down his arms. "Oh, my God," he whispered when the moan became a scream, starting deep inside her and rising wild and terrible with a raw pain that slashed at his heart.

Her scream quieting to a whimper, Rebecca whirled and, in the blink of an eye, disappeared into the cabin. Cody stood frozen while cold shudders twisted over his shoulders and into his gut. He longed to follow her, but he knew better than to try. Good intentions weren't enough, not today.

Her eyes had told him that she had wanted everything he was offering. But there was something inside her that was stronger than them both, and today that something had won.

Cody forced himself to turn away. He pushed open the screen door that led to the backyard and walked out into the night. Hot and breathlessly quiet, it waited for him like a comforting balm.

Embraced in the sensuous arms of a sultry southern night, Cody was almost tolerant of the painful ache in his groin. With each step, the throbbing reminded him that there would be other nights, and one of those nights, Rebecca would come to him. He was sure of it.

Rebecca's head throbbed with pain. She swallowed two aspirin and then held the glass of ice water against her forehead. Tremors of anxiety still rumbled through her periodically, though the crying, blessedly, had long since stopped.

She had even slept for a while only to awaken in a sweat, panting from the effects of a nightmare that had instantly receded from memory once she was awake. The one thing she truly didn't want to think about, and the one thing she knew she would have to confront sooner or later, was Cody.

She didn't know how she would ever face him again after the way she had acted. There was no explanation she could offer for her blind panic, nothing she could say that would make sense.

Pain throbbed in her head again as she remembered the look on Cody's face when he had reached out to her. She had never seen such patience, such tenderness and understanding in another human being. He had offered her everything she so desperately needed, everything she longed for, and she had screamed in terror and run away.

Wearing nothing but an oversize T-shirt, Rebecca tiptoed on bare feet across the room. Matthew lay on his side, a new trick he had just learned. He slept peacefully with a tiny fist in easy reach of his mouth.

Rebecca stroked her fingers lightly over the velvety skin of his leg, and covered him again with the sheet he had kicked aside in a restless moment. Leaving him to sleep, she tiptoed to the front door and pulled it soundlessly closed behind her.

Even in the predawn darkness, the air on the porch would have been hot enough to raise a sweat if it weren't for the slow breeze that shuffled past. Rebecca eased into the porch swing and shoved off with the tips of her toes while a deep, sad loneliness settled over her, made all the worse by a sinking feeling of hopelessness.

For a few minutes the evening before, when she had reached out to Cody and he had pulled her into his arms, she had felt young and innocent and alive again in a way she hadn't felt for a long, long time. She had wanted him to kiss her. She had ached for it.

In one trembling moment of anticipation and surrender, when he had held her close and his parted lips had slowly lowered toward hers, she had felt a new, better world opening for her. And then it was gone, and she had felt nothing but a blind, awful terror and a rage that had overpowered everything else.

All that was gone now—all the anger, all the hope—and she was alone. Silent tears coursed down Rebecca's cheeks at the thought of never being able to enjoy the touch of a man without panic, never being normal again with a normal woman's feelings. She didn't want to be like that. She didn't want to be a lonely, empty woman with endless years of solitude stretching before her, years with Matthew as her only comfort and her only child.

Rebecca crumpled against the pillows in the corner of the swing, and her fingers closed around the metal chain that suspended the swing from the ceiling. Sobbing aloud with despair, she remembered the dreams she once had that were for so much more. A husband and children, a home filled with laughter and love. She had so much to give, so much she wanted to give and so much more that she needed. She didn't want to be this way.

Chapter Seven

Rebecca sat in the rocker on the front porch. The evening light had begun to soften, but was still strong enough to work by. Dressed in shorts and a cotton camp shirt, she was almost comfortable in the shade of the porch, fanned by a western wind brisk enough to ruffle the leaves of the trees.

With her bare foot, she rocked the cradle where Matthew lay contentedly studying the string of toys that dangled above his head. In a basket beside her rocking chair was a mound of satin pillows trimmed in lace, calico pillows with eyelet ruffles and scented sachet pillows, plain and fancy.

Working steadily, Rebecca lifted an unfinished pillow from a basket to the left of her, hand-stitched the closing seam and dropped the finished pillow into a basket on the right. After a weekend of nonstop work to get the rose-garden wall hanging ready for the gallery, the finishing touches to the pillows were almost a vacation. With them done, she would have another full load to take into San Angelo in the morning.

She tapped the cradle rocker with her foot some more and paused in midstitch to cast an anxious eye at the long, empty road that connected the isolated cabin with the outside world. After his knocks went unanswered on Friday and again on Saturday, Cody had slipped a note under the cabin door Sunday morning saying that he would be off work Sunday and Monday and she should call if she needed anything.

Rebecca hadn't called, and she still wasn't sure she wanted to face him after the debacle of Thursday night, but with Monday drawing to a close, she was more than a little worried about her truck. It was supposed to have been ready today, and she needed it tomorrow. If Cody was trying to force her into calling, he might have hit upon a surefire tactic.

Dropping another completed pillow into the basket, Rebecca leaned in the other direction and retrieved one of the remaining pillows from the unfinished pile. As she straightened, her gaze moved past Matthew, who was dozing in blissful oblivion to the worries of the adult world, past the western horizon, where the first pale blush of the setting sun stained the sky, to the dirt road, where a dust cloud swirled skyward in the wake of a high-speed dark blob.

Rebecca froze while her stomach knotted itself into a hard cramp that drove the breath out of her at the same time it pulled her forward into a pained tuck. Gasping, she dropped the pillow back into the basket and eased herself out of the rocker. Then she hobbled forward a few steps and, with one hand clutching her midsection, braced herself against the porch post with the other hand.

While she struggled to catch her breath, she watched the dust cloud blossom larger. The dark blob took on the shape of a pickup truck, its color still indistinct. Rebecca massaged her stomach while she arched her back, trying to force the cramp to relax.

By the time the wine red of Cody's pickup had emerged clearly from the haze of dust, she had taken her first deep breath without groaning in pain. Discounting a subtle list toward the porch post, Rebecca stood upright, with only the fading ghost of a pain to vex her as she watched Cody pull into the graveled parking space next to the cabin.

She still didn't know what she was going to say to him, but at least she could greet him without the distraction of a full-blown panic attack. Rebecca couldn't, however, control the pounding of her heart when Cody exited the truck or still the rising flutter of her nerves while he slowly circled behind the pickup, keeping his face turned toward her the whole time as if to assure himself that she wasn't going to run away again before he reached her.

The cowboy hat he wore was pulled low on his forehead, and mirrored sunglasses hid his eyes. With Cody's mood effectively hidden from her, Rebecca tried to draw a deep breath and realized she was beginning to tremble. Instead of a uniform, he wore blue jeans, formfitting and faded with age. His shirt was a plain white, unbuttoned at the neck, with the long sleeves rolled back to his elbows. Other than that, everything about him reminded her of her first glimpse of him a week earlier.

Cody stepped onto the edge of the porch and stopped. The cowboy boots he wore were unadorned and work roughened. Wordlessly he removed his hat and ran his fingers through his hair, shaking loose the sweat-dampened locks. He tossed his hat onto a small, square table at the back of the porch, removed his sunglasses and dropped them into his hat.

When he turned to Rebecca, his gaze showed no more expression than it had with the sunglasses. "If I promise not to come any closer, do you promise not to bolt?" he asked.

Rebecca nodded, heartsick to realize that the fragile bond that had grown between them in the past week was shattered, and she was the one who had shattered it.

"I guess you got my note yesterday," Cody said. He stood with his feet apart, his weight balanced evenly, as unmoving as a stone statue.

Not sure she could trust her voice, Rebecca nodded again. She wanted to apologize, but she didn't know how to begin. An apology wouldn't be worth much without an explanation, and there was nothing she could say that would explain or change what had happened between them.

She had wanted him then, and if the ache inside her was any indication, she wanted him now, but she could never tell him that any more than she could tell him how much she wished things could be different between them.

"You still planning to go into San Angelo tomorrow?"

Rebecca started to nod and saw Cody stiffen. From halfway across the porch, the anger in his eyes was apparent, and his jaws flexed with the obvious grinding of his teeth. He probably thought she was giving him the silent treatment on purpose, and she had to admit that in his shoes, she might have felt the same way.

Over the past few days, she hadn't said much aloud, not even to Matthew, but for Cody, she would try. "Ye—" Rebecca started to say, and stopped when the word descended into a garbled croak. Clearing her throat, she coughed and tried again.

"Yes," she answered distinctly on the second try.

The flaring anger in his eyes wavered, then hardened into determination. "Would you be willing to use my truck again?"

The question hit Rebecca like a punch, and her already tender stomach tightened. Her grandfather's pickup wasn't fixed yet. The damage was probably worse than Cody had told her, and if they weren't able to fix her truck, she didn't know what she would do, but she knew there'd be no one to blame but herself.

"Rebecca?"

"My truck isn't ready?" she practically whispered.

"The part hasn't come in yet. It'll be in later this week probably. You know how it is when you live this far out in the middle of nowhere. It takes twice as long to get anything fixed."

"That's all? They didn't find anything else wrong?"

"I know you were counting on getting your truck back. I'm sorry."

"That's okay." She took a deep breath and felt relief wash through her. "I'm just glad that's all it was."

"So I guess I'll just drop my truck off here tomorrow morning, as usual."

"Thank you." Rebecca almost choked on the words. Not because she didn't mean them, but because they were so inadequate. She was already more deeply indebted to Cody than she could ever repay. "I'm really sorry to have to borrow it again."

"I don't mind, Rebecca." He gathered up his hat and glasses, holding them in his hands as he turned back to face her. "You know," he said haltingly, "I've kind of missed Matthew these last few days. Do you think it would be okay if I spent just a few minutes with him tomorrow evening?"

"Oh, sure," she said, eager to offer anything that she could. "I think he's missed you, too."

"Good." Cody bobbed his head and stepped backward off the porch. He pulled his hat low on his forehead again and slipped on his sunglasses. "See you tomorrow, then."

He twirled on his heel and strode back to his truck. Rebecca watched him drive away with a queasy sense of grief building inside her. She had lost him, and she would never have believed it could hurt so badly to lose something she had never meant to possess in the first place.

Rebecca pulled through the circular drive in front of Margaret's house and stopped with the nose of the pickup pointing toward the road. All the way back from San Angelo, her emotions had swung like a pendulum from elation to depression and back again.

During the past week, Simon had sold one of her wall hangings, a primitive farm scene that was 180 degrees away from the garden scene in style and feeling, but it was one she had been equally proud of, and the hefty check Simon had given her today confirmed her own instincts. Furthermore, he had loved the rose garden quilt, and was planning to ask even more for it. He already had a buyer in mind.

From that high point, she had gone to her group session and had cried almost all the way through it in spite of the doctor's assurances that Rebecca had made real progress toward working her way through the volatile emotions she still had bottled up inside her. The group itself was split in its reaction which echoed Rebecca's own opinion. If this was progress, she wasn't at all sure she wanted to make any more of it.

Leaving the pickup, she trudged up the porch steps and was greeted at the front door by Coco, Margaret's cat, who made a sensuous circle around Rebecca's ankles, purring and dusting Rebecca's legs with a long, feathery tail.

"Coco, you flirt." Rebecca stooped and lifted the big orange tabby into her arms. Coco turned up the volume on her purrs as she scrubbed the top of her head under Rebecca's chin. "Ooh, Coco," Rebecca murmured, snuggling her face against the soft fur of the cat. "You're such a lover."

Rebecca opened the door and went inside with Coco in her arms. Once the door closed behind them, Coco coiled herself into a spring and leapt out of Rebecca's arms to dart into the kitchen where the food bowl was.

"Traitor," Rebecca called to the cat's retreating back.

Margaret put down the magazine she had been leafing through and looked from Rebecca to the kitchen with an indulgent smile. "Coco's only loyalty is to her stomach. She's very sweet with Matthew, though. It's a good thing, too, because once he learns to crawl, he's going to drive her crazy."

Rebecca stared toward the kitchen, her brows drawn in thought. Before Coco had appeared outside the door, Rebecca's mood had been despondent, and with the soft brush of fur against her leg, the sadness had lifted and been replaced with laughter.

"What are you thinking, dear?" Margaret asked.

"I was just wondering." Rebecca turned her gaze from the kitchen to Matthew, who lay on his stomach on the floor, trying to push himself up with his arms and craning his neck in the direction the cat had disappeared in. "I was just wondering if I should start thinking of getting a pet for Matthew anytime soon."

"I think Matthew's a little young yet." The older woman pushed herself up from the couch and started toward the kitchen. "You look parched. Why don't I get you a glass of this fresh iced tea I just made. Are you hungry?"

Rebecca knelt down on the blanket beside Matthew. "I don't have time to eat here this evening. I've got to get the truck home before Cody gets off work."

She rolled Matthew over, lifted his shirt, put her mouth against his belly and blew. The act made a disgusting noise but sent Matthew into as close to a fit of joy as he could get at his tender age. His legs kicked, his arms waved, and he gave her a wide, toothless grin and a gurgle. She repeated the act, and he repeated his display of surprised glee.

What she wanted to do was to pick him up and cuddle him, but he was happy where he was, and she had been a mother long enough to know that if a baby was happy, you left well enough alone. Looking around for a toy to hand him, Rebecca came upon a small, red-and-white polka-dot stuffed toy with long floppy ears. It looked brand-new, homemade and suspicious.

In all the time she had been leaving Matthew here, Margaret had been content to let him play with the toys Rebecca brought for him. Why, all of a sudden, was there a new toy among the others?

"Here's your tea," Margaret said, extending a tall, icy glass toward Rebecca.

"What's this?" Rebecca held up the rabbit thing with one hand as she took the tea with the other.

"Oh, that." Margaret cleared the magazines off of the couch, stacking them on an end table before she sat back down. "Dora brought that over."

"Dora?" Shock mercifully covered the horror just beneath the surface of Rebecca's voice. She dropped the rabbit.

"Uh-huh." Margaret nodded and took a sip of her tea. Finishing with a satisfied swallow, she said, "She dropped by a couple of weeks ago and was quite taken with Matthew. So she made that rabbit for him and brought it by today."

"I despise that woman," Rebecca said between gritted teeth.

"I know, dear. She's horrid." Margaret tipped her head and said with the gentlest of reprimands, "But she *is* my friend."

"Do I have to take it home with me?"

"You'll hurt her feelings if you don't."

Rebecca bit off her opinion of Dora's feelings an instant before it was out of her mouth, but privately Rebecca wasn't at all sure the woman had any feelings. Dora had shown all the warmth of a pit viper to Cody after he'd lost his parents and needed a mother's love more than he ever would in his life. Rebecca had been a child at the time, but with a child's eyes she had seen through to the cold heart of a selfish woman.

"How many times has she been here to see Matthew?" Rebecca asked.

"Only twice, and the first time she didn't even know he was going to be here."

"If she comes back again, I want to know."

"Of course, dear. If you'd like, I could arrange for Matthew to be sleeping whenever I see her drive up. He's such a nice, quiet baby, if I put him to bed in the back, Dora would never know the difference."

Rebecca laughed and began to relax. "We'll see. If it looks like she's going to make a pest of herself, we might try that." As a concession to Margaret's friendship with Dora, Rebecca added, "It's not that I think she's such a bad person. It's just that I don't think she's very good with children. At least, not based on the results I've seen, and quite frankly I just don't want Matthew being influenced by her."

Margaret hooted, a loud, boisterous laugh that rang out whenever she found something particularly ludicrous. The raucous sound perked Matthew's interest, drawing his head toward the laugh as he rolled his eyes in search of the source.

"Not to disagree with you, dear," Margaret said, "but don't you think he's just a little young to be scarred for life by a half-hour visit from Dora Lockhart?"

"Okay!" Rebecca set her tea glass on the floor and held up her hands in a gesture of surrender. "I'll be honest. I can't stand the woman, and if she starts hanging around Matthew, then she's going to end up hanging around me." Even to herself, she had to admit that the excuse was at least half-true.

Dora Lockhart was bad news, and Rebecca knew better than to stand still when bad news started sniffing around in her direction. And the thought of Matthew's grandmother taking a sudden interest in him sent cold chills down Rebecca's spine.

"Fair enough," Margaret agreed. "Now, about the idea of you getting a dog."

"Dog? I didn't say anything about a dog."

"Well, maybe it was me, then. Anyway, it was one thing for Henry to be living out there in that cabin all by himself, but it's another thing entirely for you and that baby to be alone and unprotected."

"Granddad's .22 rifle is on a rack on the wall, right where he left it."

"Pish-posh. Now, Silas Vogner has a nine-month-old pup he's been wanting to get rid of. It's gonna be a nice, big dog, and it'd be good protection for you. And in a couple of years, it'd be something to keep Matthew company out there all alone with no other kids around to play with."

Rebecca opened her mouth to say no and then stopped. "What kind of dog is it?" The question surprised her almost as much as it did Margaret, who had to abandon her next argument without warning.

"Part golden retriever, part big, speckled stray."

"I don't know. Let me think about it."

"Well, don't think too long. Silas has told practically everybody in the county about it."

"Why'd he wait until it was nine months old to want to get rid of it?"

"He didn't. It's the last of the litter, and he's been stuck with it for about seven of those nine months."

"I guess I *had* better hurry, then. A deal like that won't wait more than another year or two probably."

"It's bad manners to sass your elders, Rebecca Carder."

Rebecca stood and leaned over Margaret to kiss the dimple in the other woman's smile. "Yes, ma'am. I'll remember that. I guess I'd better be going now."

"You think about that dog. I worry about you."

"Yes, ma'am." Rebecca kissed her again and straightened. "I appreciate that."

Matthew's sleepy eyelids fluttered open, and he sucked vigorously on the bottle for a little more than a minute before his mouth slowed and his eyes drooped closed again. Rebecca rocked slowly and smiled down at him. All in all, today had been a good day, and she had a feeling that the best was yet to come.

Vegetables from Margaret's garden had come to be one of the main dividends from Rebecca's Tuesday outings. At the moment, a pot of collard greens simmered on the stove. The last of the delicate pink surprise lilies that had grown by the picket fence were now in a vase on the coffee table. Light, softened by lace curtains, streamed in through the windows, casting a glow into even the deepest corners of the cabin.

She felt relaxed, eager and confident. Tonight she would apologize. She owed Cody that much, and even though they could never be more than friends, she wanted them to at least be that.

His eyes closed in deep slumber, Matthew stopped sucking altogether. Rebecca lifted him to her shoulder and continued to rock while she patted his back and breathed in the sweet, clean scent that was his alone. One short week ago, this had been all she needed, all she wanted, and she had been content. Now she found herself listening for the sound of Cody's arrival and watching the clock tick off the minutes until the sound of his boot heels echoed on her porch.

In the space of one short week, what had been enough was no longer enough. Cody had come to mean too much to her. She didn't know how it had happened, and she didn't know how to change it. She wasn't even sure she wanted to change it.

A board creaked on the porch outside and yanked Rebecca's rambling thoughts back to the present. She slid her arm under Matthew's diapered bottom and cupped her hand on the back of his head, holding him firmly against her as she rose and went to the window behind the dining table.

Peering through the lace curtain, she saw a lanky yellow dog standing in the middle of her porch. His long, feathered tail wagged gently as he faced the cabin door, panting through what looked like a smile. A leash arced from his neck toward the other side of the door, where it disappeared from her view. Rebecca leaned closer to the window and could just make out one leg of a pair of blue jeans when a knock on the door brought her upright with a scowl.

She walked to the door and paused with her hand on the bolt. "Who is it?" she demanded.

"Cody."

"Cody?" *With a dog?* She unbolted the door and threw it open. Blocking the threshold with her body, she pointed to the dog. "What is that?"

Cody frowned and looked from her to the dog and back again. "Margaret sent him over," he said in a voice that grew more cautious with every word. "I thought you were expecting him."

"Margaret sent him?" Suspicion turned to shock, and irritation to the beginnings of real anger. "That's not Silas Vogner's dog, is it?"

"I'm afraid it is. You weren't expecting him?"

"No. I wasn't expecting him."

"No wonder she insisted on sending this fried chicken." Cody lifted the hamper he held in his left hand. "He seems like a really nice dog."

"How could she do that?" Rebecca looked from Cody's face with its expression of sympathy to the dog, who smiled up at her with adoring brown eyes while wagging vigorously. "What exactly did she say?"

"Uh . . ." Cody's brows puckered with thought as he began slowly, "She said that the two of you had discussed the dog, and I was to bring him over so you could spend a few days with him and see how you liked him."

"She could have at least called," Rebecca grumbled. Her gaze kept going back to the dog, and with each glance, her resolve weakened. "He is cute, isn't he?"

"He seems really friendly, too." Cody looked down at the dog. "And so far he hasn't barked much, so he may not be one of those who raises a lot of racket for no reason at all."

"What's his name?" She hated to be such a pushover, but she was beginning to think she might keep him, just for a night or two.

"Junior."

At the sound of his name, the dog's ears perked, his tail grew still and he lifted his head to Cody in an attitude of waiting.

"I guess that's his name, all right," Rebecca agreed. "Did anybody think to send dog food?"

Cody nodded. "Food. Bowls. Some rawhide chews, and a meat bone that looks like it came off a dinosaur. Also a chain so you can leave him outside if you want. If you let him loose before he gets settled in, he'll probably try to go home to Silas. Are those greens I smell cooking?"

"Fresh from Margaret's freezer."

A crooked smile eased up one corner of Cody's mouth. "She also sent along some corn bread she claimed she forgot to give you earlier. And corn on the cob, already cooked and buttered."

"She gave *me* a peach cobbler to bring home," Rebecca said. "Do you get the uneasy feeling that Margaret might be doing a little matchmaking?"

Cody's smile grew as he shook his head. "I swear, if her cooking wasn't so good, I might end up resenting the way she tries to run other people's lives."

"She does make a person feel sort of setup sometimes, doesn't she?" Rebecca asked with a soft chuckle that banished the last of her lingering resistance.

"That she does," Cody agreed. He held up the picnic basket again. "Does this mean I get to come inside?"

"Sure." Rebecca stepped back out of the doorway. "Do you suppose Junior's housebroken?"

"Uh, let me see." Cody searched through his memory for whatever else Margaret might have said. "He's had all his shots. He minds well, he's housebroken and, oh yes, he was flea dipped just last week."

"Well, old Junior is beginning to sound like the perfect dog. I guess you might as well bring him in with you."

Cody swept off his hat as he entered. "Junior and I would both like to express our gratitude for your hospitality."

"Think nothing of it."

Rebecca closed the door again and went to put Matthew in his crib. Cody unsnapped the leash from Junior's collar, and the dog immediately collapsed with a thump in front of the door. His tail flopped twice when Rebecca walked by on her way to the kitchen. Then he laid his head down on his paws and nothing else moved but his eyes, which followed Rebecca and Cody with interest as they bustled around in the kitchen, preparing Margaret's bounty for the table.

Chicken bones, corn-bread crumbs, pot liquor and corn cobs were all that remained of the feast as Rebecca dished up cobbler and poured two cups of after-dinner coffee. Cody stood behind her, waiting to help carry the dessert to the table.

"That dog snores," Rebecca whispered.

Cody looked to where Junior lay stretched out on his side in front of the door. "He has kind of a nice, steady rhythm to it, though."

"I guess I shouldn't have expected any sympathy from a man." Turning to hide her smile, she picked up her coffee and cobbler and walked to the table.

"Are you suggesting that I snore?" Cody demanded as he followed behind her.

"Well, coming from a family with a father and three brothers, it *is* my educated opinion that all men snore at one time or another."

He set his cup and bowl on the table and slid into his chair. "Not me."

Rebecca smiled around her cup of coffee. "I guess I'll just have to take your word for it."

Cody's brows went up. He coughed and quickly took a bite of cobbler, making unintelligible grumbling sounds as he chewed.

Her eyes narrowing, Rebecca watched him. She could almost feel his need to say something that he seemed determined not to say. All through dinner they had stuck to safe topics. She hadn't apologized, and he had pretended that their kiss and its aftermath had never happened. But they were running out of safe topics, and every time she looked at him, all she could think about was how his lips had felt on hers.

"I beg your pardon?" she asked in a voice gone suddenly wispy.

"Bad joke." He held up one hand and shook his head as if embarrassed she had heard him. "It's not worth repeating."

"Oh." Her mind raced on to a topic she had been avoiding for days. "Well, I've been meaning—"

"What I said was—"

They both started and stopped at the same time, their words coming in a spurt and the silence that followed lying like a stone between them. "Sorry," they both said at once.

Rebecca winced as silence fell again. "You go ahead," she whispered quickly.

Cody shook his head. "It *really* wasn't worth saying the first time. Just a tasteless remark about having the opportunity to prove that I don't snore."

"Oh." Slowly the full meaning of his words sunk in, and Rebecca sat straighter. "Oh."

"Uh." He spread his hands, palms up, and frowned while his expression went from pained discomfort to just plain pain. "I don't want to upset you, but do you think we could talk for just a minute about last week?"

Rebecca drew in a deep breath and let it back out. "I've been meaning to apologize to you."

"I don't need an apology, Rebecca," he said quietly. His eyes gazed into hers steadily. "All I'd like to know is what happened. I don't know what I did."

"You didn't do anything."

"Well, obviously I did. I just don't know what it was. One minute we were kissing, and the next minute..." He stopped and studied his hands as if he could find the right words there. "If I'd been a cop who walked up on that scene," he said, approaching the subject from a new angle, "I would have found a woman who was running from a man in terror. And if the man had told me that all he had done was kiss her, I don't think I'd have believed him."

Cody stopped looking at his hands and lifted his gaze to Rebecca again. "Do you understand what I'm saying?"

"I overreacted." She still hoped beyond hope that he would just let the whole subject drop. As unfair as it was to them both, she knew she could never tell him the truth.

"No, I don't think you overreacted, but I don't think your reaction had anything to do with me, either. I think you were reacting to something that I reminded you of when I kissed you." His eyes narrowed and he leaned forward, bracing himself on his forearms. "But you're not going to tell me what that something is, are you?" he asked quietly.

"No," Rebecca answered, barely above a whisper. "No, I'm not."

"Okay." He nodded. "I can accept that. I may not like it, but I can accept it."

"I'm sorry."

"You don't have to be sorry, Rebecca. Believe it or not, I understand. For years after Brenda left, I couldn't talk about what happened. Hell, I could barely think about it. I had friends trying to set me up with dates, giving me the old routine about if you fall off a horse, you have to get back on. But I couldn't do it. The idea of getting near another woman sent me into a panic attack. All I wanted was to be left alone. I needed time to heal while I tried to put my life back together again."

"You think that's how I feel?"

"One way or another, yeah, pretty much. Remember, I've known you a long time. I know your family. In their eyes, you could do no wrong."

Rebecca looked up in surprise. "What?"

"Jessy could raise hell all day long, and nobody lifted an eyebrow, but Rebecca, you were the family saint. And you tried so hard to live up to that expectation. It couldn't have been easy for you to tell them you were pregnant and not married. Knowing your parents, they wouldn't have made it easy for you."

Remembering so much more than Cody could ever guess, Rebecca felt tears swell in her eyes. Her parents, her whole family except for Jessy, had been devastated by the news of her pregnancy and then angered by her stubborn and unreasonable refusal to name or consider marrying the father.

Rebecca's whole life had been spent living up to her family's image of her, and in one announcement, she had shattered everything that she had been to that point. That day, she began her life again. Pregnant, unmarried and defiant for the first time in her life, she became a new person, with secrets and pain and fears that no one else could know or understand.

Eventually, one by one, her family had come to accept what they couldn't change. Her brothers, bless them, had been the first to join Jessy in respecting Rebecca's decision whether they understood it or not. Within a few months, her mother had come around, and now, not quite a year later, even Rebecca's father was beginning to thaw. But the pain, for everyone, would be a long time healing.

"From the long silence," Cody said gently, "it must have been even harder than I imagined."

"It was pretty tough." Fatigue dragged at her voice.

"Do you still love him?"

"Love?" Surfacing from the depths of her thoughts, Rebecca blinked in confusion. "Who?"

"Like I said, I've known you a long time. I know the way you were raised. You wouldn't have a child by a man you didn't care about. So there must be some other reason you're not married to Matthew's father, and it doesn't take a genius to figure out that whatever that reason is, it's still painful to you."

To her very core, she longed to shout out how wrong he was—that the only reason she'd had the baby was because of the way she was raised; that the only reason she was able to love the baby was that some power inside her clearly divided the child from his conception; that every time she thought of the father, something cold and frightening twisted inside of her.

"Then it's true," Cody said finally. "You do still love him."

Trembling, Rebecca gazed at him with eyes that begged him to stop. Painful memories ripped at her, dragged to the surface by Cody's accusations, accusations she could neither confirm nor deny. She couldn't tell him the truth, and she was tired of living the lie that her silence encouraged.

Poor Rebecca, everyone must think, *she didn't even know he was married,* or maybe it was *poor Rebecca, jilted at the altar,* or *the marriage was annulled,* or—It could be anything. The list was endless.

"Rebecca." Cody leaned across the table and captured her hand in his, startling her out of her reverie. "Do you?" he asked urgently. "If you do, tell me. I—I need to know."

Rebecca tried to pull her hand away, but he only tightened his grip. "I don't know," she said, pulling as far away as she could while the determination in his eyes only intensified. "I'm not sure of anything anymore. I need time. I—"

She tugged at her hand again, and he released her. Freed, she sprang from her chair and put a safe distance between them before she turned, with her back to the fireplace, and faced him again. "You said you needed time once. So you must know how I feel."

"It wasn't love that I needed time to recover from." His eyes never wavered from hers. "What is it you need time to recover from, Rebecca?"

"It doesn't matter."

"Yes, it does. It matters to me."

"Why?" she challenged. "What difference would it make to you if I'm in love with another man?"

Cody rose from the table slowly. "If you're in love with another man, then I guess I'd just be wasting my time if I stayed around here any longer."

Rebecca lifted her chin defiantly and stared back into his unblinking gaze. "Then I guess you'd just be wasting your time if you stayed," she answered evenly.

"I'm sorry to hear that."

"I'm sorry for a lot of things." Tears stung her eyes, but she would be damned if she cried in front of him. He had left her no choice.

With a nod of dismissal, Cody turned and walked across the room and out the door, slamming it behind him. Junior stood facing the closed door, whimpering for the man he came with to return and take him, too. Rebecca whirled around and grabbed the mantel of the fireplace with both hands, practically hanging on it as she released huge, angry sobs that reached back over the past year and dredged up every moment of despair she had faced with bravery and dry eyes.

She was tired. She was hurting. And she was angry. Deeply, fiercely angry with herself, with Cody and with life. He was everything she'd ever wanted, and he wanted her. He had as much as said it, but she was too scared to take the chance, and he was too impatient to give her time.

Well, damn him. She'd gotten along without Cody Lockhart before and she could get along without him now. She was just fine here in her little cabin, all alone, with just her work and her baby. She was fine—just fine.

Chapter Eight

Rock and roll's ungentle rhythms blasted from the cassette player sitting on the floor in front of the fireplace. Dressed in leotard and tights, Rebecca lay on an old quilt on the floor with her fingers laced behind her neck and her knees bent. On the count of three, she released her breath in a huff and curled forward, tightening her stomach muscles in a tummy crunch as she raised her shoulders off the floor and held the position while she counted slowly to five.

Curling back down, she drew in a deep breath and counted to three, then repeated the crunch. On his back beside her, Matthew watched her every move with his toothless grin spread wide in amusement.

"Just wait, kiddo," she whispered breathlessly. "Your time's coming."

Matthew waved an excited arm in response, then pounded his heel against the quilt, and Rebecca laughed with him as she painfully worked her way toward her fiftieth crunch. Her threat was idle, and they both knew it. Matthew loved his exercise period, laughing with delight while his mother gently led him through his leg bicycles and scissors and his overhead arm lifts.

Rebecca wished she could have such a good attitude. The only reason she exercised at all was that Jessy was due for another visit soon, and Rebecca hoped to forestall any more remarks about how motherhood had certainly filled her out. Having a model for a sister wasn't always easy to take, especially one whose legs had always been longer and whose body had always been slimmer *and* curvier.

"Forty-five, two, three, four, five." She relaxed again and took another deep breath, grateful that there were only five crunches to go, even if the last five were the hardest. She hated exercising, but she had to admit that after it was over, she was always glad she had done it.

"Forty-six, two, three, four, five." Groaning with relief, Rebecca lay flat on her back and breathed. The last of the baby fat that had clung to her waist and hips had melted off over the past month of steady, hard exercise.

"Forty-seven, two, three, four, five." The slow, controlled curl down from the crunch had become more like a fast collapse, and the deep, steady breath afterward was now several quick gasps, but fifty crunches now weren't as hard as twenty had been a month ago, when Jessy had first goaded Rebecca into trying.

"Forty-eight, two, three, four, five." And as much as Rebecca hated to admit it, Jessy had been right. Lumpiness had become lean. Soft had become firm. Padded had become well-rounded. In fact, Rebecca was gradually coming into possession of a body to be proud of, and she sometimes wondered if that hadn't been Jessy's true aim all along.

"Forty-nine, two, three, four, five." Whether Rebecca's mind was ready for the change or not, physically she could feel herself coming alive again. She no longer shunned her reflection in a mirror. She no longer turned out the lights to dress and undress. And she no longer hated her body and what it had brought her to.

"Fifty, two, three, four, five." With a gasp of relief, she flopped onto her back and lay there, arms out-flung, chest heaving.

The fingers of her right hand brushed the downy softness of Matthew's hair, and Rebecca turned her head to look at him. Then she rolled onto her side and pulled him into her arms. His smile spread wide over toothless gums. His eyes danced with adoration. She was his world. She fed him, played with him, cared for him. She was his life, complete and fulfilled, and a month ago, he had been her life, or all that she had needed or wanted in life.

Tears of loss stung Rebecca's eyes as she stared into the laughing face of her son and realized that that was no longer true. She wanted more. She wanted a man, and not just any man. She wanted Cody. She wanted him to kiss her, to touch her, to make love to her. She wanted him to still the pain and anger inside her. She wanted to lie in his arms and know that she never had to be afraid again.

Rebecca stroked the tip of her finger over the velvety skin of Matthew's cheek. "Mommy wants miracles, doesn't she, sweetheart?" She held him closer, trying to fill the empty ache in her heart with his unquestioning love. "Mommies don't always get what they want, do they?" she whispered as she pressed her lips against his forehead.

Junior's rumbling growl slowly penetrated the thumping of the music and caught Rebecca's wandering attention. While the steady surge of her heart increased its tempo again, she carefully slipped her arm from under Matthew and rose onto her elbow.

Nine days had passed since she and Cody had talked. She knew because she had counted each day, listening to him come and go morning and evening, wishing she had something more to offer him than empty desires she couldn't fulfill. Each day she hoped he would be the one to break the silence.

Looking toward the door, Rebecca saw that Junior had abandoned his prone position and sat at attention with his eyes focused on the door and his ears pricked. With growing disquiet, she left the quilt and went to turn off the tape player.

In the silence that followed, she held her breath as she listened for the sound that had alerted the dog. She had almost decided there was nothing to hear when the porch creaked under the weight of a footstep and Junior rose onto all fours, hair bristling, and let loose with a string of barks, deeper and more serious sounding than any Rebecca had heard from him in the week and a half he had been with her.

More footsteps followed, too light and quick to be a man's, which left her both sad and glad. Sad that it wasn't Cody, and glad that it wasn't any other man. Cheered by the furiously wagging tail that accompanied the ferocious barks, Rebecca relaxed and went to the window to see what manner of intruder lurked beyond the door.

As she pulled back the lace curtain to look, a firm, almost demanding knock coincided with Rebecca's horrified gasp. Dropping the curtain as if it burned her hand, she staggered back from the window and cast hopelessly around the cabin's interior for an adequate place to hide.

"Rebecca! Rebecca, dear, I know you're inside," Dora's syrupy shrill voice called out. Another series of knuckle raps followed.

Cornered, Rebecca tried to convince herself that she was imagining things. She hadn't seen Dora in years. The woman outside could be anyone.

"Margaret warned me that you might not answer," Dora called. "But I've brought you something, dear."

Rebecca released her fear and loathing in one quick, strong shudder, then stiffened her back and faced reality. There was no mistaking the sprayed, blond hairstyle that hadn't changed in a decade, or the short, plump body that made its owner seem disarmingly soft and warm at first glance. Nor was there any mistaking the voice that wrapped fishwife nagging in cotton-candy sweetness. The woman outside was Dora.

"Rebecca?" She pounded harder. "Rebecca!"

Pasting what she hoped was a smile on her face, Rebecca marched to the door, grabbed Junior by the collar and pulled open the solid-oak cabin door. "Dora. What a surprise."

"Why, Rebecca, dear, I hope I haven't interrupted you."

The insincerity in Dora's voice was almost enough to make Rebecca gag, but the insincerity in her own voice was even worse. She and Dora had never brought out the best in each other. They had crossed swords at every encounter she could remember, and time seemed to have changed nothing. "Not at all, Dora. Please, won't you come in?"

"Well, I can only stay a minute." The words were hardly out of Dora's mouth before she was across the threshold and heading for the kitchen. "I brought you some of my gooseberry cobbler. Your granddaddy always said nobody could make a gooseberry cobbler like mine." She opened the refrigerator and slipped a plastic container inside. "You can give me back the bowl later," she said, turning and starting back across the room. "And wait'll you see what I brought for Matthew. Where is little Matt?"

Seized by a sudden fear that Dora was about to trample little Matt without ever seeing him, Rebecca hurried to the quilt and scooped him up. "Right here."

"Ohh," Dora cooed, holding out her arms as she advanced toward Rebecca, "there's little Mattie. How's my little Mattie today? Here's your Auntie Dora, come to bring you something. Come to Auntie Dora, my little baby."

Without asking if Rebecca minded, Dora gathered Matthew into her arms and walked away with him, chattering to him in baby talk that was as grating as it was indecipherable. Teeth bared in a silent snarl aimed at Dora's back, Rebecca argued herself out of a brief but strong urge to knock down the baby snatcher and take Matthew back.

As Dora sat on the couch with Matthew in her lap, Junior took up a position at the end of the coffee table, his stare fixed on the newcomer and the child he had developed a mutual fascination for.

"What is this dog doing?" Dora demanded.

"Watching." Rebecca made a mental note to give Junior an extra treat after supper. "He and Matthew sit for hours just looking at each other. I think Junior's becoming very protective of him."

"Junior?"

"The dog. That's his name." Rebecca turned away and went to look out the window to keep from grinning openly at Dora's discomfort.

"Well, can you make him stop?"

"Oh, I don't think I should," Rebecca answered mildly. She turned halfway around to look over her shoulder at Dora. "I got him as sort of a guardian for Matthew, and I think he's doing rather well, don't you? So long as you don't make any threatening movements, I don't think Junior will do anything but just watch you."

Dora huffed and glared at the dog. "Well, do you think he'll let me up to get my purse?" she demanded, on the edge of exasperation.

"Junior." Rebecca snapped her fingers and motioned for the dog to come to her. The game had gone on long enough, and she was in danger of becoming ashamed of herself. She did want Junior to protect Matthew, but she didn't want him to intimidate houseguests who were welcome. Of course, Dora wasn't really welcome, but Junior couldn't be smart enough to know that, and if he was, Rebecca didn't really want him to make it so obvious.

Reluctantly, and with frequent glances to monitor Matthew's whereabouts, Junior rose and trotted to Rebecca's side. She reached down to pet him, and he shoved his head against her hand, nuzzling her to apologize for anything he might have done wrong and to make sure she wasn't upset with him.

Rebecca bent over and scratched him behind the ears with both hands. "That's a good boy. Yes, that's a good Junior." A little voice in the back of her mind warned her that she sounded almost as silly as Dora had earlier. "It's okay, boy," she said, trying to reach a middle ground between affectionate and nauseating. "Dora's a friend. She's not going to hurt Matthew. You can watch her, but you don't have to scare her."

Junior licked Rebecca's chin and panted his healthy-smelling doggy breath in her face. When she released him, he whirled around and trotted back to the coffee table to take up his position again, but he seemed less tense this time.

Rebecca looked at Dora and shrugged. "You might try petting him."

Dora sniffed and rolled her eyes. "I'll take my chances. But why don't you come sit over here?" She patted the empty end of the couch. "He probably wouldn't be so worried if you were closer to Matthew."

Feeling as if a small battle had been won, Rebecca smiled and walked to the couch. She would have to call Margaret this evening and thank her for sending over Junior. He was still just an overgrown puppy, a little clumsy and occasionally dumb, but he was loving and gentle and fun—and he had just come closer to making Dora back down than Rebecca had ever seen anyone come.

"Would you just look at this boy's fingers," Dora said, holding out one of Matthew's hands to Rebecca. "I haven't seen fingers like this on a baby since J.D. was born. Long, long fingers. Born to be a pianist, or a surgeon."

While Dora displayed the baby's hand as if she had sculpted it herself, all the triumph drained from Rebecca until she was left with nothing but the hollow fear of a trapped animal. Alone and defenseless, she heard the approach of the hunter.

"J.D.'s hair was like this when he was little, too." Dora's voice softened with nostalgia as she combed her fingers through Matthew's strawberry blond fuzz. "It got darker as he got older, but when he was about two, his hair was as red as a brand-new copper penny. He was so cute." She drew in her breath with a catch.

If it were any other mother talking about any other son, Rebecca might have found the moment touching. She might have even felt a little sorry for Dora. But all Rebecca could see was a mama snake talking about a baby snake, and all she could feel was revolted. She could barely control the urge to shiver.

"You haven't seen J.D. in a long time, have you?" Dora asked.

"No." Rebecca almost choked on the question *and* the answer. "No, I haven't." She should never have encouraged Junior to be friendly. Dora might have left by now.

"He's just as handsome as he ever was. And such a lady's man. I think Cody's always been just a little bit jealous of him. Not that I really blame Cody for feeling that way. J.D.'s always had such charm, and Cody's always been, well, just a little unpolished, you might say."

Rebecca bit her bottom lip and turned her head in the other direction to stare toward the bedroom. She couldn't believe she was sitting in her own living room listening to this hateful, deluded woman talk about her warped, twisted son as if he were a paragon while slamming Cody, who was without a doubt one of the best-looking, best-built and nicest men on the face of the earth. She had to get Dora out of her house, and fast.

"How's Reever?" Rebecca asked, slowly turning back to face Dora.

"Just fine. He was working on your truck when I left."

"My truck?" Too many surprises were coming too quickly. Rebecca had never asked Cody where he had taken her pickup. She had just assumed it was at a mechanic's shop.

"Well, your granddad's truck, actually. He and Reever used to spend days working on that old thing, getting grease all over my yard, scattering parts around until it just looked like a junkyard out there. No offense, but when your granddaddy passed away, I thought all that would end. I guess I was wrong. Now Cody and Reever are out there doing the same damned thing, excuse my French."

"Cody? Is working on my truck?"

"Well, of course, Rebecca." Dora's expression clearly said that she thought Rebecca was being a little dim-witted. "Who did you think was working on that old pile of junk? Everyone in the county knows that you and this poor little baby are practically destitute."

"What?" Rebecca gasped.

"Well, now, dear, I know no one's wanted to say this to you, but I feel almost like a mother to you since I've known you practically from the cradle. The fact is that quite a few of the ladies in my circle are more than a little worried about you living out here all alone, with no husband around to take care of you. Of course, a lot of this is just an assumption on our part. It could always be that we're worrying for nothing."

"It couldn't be that you're fishing for details of my personal life, could it, Dora?"

"Oh, goodness, no, Rebecca. I wouldn't do that. Of course, if you ever needed another woman to talk to..." Dora's voice dropped confidentially. "You know, someone you could unburden yourself to, I would consider it an honor to be that someone, dear."

With visions of volcanoes erupting inside her head, Rebecca stared dumbstruck at Dora. The woman's conceit was exceeded only by her nerve. Could Dora actually believe that a few insincere words would have Rebecca spilling her guts about her marital status and Matthew's birth? Could Dora possibly think that any of it was any of her business? Could Dora have guessed the truth and just be fishing for a reaction?

Rebecca put a hand to her head and tried to still her spinning thoughts. Panic wouldn't help anything. Whatever Dora guessed, she couldn't prove anything, and there was already so much gossip going around that a little more couldn't hurt much.

Roots ran deep in Concho County, and family counted for something. For now, people were curious about Rebecca Carder and her illegitimate son, but the Carder family went back for generations. And in time, that was all anyone would remember.

Her emotions under control again, Rebecca answered quietly, "Thank you for your offer, Dora. I'll remember that if I ever feel the need."

"Well, that's good, dear. You just do that, now. Well, looka here, Rebecca. I think little Mattie's gone to sleep on me."

"I guess you must have relaxed him."

Dora's laugh was short and hard, more like a bark. "I guess he must like magpies." As she spoke, Junior looked at her and made a huffing sound in his throat. Dora cast a sidelong glance at the dog and held Matthew out toward Rebecca. "Here. Maybe you'd better put him to bed. I still don't trust that animal."

Gathering Matthew into her arms, Rebecca cuddled him to her all the way to the crib. She didn't want to put him down, and she didn't want to have to talk to Dora anymore.

Rebecca's nerves were raw and her patience was in tatters. She wanted to take a long soak in the tub and then lie down for a nap. She had a crib quilt and a matching set of accessories to finish by Tuesday, and thanks to the check she had gotten from Simon, she was ahead financially for the first time since she had moved into the cabin.

"While you're up, dear, why don't you bring me that shopping bag by the door, and I'll show you why I really came by today."

Oh, great. More surprises. Rebecca pulled a sheet over Matthew and left him blissfully undisturbed by the events around him. She lifted the shopping bag as if it contained a bomb and carried it to Dora.

With Matthew no longer in the arms of a stranger, Junior took up his usual watch post by the door and settled in for a nap.

"You really have to do something about that dog, Rebecca." Practically snatching the shopping bag away from her, Dora spread it open and reached inside. "Now, come on around here and sit down." She patted the couch beside her. "You really can't let him go around threatening your houseguests the way he does. A dog needs to know his place."

"He's just a puppy, Dora," Rebecca answered, taking her indicated place on the couch. "And he's only been here a week and a few days. I'm sure he'll relax after he's been here a while longer."

"All the same, I'd keep an eye on him if I were you. Now, here." Dora lifted a sunsuit from the shopping bag and held it up for approval.

"Why, that's very nice, Dora." And it was. Wide straps crisscrossed the back and buttoned into the square bib front. The short pants were elasticized at the waist and around the legs and full enough to accommodate the fattest diaper. The print was of multicolored umbrellas, opened and floating at all angles across a pale green background.

Dora laid the sunsuit on the couch between them and pulled out another and another and another. Blue with white elephants, yellow seersucker and red with navy polka dots. All simple, comfortable and suitable for a little boy who would soon be more active.

"Oh, Dora, they really are darling," Rebecca said with more genuine enthusiasm than she had felt all afternoon. "Where did you get them?"

"I made them." For once Dora sounded almost humble. "The patterns are old, and they take so little fabric. I hope you don't mind, but I know at this age you just can't have too many clothes."

"Oh, boy, is that right," Rebecca agreed, glad no one else knew how often Matthew went with just a diaper because everything else had gotten dirty without her realizing it.

"I hope you won't mind if I make him a few more. I still have some scraps that aren't big enough to do anything else with."

Rebecca really looked at Dora for the first time that day. "I think that's very nice of you, Dora. I wouldn't mind at all." Unlike Margaret or Rebecca's mother and father, who were in their sixties, and unlike Reever, who was nearly that old, Dora was probably not more than fifty. She had still been young when Rebecca had been a child, though it hadn't seemed that way at the time.

"You're very lucky, Rebecca," Dora said as softly as her brassy voice could get. "Matthew's a wonderful little boy, and you've got his whole life ahead of you. I had always wanted a big family, but unfortunately I had complications with J.D., and he was the only one I ever got to have."

"Oh, Dora, I'm so sorry." Instinctively Rebecca reached out to put her hand over Dora's, offering comfort without stopping to think. "I never knew."

Dora smiled and patted the hand that covered her own. "You were too young, dear. And J.D. never knew. I thought as long as he had to be the only one, it might be best for him to think I wanted it that way."

Junior uttered a soft, huffing bark and clambered to his feet to wave his tail in the direction of the door.

"More company?" Dora asked, twisting to stare at the dog. "You certainly stay busy around here."

"Not usually," Rebecca answered with a frown. Before she could reach the window to check on the identity of the newest arrival, there was a knock at the door.

"Rebecca?" Cody called out, and tapped at the door again. "I bring you glad tidings of old Fords."

Laughing at the sound of a relaxed and cheerful Cody, Rebecca pulled the door opened and leaned against it. "What?"

He dangled the keys to her truck in front of her while Junior danced around their feet, tail wiggling furiously with the thrill of greeting someone he knew and liked.

"It's ready?" Rebecca cried, and reached for the keys, far happier to have Cody back and friendly than to have her truck back and running.

"Yes," Cody answered, and pulled the keys back out of her reach. Holding them above his shoulder, he grinned down at her. "Don't I get a kiss for all my hard work and generosity? Just one little peck?"

Rebecca's eyes widened and her smile dimmed when she remembered who was inside. "I don't think right now . . ."

"Well, well, well," Dora said from not very far away. "Imagine my surprise."

"Dora." The laughter left Cody's eyes. He lowered the keys into Rebecca's hand and squeezed her limp fingers closed around the key ring. "Why didn't you tell me?" he asked under his breath, looking none too happy.

"I was trying," Rebecca answered in a whisper.

"Not hard enough," Cody said, and stepped around her into the cabin. "Been here long, Dora?"

"Just long enough, I'd say." Her eyes flashing, Dora turned her brittle smile from Cody to Rebecca and back again.

"Lucky me," Cody answered coolly.

He prowled across the room, picking up the quilt, folding it and laying it on the hearth, then moving on to the refrigerator to pour himself a glass of iced tea. He looked at home, too much at home, and far more familiar with the place than he ever seemed when he and Rebecca were alone.

Cody's performance was obviously for Dora's benefit, but Rebecca couldn't help wondering if it would end up being at her own expense. If she were a piece of property, the signs he was putting up would read Posted. No Trespassing. But she wasn't a piece of property and she didn't appreciate Cody's high-handed attitude.

"I'll take a glass of that while you're over there," Rebecca called to keep him on the other side of the room a while longer. "How about you, Dora?" she asked as she started toward the kitchen to intercept him.

"I don't think so," Dora answered smoothly. "I have a feeling I've already overstayed my welcome."

Cody lifted his head from his task of pouring a second glass of tea. "Please, don't leave on my account. Rebecca and I can always wait a little while to get down to anything really private."

Rebecca skidded to a halt in front of him, face-to-face with the muscled expanse of his chest. "What are you doing?" Her words burst out between clenched teeth while she tilted her head back to look up at him.

"I'm making sure everyone understands the way things are."

"I haven't been roped and branded by you, and I'll thank you not to go around giving people the impression that I have been."

"You have not been roped and branded by me *yet*." He stared down at her with eyes that were glitteringly hard.

"And *what* do you mean by that?" Unable to get her spine any straighter, Rebecca threw back her shoulders and tossed her head in indignation.

Cody's eyes were diamond bright and filled with enough determination to make Rebecca's heart pound just to see it.

"I mean," he said quietly, "that the fire's built, the brand's heating and the rope's in my hand." With his arm, he pushed away the tea and leaned back against the edge of the counter. "And it's only a matter of time."

"Cody, you—I—" Cold chills chased hot flushes across her skin and joined the breathless pounding of her heart. "What are you saying?"

"Well, excuse me!"

Dora's indignant huff and the heavy stomp of her heels across the floor barely made an impression on Rebecca's reeling mind. She was too intent on the ice blue flame in Cody's eyes as his fingers bit possessively into the backs of her arms and he pulled her toward him.

"I'm saying that regardless of what some people might think—" his aqua gaze flickered toward the door, then returned to Rebecca with a heat that seared her "—you're not J.D.'s girl and you never were."

"J.D.'s girl!" Stunned, she tried to move away from him, but he wouldn't let her.

"That's what Dora says." His voice was as soft as a whisper.

Rebecca drew in a full breath and expelled it with the word, "What?" Anger whooshed through her like the blast from an incinerator.

When the front door slammed shut with a force that echoed through the room, she twisted toward the sound, eager to call Dora back and demand an explanation. But again Cody's grasp tightened, and he gently but firmly turned Rebecca back to face him.

Still whisper soft, he said, "But I don't believe it." His hands slid over the bare skin of her arms to her shoulders. "I *won't* believe it." His fingers slipped under the narrow straps of her leotard and massaged the soft flesh over her collarbone. His thumb stroked a path up the side of her neck and along her jawline while his fingers slid into her hair and guided her face closer to his. "I can't believe it."

Outside, Rebecca heard the sound of a car start. Then Cody's breath was warm and light as a feather on her face, and everything else faded to insignificance. His lips moved against hers gently, tenderly, then harder, until his mouth tore away the polite pretense of patience and demanded full possession now.

All the longing Rebecca had kept bottled up for a month, a year, a lifetime, came rushing out to greet him. Her hands slid over the crisp fabric of his uniform shirt, eagerly searching out the hard muscles underneath as Cody guided her closer.

Spreading his legs, he slid lower against the counter until his towering height was lessened and his body aligned with hers in all the most tantalizing places. He held her loosely in his arms, her hip braced against his thigh, his lips locked on hers in a kiss that said more than words could ever say.

Shivers of anxiety mingled with the flames of passion that consumed her, while a tiny, fading voice whispered warnings of danger, danger in the silent promise of his kiss, danger in the forgotten needs he aroused in her. But Rebecca didn't listen, and the voice died as she moved closer, returning his hungry kiss measure for measure.

Cody's arms tightened around her, gathering her against him. While one hand held her safe in his embrace, the other glided down the sleek curves of her back to the tapered hollow of her waist and on to the rounded flare of her hips, all encased in fuchsia nylon that conformed to her body like a second skin.

Almost purring, Rebecca moved against his hand, relishing the warm, strong touch against her starved body, all the while waiting for the fear to start and for the memories to come rushing back and send her running for shelter.

His kiss trailed over her face and down her neck as his hand began a return journey of slow exploration while the panic that Rebecca waited for never came. Instead, there was only a deep, burning fire that spread outward from her core, sending flames licking along her thighs and across her chest, down her arms and past her knees until her hands tingled and her head spun and she forgot that there had ever been a time when she was afraid.

A moaning, soft and low, began in Cody's throat as he tightened his thighs around hers and his thumbs slipped under the straps of her leotard and the elastic lace bra underneath it. In one long, slow motion, he peeled the straps over her shoulders and down her arms, revealing the tops of her full, white breasts.

Pausing, he lowered his head and trailed a line of kisses along her shoulder, from the base of her neck to the curve of her arm. Limp with aroused desire, Rebecca dropped her head back and clutched the back of his shirt in both fists for support. In all her life, she had never felt this way, like melting taffy quivering in the aftershock of an earthquake. And if she never felt this way again, she would forever remember this one moment when she was a woman made whole and new, reborn in the arms of a man.

Cody reached behind her to unfasten the lacy bra, and Rebecca's heart stood still for a beat and then started again faster than ever, driven by an anticipation that set her aflame. With the last impedance removed, he gently edged the leotard down over the peaks of her breasts until they stood free, high and proud and blushing the palest pink under his adoring gaze.

"Ah, Rebecca," he said quietly. "You're so beautiful. You are so—"

His throat closed over his words, choking them off, and he lowered his head again to kiss the beginning swell of her breast, while Rebecca's heart raced and her trembling legs threatened to collapse. His mouth moved lower until he came to the tenderest flesh at the tip, hardened and aching, waiting for his touch.

As if her mind had been waiting for that moment to come alive again, Rebecca suddenly remembered Dora. How much had she seen, and where was she now? Passion washed away in a tidal wave of humiliation that left Rebecca cowering with shame, wishing nothing more than to run away and hide.

As her change registered, Cody slowly lifted his head and gathered her against his chest, cradling her protectively against him. "Rebecca? Are you all right? I didn't mean to go too fast for you." Without waiting for a response, he refastened her bra and began to readjust the tangled leotard top. "I'm sorry."

"Dora," Rebecca whispered in a strangled tone.

"Dora? What about her?" He brushed back the hair Rebecca was trying to hide behind.

"Where is she?"

Cody lifted her chin until he could look into her eyes. "Sweetheart, Dora left a long time ago."

"Are you sure? You saw her?" Through the chaos of unreasonable guilt swirling inside her, Rebecca struggled to regain her equilibrium. She vaguely remembered the sound of a car driving away. That *was* Dora, wasn't it?

"Of course I saw her. You don't think I would try to make love to you in front of her, do you?"

Blushing furiously, Rebecca said in the same strangled voice, "I forgot all about her."

A look of pure joy spread over Cody's face, pushing aside the concern that had been there. "Well," was all that he said.

Shy and embarrassed now that the moment of mad passion was a memory to all but her quietly throbbing loins, Rebecca didn't know what to do or say. She couldn't remember yesterday, she didn't want to think about tomorrow, and polite conversation was definitely out of the question.

"If I offended you earlier, I didn't mean to," Cody said. "One way or another, I seem to put my foot in my mouth every time I get around you. Actually I came here to tell you that I've been giving some thought to what you said, and if you need time, you've got it. Although you wouldn't know it from my actions this afternoon."

Relieved even if she couldn't clearly recall what their previous confrontation had been about, Rebecca answered him with a tremulous smile. "Thank you." As an afterthought, she added, "Would you like something to eat while you're here?"

"Thanks, but I've already eaten. I just dropped the truck off on my way to work. I've got a ride coming by any minute now."

"You're working a later shift today?"

"Yeah. For the next week." A honk outside brought him to attention. Cody retucked his shirt in the back and smiled down at Rebecca while he adjusted her straps on her shoulders one more time. The backs of his fingers brushed lingeringly against her skin.

Gently he caught her chin in his hand and lifted her face toward him as he leaned down and kissed her softly on the lips. "I'll try to drop by this weekend sometime," he said. When the horn sounded again, he strode across the room, stopping at the door to look back briefly, and then he was gone.

As the door closed, Rebecca sagged against the counter and brought her hand up to hide her face. "Oh, my goodness," she whispered. "What have I done?"

Chapter Nine

The night was quiet except for the soft patter of rain. With the air conditioner off and all the windows open, Rebecca listened to the sound she had been waiting over a month to hear and pretended that the rain had brought a cool, refreshing breeze with it instead of a muggy stillness that sat over the air like a blanket of wet wool.

Dressed in one of his new sunsuits, Matthew lay on his stomach a short distance away, kicking his feet and waving his arms in a determined effort to reach Junior, who was curled at the edge of the pallet. On his stomach, with his chin resting on one paw, the dog wagged his tail encouragingly and remained just out of reach.

Rebecca rested her busy fingers for a moment and smiled at the scene of happy domesticity at her feet. Friday evening she had driven her newly repaired pickup down to the low-water bridge and hammered a Closed For The Weekend sign into the middle of the road. When she had re-

turned home, she had unplugged her phone from the wall
and settled in for a weekend without disturbances.

Life was moving too fast, and her carefully planned ex-
istence was unraveling at a frightening pace. In the past
month, she had broken every rule she had laid down for
herself and her return to Eden. She not only hadn't stayed
away from the Lockharts, but also she now seemed to be
allowing them to invade every facet of her life. Reever had
become her mechanic. Dora was fairy godmother to Matthew, and Cody—well, Cody—

Rebecca sighed at the thought of him while a slow, syrupy heat crept into the pit of her stomach and trickled
downward. The mere contemplation of Cody left her dazed
and confused.

Her feelings for him were hard to define and too real to
ignore. He was a friend she couldn't afford to have, a lover
she wasn't emotionally prepared for and a danger she
couldn't seem to stay away from. Worst of all, just being
with him made her feel happier and more alive than she
could ever remember feeling. One thing was certain—so
long as she was around him, she would never start thinking
clearly again.

The bleating of a car horn on the road outside snapped
Rebecca out of her reverie and brought her to her feet just
behind Junior, who was up and out the open door like a
shot. As she reached the doorway a few steps behind the
dog, Rebecca remembered Matthew and went back to move
him from the pallet to his carrier seat, where he would be
safe, out of the way and mobile.

Then she raced onto the front porch and across the yard
to retrieve Junior from the middle of the road, where he had
taken up a stance. The rain that had seemed like such a light
shower inside the cabin felt much heavier pelting her unprotected head and shoulders. She tugged at the dog's collar and struggled to drag him out of the road in spite of his
determination to defend the homestead, whether she wanted
him to or not.

"Junior, damn it," Rebecca huffed. "Come on back to the porch. It's wet out here."

Through rivulets of water that rolled across her forehead and into her eyes, she squinted in the direction of the headlights bouncing over the rutted road toward her. The lights blinked off and on, and the horn bleated again while the obviously small car made slow progress toward her.

With an intuition that was seldom wrong when it came to her twin, Rebecca knew without knowing how that the car was Jessy's Alpha Romeo. Watching the headlights of the little sports car nosedive into a pothole and bounce out again, Rebecca thought of her sister, who abhorred anything less than a four-lane highway, and winced.

Wanting to get out of the road before Jessy drove over them, Rebecca tugged at the dog's collar. "Come on, Junior." She didn't really expect a response, and when she tugged again a second time, harder, Junior surprised her by turning immediately toward the porch.

Her wet fingers slipped off the collar, and his sturdy body slammed into the side of her knee as he turned, knocking her off balance and sending the slick soles of her tennis shoes skidding through the even slicker mud at the side of the road.

Rebecca's heels dug a trench through the mud, and her backside came down with a bone-jarring crunch, half in the mud and half in the soggy grass beside the road. Well on his way to the porch, Junior stopped and came back to see what had happened. He nudged her shoulder with his nose and licked her cheek before sitting down beside her to wait quietly for whatever was to come next.

"You could still be returned, Junior," Rebecca said grimly. "You know that, don't you?"

He leaned closer and thumped his tail happily against the hard earth.

"We really are going to have to work on our signals, fella." She patted the top of his damp head. "Because when it comes to brute strength, you're a bigger brute than I am." She gingerly flexed the tender muscles of her rear end. The side where mud squished under her seemed slightly less sore than the side resting on a wet clump of grass.

The sleek sports car splashed to a stop a yard from Rebecca's feet. The window slowly descended, freeing disembodied laughter into the night until Jessy's smiling face appeared from the gloom of the interior and the laughter was reunited with its creator.

"Quite a show there, Sis. You entertain all your guests this way?"

"Very funny." Rebecca rose with as much dignity as she could manage after freeing herself from the suction of the mud.

"Aren't you surprised to see me?"

Rebecca looked at her sister and thought of the sign Jessy had either pulled up or driven around on the first really rainy night in months. She had arrived without warning and brought chaos with her, and Rebecca felt no surprise at all. "No." She shook her head. "This seems about right."

Jessy's broad, white-toothed grin broadened. "I'd give you a ride to the house, but you're a mess. What were you doing out here anyway?"

"Trying to get the dog out of the road," Rebecca said, twisting around to inspect the streak of mud that ran down the backs of both legs.

"Have you got a hose?"

"On the side of the house by the rose garden." Rebecca wasn't sure, but she thought she could feel mud inside her shoes, as well.

"Well, I'll drive on up to the house and get it ready. Then I'll spray you down so you don't get mud all over your house."

"You'll get wet," Rebecca warned. She wiggled her foot and was rewarded with the definite squish of mud.

"Oh, and I suppose I didn't get wet standing out in the rain pulling up that dumb sign you had in the middle of the road. Don't worry. I knew enough to dress sensibly before I started out for *this* place."

Not bothering to argue that *this* place was her home, Rebecca turned and started toward the house.

"When did you get a dog?" Jessy called out.

Rebecca kept walking. "Almost two weeks ago."

"Does he bite?"

"I don't know yet," she called over her shoulder, not slowing down in her march to the house.

"Oh, well, please," Jessy answered sarcastically, "allow *me* to be the guinea pig." She shifted the car into gear, and it shot forward, digging even deeper ruts in the mud all the way to the decorative gate in the picket fence.

Trudging back through the rain, one hand firmly gripping Junior's collar, Rebecca watched Jessy exit the car and walk barefoot to the porch. A pair of high-heeled sandals dangled from her hand, and even wet, the jumpsuit that she wore clung elegantly to the long, lean curves of her body.

Jessy dropped into a wicker chair that sat against the wall and let her shoes drop with a clunk onto the floor of the porch. Focusing her attention on Junior, she clapped her hands and whistled, calling him to her.

When he tugged against his collar, Rebecca let him go without worrying. Animals, especially dogs, had always liked Jessy. She had even talked briefly of becoming a veterinarian before she had blossomed into a natural beauty at fourteen and had begun modeling on weekends for some of Dallas's better department stores.

By the time Rebecca reached the porch, Jessy and Junior were buddies. He was on his back, eyes glazed with happiness, and Jessy was on her knees beside him, scratching under his chin and across his chest and down his stomach and sides.

Rebecca stopped beside them and stared down, shaking her head. "Junior, Junior, Junior. You've got to learn to play harder to get, son, or no woman is ever going to respect you."

Jessy looked up with a wide grin. "My natural charm strikes again."

"And you," Rebecca said. "You call that dressing sensibly?"

"It's cotton." Jessy stood and shook out the wet folds of the teal blue jumpsuit. "Wait'll you see the other things I brought." Turning up the elbow-length sleeves by another cuff width, she looked up and smiled. "For a mud-splattered, drowned rat, you're looking positively radiant, Rebecca. I have a feeling we're going to have a lot to talk about over the next few days."

She stopped suddenly. Her smile softened to a glow, and her eyes misted with feeling. "By the way, I sure have missed you. Want to give me a hug before I lose all self-control and just bawl?"

"Oh, Jess, I'm glad you're here. I've got so much to tell you." Rebecca stepped into the outstretched arms of the sister who was an extension of herself and took the first deep, totally relaxed breath she had taken in a month.

So much had changed so quickly. So much would never be the same again, no matter how much they both wished it could be, but they were still, and would always be, best friends and soul mates. They complemented and completed each other. Where one was weak, the other was strong. Where one was afraid, the other dared.

"I'm *so* glad you're here," Rebecca whispered.

Jessy held her tighter and stroked her hair gently. "I know. I know. Don't you worry. Everything will be okay."

Within a few hours, the rain was gone, leaving with as little warning as it had come, and the house was once again shut up tightly. The air conditioner hummed softly in the

ague hours between midnight and dawn, while Rebecca
nd Jessy sat cross-legged on the bed, a bowl of popcorn
etween them and tall, sweating glasses of iced tea clutched
n their hands.

"So, what was with the sign in the road?" Jessy asked in
half whisper.

"You don't have to whisper," Rebecca said. "Once Mat-
hew gets to sleep, he couldn't hear the world coming to an
nd."

"So, what's with the sign?" Jessy asked in a full voice.
"You know, I tried to call all day yesterday to tell you I was
oming. By this afternoon, I decided you were either dead
r you had the phone unplugged."

"I just wanted some time to myself, without interrup-
ions."

"I don't want to seem dense, but I thought you picked
his place to live because there would be nothing but peace
nd quiet and no one would ever bother you." Jessy popped
 piece of popcorn into her mouth and chewed. "You were
arely here two months when your truck broke down and
ou borrowed Cody's. I thought I showed amazing re-
traint when I didn't ask you if you were out of your mind.
 mean, I always thought Cody was a great guy, but he *is* a
ockhart, and aren't you supposed to be avoiding them?"

"I *am* avoiding them," Rebecca answered defensively. To
low the conversation down, she dumped the handful of
opcorn she'd been holding into her mouth.

"So, have you got your truck back?"

Still chewing, Rebecca nodded. Once she swallowed, she
ould explain that she *had* been avoiding the Lockharts un-
il recently, when the whole clan had seemed to descend on
er at once.

Jessy shrugged. "Well, all I know is that I had to go out
f town on a shoot for a couple of weeks, and when I came
ack, I found you barricaded in here with a guard dog and
o phone."

"Where was the shoot?" Rebecca asked, having swallowed and being no closer to confessing all.

"A little island with black sand off the coast of South America." Jessy's expression grew dreamy as she reminisced. "White swimsuits and white evening gowns against black sand. Very classy. Now," she said, getting back down to business, "why is it so hard for you to get some peace and quiet all of a sudden? By the way, where'd you get the dog?"

"Margaret sent him over with Cody."

"Progress." Jessy's hazel eyes narrowed. "So Cody hasn't just gone away like a good little boy. Or could it be that you haven't asked him to? Rebecca, why do I get the feeling that there's something you're not telling me?"

"There really isn't much to tell." Rebecca reached for more popcorn, and Jessy stopped her hand.

"Rebecca, we came out of the womb together. Well, six minutes apart," she amended with a shrug. "Don't lie to me." Jessy's eyes narrowed to slits, and she stared hard at Rebecca. "Unless you're lying to yourself, too. And that's not like you."

Rebecca looked back at her sister and saw a mirror that made evasion useless. "You're right," she said quietly, "Part of the reason I wanted to be alone this weekend is that I'm so confused about what I want and what I feel."

"Were you just about to discover the truth when I arrived?" Jessy asked with a gently teasing prod.

Rebecca looked into Jessy's laughing eyes and smiled, "No."

"Well, here I am, all ears." Jessy spread her arms in invitation. "Tell me about it. What has you so confused?"

Taking a deep breath, Rebecca said, "I think I'm falling in love with Cody."

Jessy gasped and choked on the piece of popcorn she'd just tossed into her mouth.

Rain blown by wind gusts pounded the outside of the cabin. Inside, a steamy breeze blew from the back porch, u the hallway and across the kitchen before disappearing out the windows that were open to the front porch. The late-morning light was thunderstorm gray. Jessy stood at the kitchen counter chopping broccoli for the cream-of-broccoli soup Rebecca was cooking for lunch.

"Do you think he'll come by today?" Jessy asked.

"I doubt it." Rebecca sat at the kitchen table, Matthew in her arms and a bottle in his mouth.

"Do you think he'll be mad? About the sign?"

"I wouldn't blame him."

Jessy laid down her knife and looked at Rebecca with sympathy. "This could really turn into a mess, couldn't it?"

Rebecca winced and slowly nodded. Jessy was right, but hearing the truth voiced didn't make it any easier to deal with. Being around Cody was like playing with fire, and when you play with fire, you have to expect to get burned.

"I sure would like to see him, though," Jessy continued. "What does he look like these days? I remember him as sort of a handsome bean pole with great eyes. But I always thought he had the kind of looks that would only improve with age."

The thought of what Cody looked like these days brought a smile to Rebecca's face and a flush of heat to all of her.

Before she could answer, Jessy's teasing voice interrupted. "Look at that smile. If just thinking about him does that to you, I've got to get a look at this man. If he's not over here by tomorrow, I may have to drive over to his place, just to say 'hi,' of course."

"Tomorrow's Tuesday. I go into San Angelo on Tuesday."

"Good. I'll come along. I've got some shopping I want to do."

"I'll have a meeting to go to," Rebecca warned.

"That's okay." While Jessy's voice stayed light, her eyes grew serious. "How's that going, anyway?"

"Pretty well. It's a good group."

"Oh, I'm glad," Jessy said with a smile. "Well, look, while you're in your meeting, I can shop. Maybe I'll even buy you a surprise."

Rebecca groaned inwardly, thinking that Jessy's surprises were invariably clothes that reflected her own dramatic tastes rather than Rebecca's conservative ones. "Be gentle."

Jessy laughed. "Well, of course."

The following evening, after a long, hard day in town that had left Rebecca exhausted and Jessy wired, Rebecca was lifting a baked chicken from the oven when Jessy came dashing in from outside with Junior at her heels.

"A red truck, Rebecca," she announced, practically bursting with excitement. "There's a red truck driving up the road. Is it him?"

Rebecca carefully set the chicken down before she dropped it. "It could be," she said cautiously.

"All right!" Jessy leapt into the air, fists extended in triumph. When she returned to earth, she made three quick pumping motions with her arm at her side.

"You're going to have to act a little cooler than this, Jessica," Rebecca said with the last shred of calmness left in her body.

Immediately straightening, Jessy thrust her nose in the air and lifted her brow in haughty disdain. "But, of course, darling. I'm a model. I can strike any pose." The ice melted into a grin, and she whirled and raced to the window. "I hear gravel. The truck is stopping."

At the window, she turned and looked at Rebecca, laughing. "I feel just like I did when we used to spy on Houston and his girlfriends. Do you remember that?"

With painful embarrassment, Rebecca indeed remembered that. It was one of the many things she had allowed Jessy to talk her into that had seemed harmless at the outset. But the night they had been discovered and subjected to the wrath of their older brother, Rebecca had been deeply ashamed while Jessy had walked away unabashed.

"Get away from the window, Jessy," Rebecca ordered, her determination heightened by a sense of foreboding.

Jessy waved an impatient hand at her and turned back to the window. "This can't be Cody." Her voice was hushed by astonishment. "Those shoulders. Those arms." She dropped the curtain and turned away, fanning herself. "Rebecca, I'm impressed."

When Cody's knock sounded at the door, Jessy leapt forward. "I'll get it. Won't he be surprised to see me?"

"Oh, Lord, give me strength," Rebecca whispered.

After a meal in which Jessy talked nonstop and Rebecca and Cody gratefully listened and answered only when necessary, Cody pushed his chair back and laid his napkin on the table. "I really hadn't intended to stay for dinner, but I'm certainly glad you asked me. It was excellent."

"Oh, now, Cody," Jessy said. "You didn't really think I was just going to let you drive away again after not seeing you for all these years."

Rebecca looked from one to the other and felt torn in two. Jessy could hardly sit still from holding in all the things she wanted to say once Cody was gone. Watching her sister try to control herself, Rebecca remembered the days when boys were still strange and wonderful creatures who evoked long nights of whispers, giggles and sighs.

But when she turned from Jessy to look into Cody's eyes, Rebecca wanted only to be alone with him. To stand next to him and feel his strength envelop her, her hand in his. To watch his lips lower toward hers and feel the thrill in her heart as she waited. She had only to look at him to know that he wanted the same thing.

"Jessy, it was really good seeing you again." Cody glanced toward Rebecca. When his eyes locked onto hers and held, everything else in the room disappeared. "I've got a really big day ahead of me tomorrow. I guess I'd better be going.''

Rebecca was on her feet before the last word was out of his mouth. "I'll walk you out."

He smiled and his eyes never left her as he held out his hand.

"I'll clear the table," Jessy said to no one in particular.

Rebecca slipped her hand into Cody's. He laced his fingers through hers and all but pulled her from the room. Outside, a stiff wind rustled through the tops of the trees, but reached no lower. Twilight had come and gone. The night was dark, hot and still.

Cody pulled the door closed behind them, caught Rebecca around the waist and tugged her against his chest. "Don't ever put up a sign like that again. If you want me to stay away, tell me. I won't like it, but I'll do it."

Rebecca looked up at him, his face lowered to within inches of hers, his eyes glittering even in the dark. She opened her mouth to speak, and suddenly words didn't matter. She wanted him. Totally. Completely. The fear was gone. The anger was gone, and desire like she had only dreamed of had taken their place.

As if he read her mind, Cody crushed his mouth against hers in a kiss fierce enough to drive all other thoughts from her mind. If he lifted her into his arms and carried her to the garden to make love to her under the stars, she wouldn't utter a word of protest. Her body ached for his touch, here and now.

"Oh, Rebecca." Cody's words were a sigh against her skin as he lifted his lips a fraction of an inch from hers. "I've missed you so. If Jessy weren't here—" He rested his forehead against Rebecca's and groaned softly. His hands held the back of her head, keeping her lips within easy reach. "I don't think I have to tell you what I'd want if Jessy weren't here."

"No."

"It's all I've been able to think of."

"Me, too."

Cody lifted his head and stared hard into her eyes. "Really?"

"Really." With each movement he made, her breasts seemed to grow fuller, yearning toward him, aching for the touch of his hand, his lips, for the brush of flesh against flesh.

"How long's Jessy going to be here?"

"All week, I think."

With another groan, he dropped his forehead back to hers. "Rebecca?"

A fire burned from her thighs into the pit of her stomach, making it hard for her to think about anything else. "Yes?"

"I may have to stay away until she's gone."

"Cody." Rebecca's hands slid over his shoulders and up the back of his neck. Her fingers wove their way through his hair, then curled into fists, pulling his mouth toward hers.

"Yes?" The tip of his tongue brushed the edge of her mouth as he waited for her to speak. "What is it, sweetheart?" He caught her lower lip between his teeth and tugged gently, still waiting.

Rebecca moaned and pressed herself against him, but she couldn't say the words that would ask him to take her now, where they stood. Like a cat in heat, she longed to rub herself against him and cry out with the savagery of her need. She wanted to wipe out the past and be reborn in his arms. She wanted to forget everything but how good it felt to be loved by him.

With a gasp of pain, Cody slowly peeled her body from his and pushed her away until a foot or more separated them. His arms trembled, but he held her there. "Rebecca, don't do that again unless you're ready to do something about it." The words came with effort from a voice that was raw.

"I am."

He shook his head. "And I'm too far gone. When I make love to you, I'm going to do it right. Inch by inch. I'm going to set you on fire and put it out a dozen times over. And I'm going to know that you'll never wake up the next day and be sorry it happened."

"I won't. Not now. I know what I want."

Cody shook his head again. "You're feeling secure right now because you've got your sister here. I've got to know that you'll feel the same way when it's just you and me again. If you still want me then, give me a call, and I'm yours."

He pulled her near again and kissed her firmly on the mouth. Confusion and rejection had cooled the inferno inside Rebecca, but the warm, slow, sensuous exploration of his lips on hers ignited the fires inside her again. She wanted to be angry with him, but she couldn't be. The small part of her brain that could still reason knew that he was right. She needed more than passion, more than sex, and she needed a man who wanted more than her body. She couldn't be angry with Cody for insisting on giving her all that she needed.

Cody ended the kiss with obvious reluctance and stepped back. His hands trailed down her arms. "Good night, Rebecca."

She curled her fingers through his. "Good night, Cody."

"Call me."

"I will."

His fingers slipped through hers, and he left. Rebecca stood on the porch and watched the taillights of his pickup disappear from view. She stood for a long time in the hot, still night before the ache inside her finally faded and she was ready to go back inside.

"Well," Jessy said, "imagine that."

Rebecca turned from her own image in the mirror to look

at Jessy. "What?" Rebecca looked back at the mirror and, except for a slight shyness, was rather pleased with what she saw.

The white cotton lawn of the camisole top was as delicate as a lady's hankie. The embroidered trim was soft to the touch and more delicate still. The whole thing hugged her newly enhanced curves with the faithfulness of a lover's hands.

"My baby sister suddenly looks better in lingerie than I do," Jessy answered in a breezy pout.

"Baby?"

"I'm older by six minutes."

"You're never going to forget that, are you?"

"No. Now hurry and try on that other thing hanging on the back of the bathroom door."

"Jessy?" Rebecca turned back for one last look in the mirror. The camisole was beautiful and so were its matching tap pants, as well as the silk-and-lace teddy and the chemise she had already tried on. They were all so beautiful that they made her feel like a whole new person. But still—

Jessy paused in the midst of unwrapping one more lacy confection, looked up and smiled. "Uh-huh?"

Rebecca turned half-around with a beginning suspicion forming. "Why are you having me try these on?"

"Don't you like them?" Jessy looked disappointed.

"Well, of course I do. They're gorgeous, but I haven't worn anything like this in so long." She glanced once more into the mirror. "Actually I've *never* worn anything like this. You wear things like this."

"You look great," Jessy said encouragingly. "I think I'm jealous. You've been exercising, haven't you?"

Rebecca left the mirror and walked to the bed, smiling. She shoved aside the boxes and sat facing her sister. "Jess, you're so sweet. And so transparent. What are you up to?"

Jessy sighed. Caught in the act, it was useless to deny what Rebecca had already guessed. "They're yours."

"Oh, Jess."

"Rebecca," Jessy said sternly.

Rebecca recognized the don't-argue-with-me look in her sister's eye. "But I thought you were shopping for yourself yesterday."

"I bought some lace hose and a garter belt. It's the cutest thing, with little pink roses on it. But I've got to be honest with you, I model that stuff—" she pointed to the things that were strewn across the bed "—so much that I'm getting kind of tired of wearing them. I'm really starting to crave things like that virginal white cotton underwear we used to wear when we were about six."

"Jessy, you're insane."

"Why? I happen to like cotton."

"No," Rebecca groaned in frustration, and held up a fistful of the silky lingerie. "I'm talking about this! *Why* did you buy this for me?"

"Oh, because." Jessy stopped and cleared her throat. Her hazel eyes clouded with a frown of discomfort.

"Just because?" Rebecca's quick flash of temper cooled, and she gently smoothed out the wadded lingerie she had shaken in Jessy's face. "Jess, is there something you're trying to tell me with all this?"

"Well, yes, actually there is, but I'd rather not have to say it."

Moved by the gathering tears in her sister's luminous eyes, Rebecca put her hand over Jessy's. "I don't want you to have to hide your feelings from me. Please, tell me what it is."

Jessy sighed uncomfortably and turned her glistening gaze away. "You're just so different, Becky." Her words were little more than a trembling whisper. "There's a part of you I can't reach anymore, and it's like I've lost a piece of myself. I want to help you, and I don't know how." Her voice disappeared entirely on the last word, and she stopped to sniff back tears.

Dressed in a flimsy camisole and tap pants that had become acutely inadequate, Rebecca longed to put her arms around Jessy and offer the comfort that they both needed. But physical contact with anyone, even Jessy, didn't come easily anymore, especially when emotions were involved. Offering the only thing she had to give, Rebecca squeezed her sister's hand, then quickly escaped into the bathroom to change into the T-shirt and cutoffs she had been wearing earlier.

"I told you I didn't want to say it," Jessy called through the closed door.

In spite of her own heavy heart, Rebecca smiled. Hanging on the back of the bathroom door was a truly outrageous teddy made entirely of black nylon lace that was soft to the touch and thin as a veil.

"Oh, really now," she said, opening the bathroom door with the teddy dangling from her extended index finger. "What am I supposed to do with this?"

"Wear it under flannel in the winter. You'll look like a lumberjack and feel like a *woman.*" Jessy's voice dipped to a throaty rumble on the last word, and she leaned forward with a teasing grin, her tears forgotten.

"Tell me something, Jess." Rebecca tossed the scrap of lace atop the garment pile in the center of the bed and sat down again, facing her twin. "Do you really wear things like that when you're with a man?"

"It depends on who the man is. I've worn things like that with lots of photographers."

"Men," Rebecca insisted. "Lovers."

With a heavy sigh, Jessy flopped onto her back, bouncing the bed and scattering the lingerie into a silken kaleidoscope of peacock colors. "Oh, Rebecca, you don't really want to talk about this.'' She sighed again and ran her fingers through her thick mane of dark blond hair.

"Of course I do."

Jessy squinted her eyes closed and groaned. "This isn't going to be easy to say." She took a deep breath and blurted, "I'm a virgin."

Rebecca rocked back and waited for the punch line while Jessy slowly eased open one eye and said, "Well?"

"You're joking, right?" This woman was her sister, her twin, practically her other half. This couldn't be.

Both eyes open now, Jessy answered, "No" in a tiny voice that was more like a bleat. "But you don't have to seem so shocked."

"But how could you be? I thought— Well—" Flabbergasted, Rebecca stuttered to a halt, unable to sort out what she thought, except that she'd have sworn Jessy hadn't been a virgin since high school, when every boy they knew had circled around the fickle, flirtatious Jessy the way bees circled honeysuckle. "But, you told me— Didn't you?"

Rebecca stared at the sister she suddenly didn't know while hurt and anger replaced her bafflement. From childhood through high school, and in all the years since, she had told Jessy everything, no matter how painful or private, and all this time, Jessy had withheld this one profound secret.

"Jessy, why? Why would you lie to me like that?"

"I didn't," Jessy insisted, leaning forward intently. "I may have misled you, but I didn't lie to you."

"It's the same thing."

"No, it isn't, and I had my reasons."

Recognizing the sullen look that was stealing its way across Jessy's face, Rebecca realized that the surprises weren't over and that this confession wasn't easy for Jessy and had been a long time in coming.

"Okay." Rebecca folded her arms in front of her and leaned back to wait. "But those reasons had better be good."

"Stephen."

"Stephen?" Surprise, followed closely by curiosity, chased away the lingering traces of Rebecca's anger. She hadn't thought of Stephen in years, and remembering him now reminded her of the fresh and fickle days of their youth.

Her crush on Cody had been what dreams were made of, but Stephen had been real, someone she could reach out and touch. While she had pined for Cody in her heart, Stephen had given her her first kiss, been her steady throughout high school and taken her to the prom. In college, they had become lovers and then betrothed. Theirs was never a passionate affair, but for a while at least, marrying Stephen had seemed the natural thing to do.

Returning to the present, Rebecca shook her head in puzzlement. "Why would you lie to me because of Stephen?"

"Because, damn it," Jessy practically shouted, "I was in love with him." She took a deep breath and continued more quietly, "But he was your boyfriend, and then he was your fiancé, even though I knew you didn't really love him. Not the way you loved Cody."

Stunned and not quite believing what she was hearing, Rebecca repeated, "You were in love with Stephen?"

"Stark raving mad about him! The night you called me up to tell me the two of you had finally gone all the way, I thought I was going to die."

"We were nineteen, Jessy. You were living in New York and dating that photographer, Raoul Whatsits. I thought—"

"I know." Jessy held up her hand to stop the flow of Rebecca's memories. "You thought what I wanted you to think. Me and my stupid pride. I was so afraid you'd guess the truth that I misled you in the other direction."

"Those are called lies, Jessy."

"I never actually told you I'd slept with anyone," Jessy said defensively. "I think everybody just assumed it because I dated so many different guys."

"Maybe." Rebecca sighed, disappointed in herself that she hadn't paid more attention at the time. Jessy should never have been able to keep so much hidden for so long.

"I didn't *want* you to know, Rebecca." Jessy reached out to brush her sister's arm, reestablishing the bond that had been strained. "Whatever happened between you and Stephen, I didn't want my feelings to get in the way."

"So if you cared so much about him, when Stephen and I broke up, why didn't you go after him?"

"Well, the reason was twofold," Jessy answered slowly. "First, he disappeared too fast."

Rebecca laughed and gave her sister's hand a quick squeeze. "Well, I'm glad to hear that. I'd hate to think your reason was a noble one."

"Far from it." Jessy glanced up and quickly slid her gaze away from Rebecca's smiling face. "The second reason was guilt."

"Guilt? What would you have to feel guilty about?"

"I hate to tell you this, but I guess if there was ever a night for confession, this is it."

"Probably. I'm so tired now, I doubt that I'll remember a lot of this tomorrow." Rebecca gazed toward the windows for the first telltale approach of dawn and was relieved to see no pale glow creeping past the shutters that were closed up tight each night.

"Do you remember what you told me just a few weeks before the wedding?" Jessy asked.

"When I was afraid I was making a mistake?"

"'Terrible mistake' was what you said."

"Okay." Rebecca nodded in agreement. She remembered the conversation, and she remembered the panicked foreboding that had taken all the joy out of the wedding preparations.

"You said that you loved Stephen, but you weren't *in* love with him, and that the two of you hardly ever slept together anymore, and that you thought Stephen was feeling the same way but neither one of you had the guts to admit it."

"Yes," Rebecca agreed again. Hearing Jessy was like reliving that summer when what had been fun and romantic in high school had become stagnant and more of a duty than a joy.

"Well, you know me," Jessy said with a shrug, "the original bull in a china shop. I swear to you, Rebecca, I had only the best intentions."

Rebecca almost laughed. She had never connected Stephen's garbled phone call breaking off the engagement and his subsequent disappearance with anything Jessy might have done, though Rebecca realized now that she should have. Almost from infancy, Jessy had taken her extra six minutes of life very seriously and had considered herself Rebecca's defender against all peril, real or imagined.

"What did you do?" Rebecca asked, hoping she wouldn't regret knowing.

"I asked Stephen to dinner. I thought maybe if he and I talked, I'd be able to tell if he really *was* feeling the same way you were. I thought he might be more honest with me than he could be with you."

Horrified at the thought, Rebecca gasped. "You didn't tell him what I said, did you?"

"Oh, good grief, Rebecca, credit me with a little more sense than that."

"Sorry," Rebecca said, abashed. "So what *did* you say?"

"Well, actually we just had dinner and talked about things in general, and then he brought me home."

"And you felt guilty because of that?"

"Well, no," Jessy said slowly. "Not exactly. I felt guilty because we never actually got around to talking about you at all. And then when I turned to say good-night at the door, it was suddenly like every fantasy I'd ever had was coming true."

Jessy's voice had taken on such a dreamy quality that Rebecca knew the answer even before she asked, "He kissed you?"

"Yes. Just a little kiss at first, but then it changed, and when Stephen finally let go of me and walked away, we were both shaking like leaves in a high wind. I was so afraid you could tell what had happened that I slept on the couch that night."

"Well, I'll be damned," Rebecca said softly. She remembered the night Jessy had fallen asleep on the couch instead of in the room they shared in their parents' home. And she remembered the relief she'd felt when Stephen had called the next day to say he couldn't go through with the wedding. Rebecca hadn't needed a reason because she felt the same way, and it wasn't until after Stephen had dropped out of college and just disappeared that she even thought to wonder what had happened to cause such a sudden change in him.

Now that she knew, Rebecca felt a little guilty herself. "I wish it had turned out differently for you, Jessy. I wish I'd known."

"Maybe we just weren't meant to be lucky in love."

"Aren't we a pair? All those years, I was in love with Cody, and you were in love with Stephen," Rebecca said softly. "And all these years later, we're still in love with them, and we've never gotten them."

"At least you still have a chance. He's gorgeous, Rebecca."

Rebecca started to ask who. Then she stopped herself as the image of Cody floated across her mind, and she smiled instead. "Yes. Yes, he is, isn't he?"

"Don't lose him." Jessy took Rebecca's hand. "Don't let anything stop you. One of us, at least, has got to be happy."

"What about you? Stephen's out there somewhere."

"No." Jessy shook her head. "It's too late. I wouldn't even know where to start looking. It's up to you, Rebecca, to be happy for both of us."

"Well, I'm too tired to do it tonight. Let's go to sleep, and I'll start on it first thing in the morning."

"Good, and the first thing you need to do is to tell Cody the truth."

A cold fist of fear clenched around Rebecca's heart. "About what?"

"About everything," Jessy said, stifling a yawn. "Matthew is the spitting image of J.D., and it won't be too long before everybody starts noticing it. Tell Cody now. He's a good man, and he's crazy about you. He'll help you."

"Oh, Jessy," Rebecca groaned, "why did you have to start getting sensible now?"

"Old age. Sooner or later it catches up with all of us." Jessy rolled over on her side and tucked her hands under her head. "Good night."

Rebecca cleared off the bed, pulled back the covers and shook Jessy awake again. With the bedside lamp turned off, the pale light of dawn seemed to set the room aglow. Rebecca tiptoed into the kitchen and made a bottle for Matthew. Maybe she could nap this afternoon, but for now, there was no hope of sleeping.

She would feed Matthew while she rocked and watched the sunrise, and maybe somewhere in there she could find a solution that wouldn't leave her frozen in terror.

Chapter Ten

"Rebecca?"

Half-asleep, Rebecca was startled by the sound of a voice so close to her in the night. Thinking it was only a dream, she rolled over and was almost asleep again before she remembered that Jessy was visiting and there was only one bed.

"Yes, Jessica?" Rebecca mumbled into her pillow.

"Do you suppose if he finds out about J.D. on his own that he's going to know the difference between being lied to and just being misled?"

Groaning, Rebecca opened her eyes, rolled onto her back and stared at the black void above her head. Two days had gone by since she and Jessy had talked until dawn, and for two nights, Rebecca had lost sleep worrying about what would happen with Cody once Jessy had gone. Tonight, determined to sleep, Rebecca had refused to allow Cody's name to be spoken.

"Jess, I'm too tired to worry about it now."

"Just think about how upset you were with me when you thought I'd lied to you, and then answer that one little question," Jessy insisted quietly. "After that, I'll shut up, and you can sleep."

Rebecca clearly remembered the betrayal she had felt at Jessy's revelation and that anger had been the first reaction to that feeling of betrayal.

"No," Rebecca said, "I don't think he would understand the difference."

Cody's past had been one long string of betrayal and rejection, all by women, starting with his mother's death and ending with the loss of his daughter when his wife had left him. If any man was primed to resent even the slightest betrayal at the hands of a woman, Cody Lockhart was that man.

"I was afraid of that," Jessy answered. "Maybe before I leave, we can figure something out. I'd sure hate it if everything you've got here started blowing apart someday, and it can't be good that Dora's been sniffing around. That woman's never done anything decent in her life."

"I know it, but I don't know what to do. Other than pack up and leave, everything I can think of is just going to make it worse."

Across the top of the covers, Jessy's hand found Rebecca's and clasped it tightly. "We'll think of something. You've been hurt enough. It's time for you to get some happiness back in your life."

"I'm happy," Rebecca protested in a whisper.

"You're existing, Becky. There's more to life than taking care of a baby and making quilts. The day you make love to a man and enjoy it is the day you'll truly start to heal."

"Oh, Jess," Rebecca said with tender laughter in her voice, "I'm going to miss you when you go."

Jessy squeezed the hand that was still next to hers. "I'll miss you, too, Rebecca. You don't know how much. But you've got Matthew now, and a new life, and pretty soon, you'll have Cody. We're grown now, and some things will never be the way they used to be."

"You don't know that. About Cody, I mean. A year from now Matthew and I could be back in Austin, pestering you." A note of teasing crept into Rebecca's voice. "My future is very uncertain."

"I don't think so. I don't think you and Cody could get away from each other now if you tried. Besides, I might go find Stephen, get married and start a family of my own."

Rebecca laughed. "Well, you do look pretty maternal when you're rocking Matthew, but when it comes to diaper time, I'm not so sure you're really ready for it."

"I'd have nine months to get ready for it. I might surprise you."

Rising up on one elbow, Rebecca stared into the darkness where she knew Jessy lay. "You're at least halfway serious, aren't you?"

"At least," Jessy agreed softly. "I get lonely sometimes, and I'm not used to that. What happened a year ago took you away and put you somewhere I couldn't reach. And even though you're getting over that, the spot that's closest to your heart doesn't belong to me anymore. It's Matthew's now. I guess in a way, J.D. changed both of our lives that night, and it's time that we both got on with building new ones."

Rebecca lay back down and stared at the black space above her. She knew how Jessy felt. They were both more alone now, and life was so much more frightening than it had ever been before.

"What if I can't do it, Jessy?" Rebecca asked. "What if this is as good as it ever gets?"

"You're already there, Rebecca. You can't see it yet, but I can. You're already there."

Rebecca's thoughts were miles away when she pulled into Margaret's driveway on Tuesday. The week with Jessy had been like a vacation, exhilarating but exhausting. They had both cried when Jessy left on Sunday, as if they sensed that Jessy's prediction would come true and they would never have another week just for the two of them again.

After Jessy drove away, Rebecca had had a thousand and one things to catch up on before Tuesday, but she had fallen asleep to the sound of rain late Sunday afternoon and had slept through the night and most of Monday, with occasional periods of consciousness to care for Matthew.

When she reached her group session on Tuesday, she still hadn't decided when she would call Cody or what she would tell him when she saw him again. Jessy's warning rang in her ears and reverberated through the Tuesday session.

The sudden changes taking place in Rebecca's life had become a catalyst for the hopes and fears of many within the group. What she wasn't prepared for was that her own re-emerging sexuality would become the newest hot topic, especially after the week of soul-searching she had just gone through with Jessy.

Rebecca was only too glad to put San Angelo behind her and return to the quiet of her life just west of Eden. As she pulled in front of Margaret's house, she was disappointed to find a car was already parked in the gravel driveway next to the porch steps and blocking the fastest path to the front porch.

Pulling the truck as close as she could get it to the car's back bumper, Rebecca turned off the radio, which was more static than music, shut off the wipers, which thumped loudly from one side of the windshield to the other, and sat in the truck listening to the torrent that the skies had opened up and poured forth sometime during the afternoon.

When she had left San Angelo, the sound of the rain on the cab of the truck had been like the drumming of impatient fingers on a desktop. Now the sound was more like the pounding of angry fists. Rebecca reached for the inadequate umbrella that was lying on the floorboard and gave silent thanks for the sturdy cowboy boots she had decided to wear at the last minute.

Flinging open the truck door, she bailed out and unfurled the umbrella at a dead run. She was soaked before she had gone two steps. At the front of the truck, she drew to a halt and stared unbelieving at the set of bumpers that were almost touching and far too close together for her to get through. Tossing a curse into the rain, she dashed around to the front of the car and onto the porch.

Once there, she looked back at the car in dismay as she realized it was Dora's, and Dora was the last person Rebecca was in the mood to cope with right now. Hot, tired and frazzled, all she wanted was to get her baby and get home with as few complications as possible. After that, she wanted to get out of these wet clothes, take a long, refreshing bath and spend the rest of the night trying to figure out what to do with the rest of her life.

Leaving the dripping umbrella on the porch, Rebecca opened the squeaking screen door and went inside. Margaret, who sat on the couch facing the door, looked up and smiled.

"Wouldn't you just know it?" Margaret said. "The first good rain we get in months, and it turns out to be a regular gully washer. Hope you didn't get too wet trying to make it inside. I guess you noticed we've got company."

Raindrops rolled down Rebecca's arms and off the tips of her fingers. She nodded politely to Dora, who sat in the chair beside the sofa and had twisted around to witness Rebecca's entrance.

"In rain like this, there's not much way to stay dry," Rebecca replied in answer to Margaret's concern.

"Oh, dear, I'm so sorry," Dora said. "If I'd known you would be here so soon, I would have had J.D. move the car up so you could get closer to the steps."

Dora's mouth kept moving, but Rebecca couldn't hear a thing after J.D.'s name. Her heart thudded and then seemed to go into slow motion as all the blood in her veins turned icy cold. Instinct drew her toward Matthew, who lay on his stomach, arms flapping, feet kicking, happily unconcerned that a viper was within striking distance.

A suntanned hand, slim, with long fingers, rested on Matthew's diapered bottom. Blue-jeaned legs sprawled comfortably next to Matthew, who seemed to be enjoying the attention of the newest stranger in his life.

Slowed by dread, Rebecca struggled to force her gaze up the slim torso, clad in a white T-shirt, to the deeply tanned face that most would call handsome and the thinning blond hair that was once streaked with copper and was now slicked back neatly, like a little boy on his way to church.

The lips, which looked strange without a cigarette between them, smiled. The eyes that were the same clear blue as Matthew's stayed cold as they returned Rebecca's steady gaze. The hand that touched Matthew seemed to tighten, and that one small movement brought Rebecca out of her trance and into action.

Shaking with the icy fury that pumped through her with every beat of her heart, she walked to Matthew and knelt so close to J.D. that the hairs on her arms rose and a chill passed over her. Careful not to upset her little boy, she lifted him into her arms and cuddled him to her on the way to his infant seat, where she strapped him in.

She gathered up the few toys that were close to the diaper bag and packed them away. Margaret brought the cooler and a few more toys, which she added to the diaper bag.

"Are you all right?" Margaret whispered.

Afraid to trust her voice, Rebecca nodded.

"I'll help you carry some of this out," Margaret said, lifting the cooler and the diaper bag and leaving Matthew for Rebecca, who lifted him and squeezed out the door ahead of Margaret.

Outside, Rebecca took one look at the rain and traded burdens, leaving Margaret on the porch with Matthew while she ran to the truck with the cooler and diaper bag. When she returned, she retrieved the umbrella and settled Matthew in her arms with the umbrella over him. Then she leaned to the side and kissed Margaret on the cheek, murmuring, "Bless you."

Without a backward glance or another word of farewell, Rebecca turned and hurried through the rain with her precious burden. To get the truck door open, she had to partially close the umbrella and drop it in the wet grass at the side of the house while she used her body to shelter Matthew.

Rain soaked through her hair and into the collar of her shirt as she slipped Matthew and his carrier onto the truck seat and fastened the seat belt around him. Backing out of the truck, Rebecca slammed the door and shook herself like a drowned rat. When she turned to retrieve the umbrella, she came face-to-face with J.D., who stood waiting for her, blinking through the rivulets of water that rolled down from his unprotected head.

"I've got to talk to you." He reached out to grab her arm as he spoke.

As soon as she felt his fingers close around her wrist, Rebecca jerked her arm free and pulled back. "Don't touch me!"

"But I didn't know!" he shouted through the rain.

"Didn't know *what?*" Rebecca demanded. She couldn't believe he would try to talk to her. She couldn't believe he thought she would care about anything he had to say.

"About the baby. My God, Rebecca, what you must have been through!" He reached for her again.

She deflected his hand with her forearm and stood her ground. "What I must have been through? You son of a bitch, you know what I've been through! You did it to me! How dare you even come near me!"

"Rebecca." Suddenly J.D. grabbed her by the shoulders and tried to pull her nearer.

Doubling up her fists, Rebecca struck him frantically, hitting him in the chest and across one arm. At the same time, she whirled away from him, trying to reach the truck before he could come after her again, but she wasn't fast enough.

J.D. grabbed her wrists and pinned her arms behind her as he shoved her back against the truck. "Listen to me," he shouted with his face in hers. "You don't understand. I'm going to make it up to you."

With the weight of his body pinning her to the truck, Rebecca's jerky gasps turned to panicked whimpers. She had to get away from him. She couldn't stand to have him touching her. She had to—

"Listen to me, Rebecca," J.D. said from a million miles away. "I want to marry you. I want to be Matthew's father."

Using all the force that racing adrenaline and seasoned rage could provide, Rebecca drove her knee straight up into the delicate tissue unprotected between J.D.'s widespread legs. His breath went out of him in a startled huff, and his hands slid from her wrists as he crumpled to his knees and began to rock back and forth on the ground. A low, keening wheeze came from deep in his throat.

As he gazed up at her with wide, helpless eyes, Rebecca's fear of him hardened to loathing. This time she had done what she hadn't had the chance to do the first time, and she felt good, better than she had in a long time.

Stepping around J.D., she reached into the wet grass for her umbrella. When she turned back, she held the umbrella in both hands, keeping it between her body and J.D.'s while she leaned over him and whispered, "Don't ever, *ever* come near me or my baby again. I was your victim once, but I will never be a victim again, not for anyone. Go back where you came from. You're not wanted here."

With that, she stalked around the back of the truck, got in and backed up just enough to pull out around Dora's car.

As Rebecca drove away, her last glimpse of J.D. showed him still on his knees, hands cupped in front of him, rocking. It was a picture she wanted to carry with her.

When Rebecca reached the cabin, Junior rose from the shaded porch and sauntered out to meet the truck, his tail wagging in a slow, easy greeting. His friendly face seemed to smile up at her as he trotted next to her, back and forth to the house, until everything was unloaded and everyone was safely inside.

With the pickup locked and Junior beside her, Rebecca bolted the cabin door and pulled the curtains closed. The returning tremors of fear that had stalked her during the drive home were rapidly degenerating into blind panic. The more she thought of what was to come, the closer she was to unraveling totally.

She had never thought it would come to this. Remembering the bitterness J.D. had harbored toward Eden and all the people in it, Rebecca had believed this was the one place she would never see him.

And if by some fluke he ever did return, she had thought his guilt would keep him away from her. What she had forgotten was that J.D. never bothered with emotions like guilt. When he wanted something, he took it, and he didn't worry about the consequences until they caught up with him.

Now that he was back, Rebecca wasn't sure if she believed what he had said or not. A shiver of cold terror ran through the pit of her stomach and up the back of her neck at the thought that J.D. could be crazy enough to think she would marry him, or let him claim any rights in Matthew's life.

A loud cry from Matthew cut short the wave of panic that swept through her and brought Rebecca around in search of her son. She found him, still strapped into his carrier, sitting on the floor midway between the front door and his crib. A worried Junior hovered nearby. The affectionate nudge from a wet nose, which normally sent Matthew into spasms of mirth, now just irritated him further.

A wildly swinging fist parted the fur just below Junior's collar, and the dog shifted sideways. His sad brown eyes seemed relieved by Rebecca's arrival on the scene. Repentant, she freed Matthew from his prison and carried him to the old wooden table she used for changing him.

Murmuring soothingly, she stripped him down, wiped him off and dried him, put lotion where the heat chafed him, rubbed the angry tension from his muscles and tickled him into a good mood before she redressed him. Then she put him on a floor pallet and ran to the bedroom to strip off her own wet clothes and shrug into an old chenille robe that was warm, comfortable and far from elegant. Pattering back into the living room on bare feet, Rebecca carried Matthew with her into the kitchen to heat his bottle.

When they settled down into the rocking chair in front of the fireplace, Rebecca was almost cold enough to light a fire. The scene at Margaret's and a thorough soaking had taken their toll, stressing her mind and body to their limits, and the softest of tickles had begun to scratch at her throat when she swallowed.

Matthew sucked greedily at his bottle while she held him closer than normal and watched the changing emotions on his face. From avid to content to sleepy to sound asleep and as limp as overcooked pasta, he slipped through the stages that never failed to bring a smile to Rebecca's face. Sometimes she envied him the simplicity of his life. And for all the times when the burden of his needs grew heavy, there were more times when having him to care about and care for was all that kept her going.

She leaned down to him and laid a kiss on his brow, then brushed her cheek over the soft curls of his telltale red hair. "Oh, Matthew," she whispered, and pressed another kiss against his temple. When she straightened, she slipped her index finger under his palm and lifted his hand out of the folds of his blanket. Long fingers curled around hers, holding tight. "Why did you have to look so much like your father? I know Margaret noticed. It would take a blind man not to see with J.D. sitting right there beside you."

Rebecca squeezed her eyes shut against the hot sting of tears as she pulled her little boy closer. Grief pounded in her heart. Dora had seen it, of course. It was she who had called J.D., and he had returned to claim his son. There was no other explanation.

Silent tears ran down Rebecca's cheeks as she carried Matthew to his crib and laid him down. When she turned toward the door where Junior lay keeping watch, he lifted his head in greeting and thumped his tail against the floor twice.

"What am I going to do with you, fella?" She knelt beside him and scratched his head while his tail pounded the floor steadily. "Huh? You don't have any idea, do you? Well, neither do I. Maybe I can drop you at Cody's on my way out of town. You like him, don't you?"

In answer, Junior nuzzled closer and wagged harder. "I know," Rebecca whispered. She leaned toward him and rubbed her cheek against his head while her tears continued to drip. "I don't want to leave you, either. But I don't know what else I can do."

Her heart was heavier than ever when Rebecca stood and walked to her bedroom. Reaching into the closet, she pulled out a suitcase and spread it open on the bed. Then, without paying much attention to what she packed, she began to pull clothes from hangers at random and drop them into the suitcase. When the pile looked like a small mountain, she went back to the closet and took out an overnight case and began to fill it with articles from the bathroom.

After half a dozen trips from the bathroom to the bedroom, Rebecca stopped and looked down at the jumble of items in the case. Toothpaste, no toothbrush. Cream rinse, no shampoo. Cotton balls, astringent, cleanser, blusher, no makeup, no moisturizer, no lipstick. Two kinds of dusting powder, but no deodorant.

When she turned her gaze to the suitcase full of clothes, she saw only disorder and confusion. An hour of packing, and she had accomplished nothing but a mess. Rebecca pushed the overnight case aside and sank down onto the bed. As she lay there, sanity slowly returned, pushing aside the haze of despair that had sent her rushing into flight.

She had nowhere to go and too much invested here to give it up without a fight. This cabin, this land, was her home. She had weeded and hoed and fought to reclaim its garden from the wild. She had scrubbed and polished and molded its stark interior into a cozy haven. And if she let J.D. run her out, she would just be making herself a victim all over again.

Her spirit fortified with new determination, Rebecca sat up and smiled. She had her home back. She had her life back. She didn't have to leave. But she did have to do something about her wet hair.

Fishing through the overnight case for her comb, Rebecca walked into the bathroom to unplait the French braid that held her hair out of the way. In front of the mirror, she combed her fingers through her hair first, shaking loose the waves that fell around her shoulders and down her back.

As she raised the comb to her hair, a hard sneeze surprised her. A second one doubled her over, and a third one sent her scurrying for a tissue to stem the flow of her suddenly watery eyes and runny nose. At the same time a fourth sneeze shook her to her toes, a determined knock sounded at the door and set a startled Junior to barking.

"Oh, damn." Grabbing a second tissue, Rebecca looked around for her slippers, which were nowhere in sight. She peered into the closet while the knock at the door grew more demanding and Junior's barking grew more threatening.

Trying to think, Rebecca turned and shoveled through the pile of clothes in the suitcase. When she was through, the once-tall mountain looked more like a broad, flat mesa, but she was still barefoot, and Matthew had begun to make the low, sputtering cries that signaled he was waking and wasn't very happy about it.

Rebecca gave up her search and dashed across the room to the door. "Be quiet," she snapped as she grabbed Junior by the collar and pulled him to the side while she unbolted the door and swung it open, too irritated to care who was on the other side.

Cody, in full uniform, paused with his arm raised to pound again.

Stunned and pleased to find that it was Cody and not one of several unpleasant alternatives, Rebecca smiled and released her grip on Junior. "Well, hello."

"Are you okay?" Cody asked, clearly agitated.

"Sure, I guess." Her own smile wavered uncertainly as she backed away to allow him room. "You want to come in?"

Cody swept by her and went to stand in front of the fireplace. As he turned to face her, his rigid stance and the hat held stiffly in front of him did nothing to relieve her sudden anxiety.

"I know I said that I wouldn't be back until you called." Cody's eyes studiously avoided her, fixing instead on the wall behind her. "But it couldn't be helped."

"That's all right. I—"

Before she could finish, he lowered his gaze to her face and said softly, "I'm afraid this is official, Rebecca."

"Official?" She fought a nervous impulse to laugh. He had to be kidding. This was all an elaborate joke to sidestep his promise to wait until she called him. And it wasn't even necessary, because she would have called him on her own, if not tonight, then tomorrow.

"Dora filed a vehicular-hit-and-run complaint against you."

"A what?" Laughter strained to be free as Rebecca leaned toward him, certain she hadn't heard him right.

"I checked your truck on the way in here, and I'm afraid that the paint smears on your right front bumper are going to match up to a dent on the left rear fender of Dora's car."

"Oh, my goodness." Rebecca lifted the tissue to her nose to stop a sniffle that had nothing to do with emotion. "Do you mean I hit her car when I pulled out? I could have sworn that I cleared it."

"Then you *were* there?" He seemed none too happy about her confirmation.

"Well, sure, when I picked up Matthew." She brushed the back of her hand across her forehead and blinked at him with eyes that had begun to burn. "It was raining cats and dogs, and I guess I just didn't back up far enough before I tried to pull out around Dora's car."

Rebecca hoped she didn't sound as vacant to Cody as she did to herself, but she was really beginning to feel tired. He must have noticed, though, because when he pulled a small notebook from his pocket and motioned toward the sofa, his manner was almost apologetic.

"Would you like to sit down?" he asked gently. "I'm afraid I'm going to have to ask you some questions."

Rebecca managed not to sigh aloud. "Could you wait a minute while I find my slippers?"

"Go ahead."

She padded across the living room, past the crib, where Matthew was sleeping quietly again, through the bedroom and into the bathroom. There, she glanced at her pale face in the mirror, noting the bluish smudges under her eyes and the still-damp waves of her hair. She looked awful, but she didn't feel good enough to care. When she turned around, she found her slippers behind the door.

With warmer feet, Rebecca walked back into the bedroom and past the long, narrow closet that was the only partition between the bedroom and the living room. When she reached the end of the closet, she found herself facing Cody, who was standing a few feet in front of her, notebook open and staring at the suitcases that were visible on the bed.

"Were you going somewhere?" he asked in a voice that was much less kindly than it had been moments earlier.

Too weak to fight, Rebecca answered frankly, "I had thought about it."

"Could you come back into the living room now?"

"Of course."

She quietly followed him into the living room with the uneasy feeling that this thing might be more serious than she had thought, and that if the officer at her door had been anyone other than Cody, she might have realized that sooner.

With that thought, a cold shiver traveled up Rebecca's back and across her shoulders. Crossing her arms in front of her for warmth, she settled into the corner of the couch closest to the door and tucked her legs under the long tail of her robe.

Cody took up his position in front of the fireplace again and said, "First, I'll need to see your driver's license and proof of insurance."

In no hurry to unwrap herself from her cozy tuck, Rebecca gazed up at him in dismay and was rewarded with yet another crack in his professional facade.

"Are you sick?" he asked, sounding more like Cody and less like Officer Lockhart. "You look flushed."

"I just got a little chilled earlier. I'll be all right in a minute." She twisted around and peered over her shoulder toward the door where the diaper bag and cooler still sat. "I'm sure what you need is in my purse, if I can only remember where I put it when I came in."

"I think I see it." Cody started toward the door. "You stay there. I'll get it for you."

Before she could answer, he retrieved her purse from the bench beside the door and returned. After he handed her purse to her, he settled onto the other end of the couch and opened his notebook again.

"I'm really sorry about this," Cody said while Rebecca began to shuffle nervously through her purse. "But Dora made an official complaint, and I've got to follow it up with a written report. If you really don't feel well, though, we could put it off until tomorrow."

"No, that's okay." Locating her wallet, Rebecca flipped it open to her license and handed it to Cody. "We might as well get this over with."

He took down the information while she continued to comb through her purse for the envelope containing her insurance verification. "You're working kind of late, aren't you?" she asked without looking up.

"Just until I get this report finished."

At the unusual tightness in his voice, Rebecca brought her head up sharply to gaze at him with a renewed sense of foreboding. "Is there something you're not telling me, Cody?"

"We'll get to that." His smile looked almost as tight as his voice sounded and left his eyes untouched. Handing her back her wallet, he asked, "You *are* insured, aren't you?"

"Oh, yes." She replaced her wallet and almost immediately withdrew the insurance verification. "Here. Do you mind if I make some tea while you do that? I think I'm getting a sore throat."

"Sure. Go ahead."

Turning away from his stiff smile, Rebecca unfolded her legs and stood, then walked away without looking back. In the kitchen, she put on a kettle to heat. The microwave would be faster, but she was in no hurry to return to the tense scene in the living room. Besides, there was something about the singing of a teakettle that added to the warm, cozy comfort of the drink, especially on a wet night.

With her back to Cody, she stood at the kitchen sink and watched the rain fall in the garden outside the window. When another shiver traveled up her back, she knew it wasn't just a cold that was getting her down. It was the memories. Memories of the last time she had seen J.D. before today. Memories of the last time she had sat in her home talking to the police.

The memory of that night and the way they had looked at her still haunted her. One young officer had watched her with sympathy, while the other, older one hadn't even tried to hide the suspicion in his eyes—reminding her that night, and forever after, that the rest of the world would look at her the same way if they knew. While some would hold her blameless, there would always be those who felt that in some way what had happened to her had been Rebecca's own fault.

More than once in the past month she had wondered what she would see in Cody's eyes if he knew, but she had never had the courage to find out. Breaking away from her uncomfortable thoughts, Rebecca took down a teacup and turned just enough for her words to carry across the room. "Would you like a cup of tea?"

"Hot tea?"

She could tell from his voice that he had looked up. "Yes."

"It's ninety degrees outside."

"I could fix you a glass of iced tea if you'd like."

There was silence, and then, "No, that's okay. Thanks, anyway."

The whistle of the teakettle relieved Rebecca of the need to reply. Moving quietly, she poured the steaming water into her cup, adding sugar and lemon while the tea steeped, and then lifted the tea bag out to drain on a china caddy shaped like a miniature teapot. All the while, her mind kept returning to her clash with J.D. outside of Margaret's and wondering how much Cody knew.

"You about through in there?"

The sharpness of his voice cut through the calm she was struggling to hold on to and set her nerves to jangling. Not answering, she lifted her teacup and walked carefully back to the sofa, where she settled once more into the corner and tucked her legs tightly under her. Lifting her downcast eyes finally, she returned Cody's steady gaze through the steam rising from her cup and offered up a silent prayer that the sinking feeling in the pit of her stomach was just her imagination.

Without looking away, Cody flipped open his notebook to a blank page and asked almost too quietly, "Now, can you tell me what, if anything, happened with J.D.?"

"What?" Rebecca's lips shaped the word, but no sound came out. To cover her confusion, she steadied her tea with both hands and lifted the cup to her trembling lips.

Cody waited, and the longer he waited, the more his eyes resembled blue-green chips of ice. The mouth that could curve so invitingly into a smile was pressed closed in a line as unyielding as granite.

Silence stretched, and Rebecca's already shaken nerves stretched with it. She could see that Cody was angry, angrier than she had ever seen him, but she didn't know if that anger was directed toward her or toward someone else.

Her mind racing, she wished that she had taken Jessy's advice and told Cody the truth. Or failing that, Rebecca decided half-seriously, she should have at least packed faster. She could have taken her baby and her dog and made a break for it while she still had the chance.

"Do you want to talk to me about this, Rebecca?" His voice sounded much more understanding than his expression looked.

Slowly dragging her scrutiny from the strip of braided rug that was visible between the couch and the coffee table, Rebecca turned toward Cody and saw that his hands no longer held the dreaded notebook and pen. Emboldened, her gaze traveled upward, noting the uniform, stretched tight across his chest, lingering on his broad shoulders, rigid with tension, and coming to rest at last on the stark lines of strain that were drawn across his handsome face.

For a heartbeat, he looked back at her in silence. Then something inside him broke. "Say something, damn it!"

"Like what?" Struggling against her feeling of helplessness, Rebecca knew that their confrontation wasn't professional anymore. If Cody had stripped out of his uniform and stood naked before her, the emotion in his voice couldn't be any more personal.

"I didn't come here to play games, Rebecca."

Afraid she was about to drop her tea in her lap, she leaned forward and eased the trembling cup onto the coffee table. The room tilted a few degrees when she straightened. "I'm sorry about Dora's car. It was an accident, and I didn't know I'd hit it, but I'm sure my insurance will cover it. Won't that be enough?"

"We're not talking about the accident now."

"What are we talking about?" The tea must be working. She had gone from cold to hot. At any moment, she expected to break out in a sweat.

"J.D. and the assault."

The room tilted a few more degrees, and Rebecca momentarily forgot to breathe. She didn't know if Cody was asking about what happened today or a year ago. Straining for nonchalance, she asked, "Am I supposed to be the assaulter or the assaultee?"

The hard line of Cody's mouth almost relented in a smile before he caught himself and straightened it out again. "You are alleged to have committed the assault." His eyes glinted with an amusement he couldn't hide.

Rebecca's eyelids fluttered closed while she waited for the room to stop spinning. She tried to remember when she had eaten last. Breakfast, probably. She couldn't recall anything since then. This couldn't all be emotional. She wasn't the type to faint. The only time she had ever fainted was the night J.D.— Suddenly cold again, she shivered, remembering that she hadn't really fainted that night, either.

"Rebecca, are you sure you're all right?"

"Oh." She lifted her heavy lids and was relieved to see a look of genuine concern on his face. "I'll be fine."

"I'm not so sure about that." He took her hand in his. "Sweetheart, I just need a statement. It doesn't even have to be a long one."

"Okay," she said in a whisper. She couldn't believe this was happening. After what J.D. had done to her, *she* was the one being accused of assault. It just wasn't fair.

"Would you like to tell me about it?" he asked once more.

"It was just a knee shot to the groin."

Cody's brow arched dramatically while the corners of his mouth twitched. Then he covered with a cough and smoothed his hand over the lower half of his face. "'A knee shot to the groin,'" he repeated, removing his hand to reveal an expression that was once again sternly serious. "*That's* what you did?"

"What do you mean?" Rebecca frowned and was instantly afraid that she had confessed to more than Cody had been aware of. "What did he tell you?"

"J.D.? He didn't say anything. This complaint came from Dora."

Feeling tricked and not liking the feeling a bit, Rebecca stared Cody down through narrowed eyes. "Listen, would you, please, just tell me what this is all about? I'm tired of playing twenty questions. You and I both know that Dora is capable of saying anything and that the truth isn't something she worries much about."

"I know." Cody leaned toward Rebecca with his forearm braced against his knee. "And I'm here trying to keep you out of trouble. But Dora wants your pretty little hide nailed to a wall, and if you keep admitting to everything she's accused you of, she may just get what she's after.''

"What do you mean?" Rebecca felt the return of real panic. Her life had already been wrecked beyond all recognition, and she couldn't take much more. "What did Dora say?"

He clenched his hand into a fist and leaned back again, looking past Rebecca to the window. "She called to report that her parked car had been hit and, as usual, she wanted to talk to me. My shift was about over anyway, so I picked up my truck and went by to take her statement on my way home."

Cody opened his fist and spread his fingers wide, flexing his hand and closing it again while his gaze roamed restlessly around the room, landing everywhere but on Rebecca.

"Well, after Dora showed me her car and told me you'd been the only one near it," he continued, "she went on to tell me about a fight you supposedly had with J.D." Cody shook his head and looked at Rebecca finally. "Naturally I didn't believe her. When she told me you had knocked him down and assaulted him while he was helpless, I almost died laughing. Then I got a look at J.D."

Rebecca cast rapidly through her memory, trying to recall how J.D. had looked when she had stormed away, but the whole scene was a blur.

"I've got to tell you that this worries me, Rebecca," Cody said quietly. "If they were to stick together on their stories, they could end up causing you some real problems."

His face looked as serious as his words sounded, and as Rebecca tried to stifle a groan of despair, she could almost hear the fearful pounding of her heart. The threat was as clear as a noose tightening around her neck. If she would agree to J.D.'s proposal and marry him, Dora would drop the whole thing. If not—

"The only part that has me confused," Cody said, sounding as puzzled as he was pleased, "is that J.D. denies the whole thing."

Rebecca's head popped up, and she looked at Cody through eyes that swam with tears she couldn't shed, because she was afraid that once she cried, she'd never stop. "What?" Her voice was so hushed she could hardly hear it.

"J.D. said he'd just fallen down. He said Dora had misunderstood what she'd seen."

Confused, Rebecca shook her head. She refused to believe that J.D. had defended her, and against Dora of all people. There was a trick being played somewhere, because honesty and nobility were character traits J. D. Lockhart couldn't even spell, much less exhibit. Whatever he hoped to gain from this, he was going to be disappointed.

"If you could see the look on your face," Cody said, "you'd understand why I have to get to the bottom of this. Because something *did* happen, didn't it? J.D.'s limping, and his face has a bruise and some scratches."

"Scratches."

Cody nodded. "Yeah. Do you remember doing that?"

Still shaking her head as if she were slowly emerging from a bad dream, Rebecca said, "No."

"How about the umbrella."

"I don't think I hit him."

"But you really don't remember, do you?" he asked gently.

"No. I just wanted to leave." The whole incident was a blur. She might have hit him. Goodness knows, she wanted to badly enough, but she just couldn't remember.

"Did J.D. try to stop you?"

"I don't want to talk about it."

"I just have a few more—"

She couldn't answer any more questions, and she didn't want to hear any more, either. Rebecca propelled herself from the couch and started toward the bedroom. The air around her was thick, and with each step she seemed to move slower, almost as if she were walking underwater.

"Rebecca."

Cody's voice was far away. When his hand caught her arm and swung her around to face him, Rebecca kept turning in a slow spiral that got darker and darker until everything finally went away and left her alone.

Chapter Eleven

Rebecca opened her eyes to the sight of Cody's face directly above hers.

"That was a very clever ploy, ma'am." He wiped her brow with a cool cloth. "Fainting to avoid unpleasant questions. It was very effective."

"Thank you." She looked around and realized that she was on her bed. Cody must have carried her in from the living room after she passed out.

"Did you eat breakfast this morning?"

"Yes."

"Did you eat anything else today?" He draped the wet rag over the bowl of water on the nightstand.

"I don't think so."

"Have you got any soup in your cupboard?" Cody stood and pulled a thin, summer comforter over her.

"I'm fine," Rebecca protested, trying to rise as he laid his hands on her shoulders and gently pressed her back down. "Really, I can do it myself."

"Maybe you can, but so can I, and I haven't already fainted once tonight. So I vote for me to do it." He walked around the bed toward the living room. At the imaginary boundary between the two rooms, he paused and turned to caution her, "Now, don't move. I'll know if you've moved, and I'll make you answer more questions."

Afraid that he might be serious, Rebecca agreed without hesitation. "I feel silly, but okay."

He left and she lay there, listening to the opening and closing of cupboard doors, to the sound of the microwave and, in practically no time at all, to the sound of Cody returning, tray in hand.

While she ate, Matthew woke, and Cody once again insisted on handling the situation. He changed him and fed him and then brought Matthew to visit his mother. Cody stretched out opposite Rebecca, with Matthew on the bed between them, and the three played and laughed as if the rest of the day had never existed.

When Matthew fell asleep again, Cody carried the baby to the crib and returned without the gun and leather holster that had creaked all evening with every shift of his position.

Rebecca smiled her approval when he sat down on the other side of the bed and stretched out without sounding like a cowboy readjusting himself in the saddle. "Does this mean you're off duty finally?"

"Yeah." He plumped his pillow and leaned back with his hands clasped behind his head. "Does this mean you're not going to answer any more of my questions?"

"Oh, no," Rebecca groaned, hiding her face behind her hands.

"I just have a few. And if you'll answer my questions, I'll tell you the rest of what Dora said."

Rebecca slid her hands away from her face and looked at him. "What do you mean? What else did Dora say?"

Cody shook his head. "I get to go first."

She closed her eyes and clenched her fists. "Okay. Go."

"Do you love him?"

Rebecca popped up like a jack-in-the-box. "Who? J.D.?" She drew back in horror at the thought. "No! Where would you get a stupid idea like that?"

"Swear it," Cody said calmly.

"Swear what? That I don't love him? Are you serious?"

"Very. Now swear it."

At the very thought, her flesh was crawling. "No, I don't love him," she said with vehemence. "I don't even like him. Once upon a time, I thought he was a friend." She threw back the comforter and stood up to pace into the shadows at the back of the room, the side that would look out onto the screened porch if there were windows. "Now I can't stand him." She crossed her arms in front of her and hugged herself for comfort. "No, I don't love him," she finally said in a whisper.

"I'm sorry," Cody answered quietly. "But I had to know."

"For your report?" Her voice was bitter from the anger that hadn't cooled.

"For myself. Dora's claim was that you attacked J.D. in the heat of a lovers' quarrel, and that he didn't want to press charges because he still hoped to reconcile."

"So you needed me to tell you that it wasn't true." Still in the shadows, Rebecca felt cold again, cold and alone.

"Yes. Sad but true. Are you angry?"

"I don't know. Are there more questions?"

"Just one." He raised up on his elbow and looked at her, standing at the edge of the shadows, uncertain of which way to go. "Were you going to call me?"

"Yes." She knew that the admission was the same as saying that she wanted to make love to him.

He didn't move. "When?"

"Maybe tonight. If not, then tomorrow."

"You're not just saying that? Because I'm here now?"

Amazed that he could seem so vulnerable, Rebecca smiled and walked from the shadows toward the bed. "No."

"I guess I saved you the trouble, then, huh?" His eyes were locked on hers, and he reached out to her.

"I guess so," Rebecca agreed as she laid her hand in his and he gently pulled her down onto the bed beside him.

"Rebecca." He caught her face between his hands and looked into her eyes. "I want you to know that whatever happened in the past is behind us now. It doesn't matter, not to me."

"No more twenty questions?"

"No more. I'm not even sure I want to know any more." He slipped one hand behind her back and pulled her closer as he guided her lips toward his. "All I care about is today, right here and right now."

Tremors of anticipation rippled through Rebecca as she watched him draw nearer, murmuring the words she had longed to hear. The shackles of the past had left her hobbled and fearful, fearful that she could never trust another man, fearful that she could never be a whole woman again, fearful that she would never feel the kind of trembling joy that she felt at this moment.

Cody's lips touched hers, and Rebecca's heart soared. She was free, with no fear, no doubt, no awful, aching pain that stretched out before her across a lifetime that was forever forfeit to the memories of one night.

His kiss deepened, softly, tenderly drawing her in, warming her where she had been cold, filling her where she had been empty, loving her without conditions. Rebecca returned his kiss with a passion that was new and strong and for him alone.

Withdrawing only slightly, Cody trailed kisses down her throat and into the hollow of her neck while his hand unknotted the belt that fastened her robe at the waist. Slipping his hand inside, he spread the robe open and laid bare the creamy mound of her breast.

He lifted his head from her throat and looked down at her, catching his breath with a sound that sent shivers of pleasure coursing through the pit of Rebecca's stomach. No man had ever looked at her with the dazed awe that was naked in Cody's eyes. No man had ever left her paralyzed in anticipation of what was to come next. Every sight, sound and touch with Cody was more than she had ever known and all that she had ever dreamed of.

His hand gently cupped her breast, lifting and weighing it with his palm. His thumb stroked the rounded edge of her nipple while his eyes drank in the sight of her with a hunger that left Rebecca aching inside. As Cody slowly lowered his mouth toward her, a sputtering, irritated cry arose from Matthew in the next room.

Rebecca's groan was of pleasure and pain when Cody's tongue gently flicked the tip of her breast an instant before he gathered in a mouthful of tender flesh and suckled for scarcely more than a second before he released her and lifted his head.

Matthew's cry rose to a wail, and Rebecca groaned again.

Cody smiled and drew in a shaky breath. "You'd better go." He stroked her cheek briefly. "We have all night."

Rebecca gathered her wits and retied her robe before rising on legs that were none too steady.

As she began to walk away, Cody caught her hand and stopped her long enough to say, "Bring him back over here to feed him."

"Are you sure?"

He guided her hand toward his mouth. "I love to watch you when you hold him." His lips nibbled at the tips of her fingers while his burning eyes watched the reaction on her face. "It's about the most beautiful sight I've ever seen." He buried a final long, slow kiss in her palm and then released her hand. "Of course, the night isn't over yet."

Blushing, with her knees weaker than ever, Rebecca went to retrieve Matthew before he worked himself into a frenzy.

For a moment, she had almost forgotten that all the passion in the world wasn't enough to hold reality at bay for long. After tonight, the same problems were still waiting for her outside her door. And after tonight, she would have more than ever to lose.

The smell of fresh coffee pulled Rebecca from a deep, billowy cushion of sleep. Rolling onto her back, she yawned and stretched with a feline thoroughness.

Her first sight when she opened her eyes was of Cody leaning against the closet wall, watching her with a steaming mug in his hand. Dressed in his uniform, with the shirt hanging loose and unbuttoned over his bare chest, he was a glorious sight in the soft glow of dawn.

"Good morning," Rebecca purred.

A smile spread across her face, and with an answering smile, Cody unpeeled his shoulder from the wall and walked toward the bed.

"Good morning yourself." He set the mug on the bedside table and leaned down to kiss her.

At the touch of his lips, memories of the night before came flooding back. Rebecca slipped her hands under his shirttail, trailing her fingers over his ribs and around his back while Cody pulled away the sheet that covered her.

His bare chest brushed against her soft breasts as he lifted his leg across her, pinning her to the bed with his body. His lips covered hers in a gentle kiss that grew harder while his hand cupped the side of her waist and moved slowly upward.

At the base of her full breast, he paused and began a tender exploration with his fingertips, around the side and over the crest, taking his time while his mouth explored hers in the same detail.

Where his body pressed against her thigh, Rebecca felt the growing proof that his arousal was as instant and complete as her own. So quickly, so simply, he touched her, and she was his with no shame and no hesitation.

Groaning, Cody pulled his lips from hers and arched his body away until his chest barely rubbed the hardened tips of her breasts. His forehead rested against hers, and his breath came in catches. "I've got to go to work. I'm going to be late."

"Not yet," Rebecca answered in a voice that was half whisper, half plea. Brazenly she followed him, pressing herself against him, offering what she hoped he wouldn't refuse.

Cody cupped her breast in his hand and squeezed gently. "I can't believe I used to know you when you could pass for a boy."

Where his thigh stretched across her, she could feel the swelling, hard and pulsing, against her leg, and she pressed closer, struggling to breathe through the thick, aching passion that filled her. She didn't wonder how she could want him so. She only knew that she did.

She moved her body against his, taunting them both with the fulfillment that was just a few inches away. "Cody," she whispered.

"I only meant to bring you coffee."

"I'm sorry."

"No apologies necessary," he murmured, and brushed his lips over the tip of the breast he still held in his hand. "Ah, Rebecca." He breathed her name in a sigh and traced the outline of her nipple with his tongue before he drew the swollen crest into his mouth and suckled with an urgency that set her aflame.

Like molten lava, the fire spilled from the tip of her breast and down its rounded slope, across the plane of her stomach and into the valley where Cody's khaki-covered thigh applied a gentle pressure that was slowly driving her beyond the edge of reason.

"Cody, Cody," she whispered close to his ear. "Please. Now."

Taking his mouth from her breast, he raked a clean-shaven cheek over the tender flesh and lifted passion-glazed eyes to hers. "Now?"

"Now."

His hands shook slightly as he lifted his body off of hers and stood to remove his clothes. Rebecca concentrated on catching her breath while she watched him turn his back and quickly shuck the uniform shirt that was already half-off. With each move he made, the broad, work-hardened muscles of his back and shoulders rippled, while the heat inside of her curled hotter and pierced deeper.

Within seconds, the belt that hugged his slender waist was unbuckled and the trousers of his uniform were peeled down past his narrow, rounded hips and over the long, hard thighs that aroused sensory memories of passion and tenderness without end.

With his back still toward her, Cody sat on the side of the bed to remove his boots, and Rebecca curled toward him, reaching out to trail her fingertips over the muscled contours of his back.

At her touch, he sucked in his breath and arched toward her while Rebecca moved closer to rest her cheek on his shoulder with her breasts against his back. Cody exhaled with a groan and straightened, pressing closer to her as he dropped his head back and twisted his shoulders around to cover her mouth with his in a kiss hungry with desire.

Her breasts raked against his back, and then his forearm, when he turned without breaking the kiss and pulled her to him. His powerful arms lifted her against him and held her while he slowly lowered them both onto the bed.

When he broke the kiss, he held himself suspended over her, his chest gently nudging the peaks of her breasts, his thighs pressing hers apart, poised as he waited.

Pushed beyond patience, Rebecca gasped and caught her lower lip between her teeth as she arched toward him, urging him where words failed. Still he waited, swollen hard and throbbing against the softness of her inner thigh, until she moved toward him and felt him slip closer.

"Now?" he asked in a choked whisper.

Her answer was a gentle thrust that brought him past the edge and into the valley. With a gasp of pleasure, Cody moved deeper, and the waiting was over.

Rebecca lay with her head on Cody's shoulder, her fingers playing over the hills and valleys of his chest, while he stroked the long locks of hair that fanned out on the bed behind her.

"Are you going to be in trouble?" she asked, repentant now that they both lay happily sated.

His chin brushed her hair. "For being late?"

She nodded, brushing her cheek against the bare satin of his chest.

"I don't think so. It's not something I should make a habit of, but for today, I don't think there'll be a problem."

"Good." She kissed the hollow below his collarbone and snuggled closer. "I'm surprised Matthew hasn't cried by now."

"He has."

Instantly alert, Rebecca pushed herself up onto one elbow. "What do you mean, he has?"

"He woke up and started fussing earlier. So I got up and fed him and changed him and put him down to play. He's probably asleep again by now."

"I slept through all that?"

Cody didn't try to hide his pleasure. "I guess maybe you were a little more relaxed than usual last night."

Rebecca laughed and laid her head back down on his shoulder. "I guess you're probably right. But it was very sweet of you to take care of him like that."

"I enjoyed it. He's a good kid." Cody moved his hand from her hair to her shoulder and pulled her closer to him. "I hate to go, but I've got to get a move on."

Rebecca looked up at him, enjoying the last seconds of the smell and feel of him next to her. She could have stayed like this forever, curled in his arms, staring into his eyes and relishing the slow heat of passion as it once more began a slow burn inside her.

She had never felt like this with any man. She had never wanted anyone else like this. Love had always been something comfortable, not a fire that burned on and on, returning hotter and brighter each time it seemed to be extinguished.

"If I lay here one more minute," Cody said, "I won't leave here at all."

"You could always call in sick," Rebecca answered with a slow, teasing grin.

He almost kissed her, and then drew back with a sigh. "You don't know how tempting that is, but no, I can't do that." He gently withdrew his arm from around her and slipped his shoulder from beneath her head. "Why don't you just pull that sheet up to your neck and lay there until I'm gone?"

As he moved toward the edge of the bed, he stopped long enough to cover her with the sheet. When he tried to withdraw his hand, Rebecca caught it in both of hers.

"Just so you'll know," she said. "I've never felt this way with anyone else."

He cupped her chin in his palm and rubbed his thumb over the soft flesh of her lower lip. "And just so you'll know. Neither have I."

Desire, full-blown and sweetly fragile, washed over her. "I'm glad."

"So am I." He slipped out of bed and walked to the other side to gather his clothes.

Rebecca tried not to watch. Every time she looked at him, she only wanted him more. But she couldn't help herself. By the time he reached the foot of the bed, her eyes were drinking in every detail of him, and he made no attempt to cover the flagrant evidence that he wanted her, once again, just as strongly as she wanted him.

He stepped into his pants and adjusted himself carefully inside as he zipped them up. Then he picked up his shirt and pulled it on, leaving it unbuttoned while he sat on the side of the bed and put on his socks and boots.

"Sweetheart." He twisted around to face her with the look of a man about to say something unpleasant.

Rebecca felt a clutch of fear in the pit of her stomach. Please, not now. Don't let anything go wrong now. She was too happy.

"I don't think I'm going to make it back tonight," he said. "With all this rain, some of the creeks are starting to flood. A few are supposed to crest tonight, and if it gets bad, we're probably going to be working around the clock." He reached out and trailed his finger down her cheek and under the curve of her chin. A slow, sweet smile lifted the edges of his mouth and lit his sea blue eyes. "So maybe it's a good thing that I was a little late this morning." Still smiling, he rose and began to button his shirt. "I'll call you if I get a chance."

With that, he turned and was gone. When the door closed, Rebecca threw back the sheet and ran to the window. Through the lace of the curtain, she watched him drive away. Even after he was out of sight, she continued to watch through the curtain and the rain.

When she finally turned and walked away from the window, she noticed that her body was tender, inside and out. Subtle aches in secret places reminded her of Cody with every move she made, and she missed him already, terribly.

She wanted him back so she could say all the things she hadn't said.

She should have told him about J.D. There was no use to keep the secret any longer, not from Cody. And she couldn't let him find out from anyone else. She wanted him to know the truth, because she loved him. And if anything happened to take him away from her now, she didn't know how she could stand it.

After a long day and longer night filled with rain and silence and little else, Rebecca awoke to a gray and gloomy dawn that promised much of the same. Clouds hung almost low enough to touch, and a fine mist seemed suspended in the stagnant air.

Matthew fretted and fussed while Junior paced restlessly from the living room to the kitchen and back. Unable to stand the claustrophobic quiet of the cabin for another second, Rebecca put Matthew in the bouncing chair Jessy had bought for him and moved him onto the front porch. Junior raced into the yard with a yip of joy and took off across the soggy landscape.

Rebecca wandered to the edge of the porch and onto the gravel path that led into the garden. Strolling through air so thick she could almost see it parting around her as she moved, she discovered a profusion of newly set rosebuds but few blooms within the steamy stillness of the rock walls. The flower beds in the center of the garden were a damp chaos of leggy perennials and thriving weeds bordered by the few rain-flattened annuals that Rebecca had set out earlier in the summer.

All in all, the garden was a mess, but a few weeks of sunshine and hard work would restore it in time for a fine crop of fall blooms. At the thought of sunshine, Rebecca glanced skyward and saw only unbroken gray. In the distance, thunder rumbled, threatening a return of the steady downpour that had marked the past week.

If the rains continued, she would have to start worrying about the low-water bridge, which was her only connection to the outside world. The force of a flash flood could take out the bridge in seconds and leave her stranded for a week or more with no way out until the waters went down and a temporary bridge could be put up.

When Rebecca returned to the porch, she found that Matthew had bounced himself to sleep and Junior was still out chasing after whatever small game he could flush out. Lifting Matthew from his chair, she carried him to bed and climbed the stairs to the loft. While she gathered up the crib quilt she hoped to have finished by the end of the day and sorted through the remaining handwork to be done by Tuesday, she listened to sounds of thunder moving nearer and tried not to worry about Junior.

An hour later, the rumbles of thunder had turned to clashes and Matthew showed signs of waking. When Rebecca heard the sound of a car splashing to a stop outside, she laid down her sewing and hurried down the stairs. Her smile of greeting faded when she reached the front porch and saw that it was Dora walking toward her and not Cody.

Rebecca's first thought was to hurry back inside and lock the door, but a second, wiser voice reminded her that it was too late to run from the inevitable. She had thought she could come back to Eden and still hold on to her secrets, and maybe she could have if the one she was trying to protect had looked just a little less like his father with each passing day.

"Rebecca," Dora said, huffing to a halt on the porch, "have you been down to look at that bridge of yours?"

"No." Anxiety swarmed in the pit of Rebecca's stomach, and she cautioned herself to calm down. The bridge couldn't be that bad, or Dora wouldn't be here now.

"Well, another foot of water, and you're not going to be able to get across it."

Looking at the ill-disguised satisfaction on Dora's face, Rebecca remembered one of the many reasons why she had never liked the other woman. Dora relished the misfortune of others and wasn't above exaggerating small problems into disasters just for dramatic effect.

"Well, thank you, Dora. I'll start keeping a closer eye on it." Rebecca edged back toward the cabin. Feeling behind her with her hand, she found the doorknob and pulled the cabin door closed before Dora could worm her way inside. "Is there anything else I can do for you?"

"Well." Like a bird in cold weather, Dora seemed to puff up before Rebecca's eyes. "I didn't come here to have a fight with you, and you may not like what I have to say, but I'm going to say it anyway."

Rebecca took a deep breath and mentally girded her loins. "I'm sorry about your car, if that's what you're upset about. Cody took down the insurance information, and I thought he was going to bring it to you."

"Oh, yes," Dora said, practically hissing. Bright pink spots the size of silver dollars suddenly appeared on her cheeks, and her eyes glittered with an emotion that looked much nastier than mere anger. "Cody stopped by with that information yesterday. And thanks to you, he took J.D. in for questioning about that little incident you caused."

"He—I don't know why." Rebecca's mind raced ahead. She hadn't heard from Cody since he'd left yesterday morning. She didn't know what J.D. would have told him or why Cody hadn't called.

"Of course you don't," Dora spit. "Just like you don't know why I'm here right now."

"No, I don't. Would you like to tell me?"

"All right, missy, I'll tell you. In case you're wondering why J.D. is here, it's because I wrote him. I took a picture of Matthew one day while Margaret was out of the room, and I sent it to J.D. along with a picture of him when he was a baby. And just what do you think happened then?"

"It's your story." Rebecca's mouth tasted sour, and her stomach rolled and tumbled like a roller-coaster ride. She had had nightmares of this day, but even her nightmares hadn't been quite this bad.

"I'll tell you what happened. J.D. caught the next plane out of Alaska. And do you know what he told me when he got here?"

"I have no idea." Bile bubbled at the base of Rebecca's throat, and her knees trembled with the effort of remaining on her feet.

Dora smiled as she closed in for the fatal thrust. "He told me about the little affair you two had in Austin last year."

"The little what?" Rebecca asked so softly that she barely heard herself. Her hand gripped the back of the chair closest to her as she felt her legs turn to jelly.

"The affair," Dora repeated distinctly. "He told me *all* about it. And you are a cruel and selfish girl, Rebecca Carder. You have lied to everyone just to spite J.D. and keep his child a secret from him and from me, his grandmother. I have a right to know that child, and he has a right to be loved and acknowledged by his father and his grandparents."

"Get off my land." Rebecca took a threatening step toward Dora, ready to do almost anything to shut off the flow of lies.

Dora stood her ground, her fist on her hip, glaring at Rebecca in defiance. "And I suppose this is all just so Cody won't find out you had an affair with J.D. first. Just so Cody won't know that Matthew is J.D.'s love child."

"Shut up!" Rebecca screamed, taking another step with her hand raised. "Shut up and get out."

Dora retreated, shouting as she backed down the sidewalk. "You're not going to get away with it, you selfish little witch. There are tests they can do that will prove J.D.'s the daddy. We'll take you to court if we have to. That baby is my grandchild, and the world is going to know it."

Rebecca leaned over the edge of the porch to pick up a piece of dead wood, ready to throw it at Dora if that's what it took to get the woman to shut up and leave. Stick in hand, Rebecca had started to rise when the nausea she had been fighting overwhelmed her, doubling her over.

She clung to the porch rail with both hands, stick forgotten, and heaved everything inside her into the boxwoods next to the steps. When she finally lifted her head and looked around through watery eyes, she found that Dora had gone.

Rubbery legged and trembling, Rebecca staggered back inside the house and sat down to make some sense of her jumbled emotions. She didn't remember being *this* upset the night J.D. had raped her, but then she hadn't been in love with Cody at the time, and she hadn't already had a day to think about how much she suddenly had to lose.

If Matthew were all she had to worry about, she could just move. Before Dora and J.D. could do anything, Rebecca, her baby and dog would be gone, but it wasn't that simple, not anymore. And it hadn't been that simple since the day her truck had broken down.

Going into the bathroom to wash her face, she changed into fresh clothes that would be comfortable and sturdy enough for battle. Pulling on blue jeans, she tucked a short-sleeved shirt of blue chambray inside the jeans. For extra protection against the uncertain weather, she added a mustard yellow vest that she left unbuttoned.

Next she went to the phone and called Margaret to ask if she would watch Matthew at the cabin while Rebecca paid a visit to Dora. Keeping busy, Rebecca went to the back of the closet and pulled out the box Jessy had left, just in case. In it were the police and medical reports from the night of the attack.

Rebecca had never wanted to keep the reports. She didn't want to have them, to see them or to think about them. But Jessy, with the foresight of a realist, had held on to them.

bringing them along on each visit, just in case. When she left this latest time, she had insisted that Rebecca keep the papers, just in case.

And like it or not, Rebecca was going to use them if she had to. Once and for all, she was going to get J.D. out of her life and keep him out. Now. Today. And then she was going to find Cody and tell him everything.

Chapter Twelve

Margaret caught Rebecca's arm as she headed out the door. "Are you going to be all right?" Concern lined the older woman's face.

The self-doubt and nagging fear that had been Rebecca's companions for the past year were gone, wiped out by a new determination and a mounting sense of urgency. She squeezed Margaret's hand and answered, "I'm going to be just fine."

"I don't think you should be going over there alone. Let me ride along with you, or at least call Cody and have him meet you at Reever's."

"No. I've got to do this myself. Once I get this mess straightened out once and for all, then I can figure out what I'm going to tell Cody." Rebecca gently disengaged her arm and backed away toward the pickup. "Please, just take care of Matthew and don't let anyone else in."

"Be careful."

"And keep an eye out for Junior. He's been gone since I let him out this morning."

Margaret nodded and waved.

"And lock the door," Rebecca called as she opened the truck door.

Margaret waved again and stood in the open doorway with folded arms, watching Rebecca drive away. Rebecca made slow progress over the rutted road. Every few seconds she turned and checked over her shoulder until she saw Margaret withdraw and the door close.

At the bridge, the rushing water of the creek lapped within inches of the road. Once the water churned onto the roadway, the bridge wouldn't be safe anymore, and any car that dared to cross would run the risk of being swept away by the deceptively powerful currents.

Rebecca drove slowly across the bridge, staring into the roiling, debris-filled creek that could continue growing higher and stronger until even the bridge itself no longer stood. The safe life she had so carefully structured for herself and Matthew was unraveling at every seam, and there was nothing she could do to stop it. What man didn't attack, nature did.

On the other side of the creek, the road improved and Rebecca accelerated. The gray blanket of clouds overhead rumbled and clashed but held their rain. Keeping her eyes on the road, she pulled her purse toward her and slipped her fingers inside the flap until she could feel the folded papers inside.

Then, with a sigh, she grasped the steering wheel with both hands and drove on. At the highway, she turned east toward Eden, then south to the ranch owned by Reever Lockhart. She tried not to think of what she was about to do as she pulled into the drive of the simple white farmhouse where she had spent so many hours as a child.

Three dogs came charging from the backyard, barking a combination of threats and greetings. Two were young dogs she had never seen, but one was an old mutt that Rebecca had known since it was a pup. Clutching her purse and its vital contents under her arm, she stepped out of the truck and called to the old dog.

"Bingo. Hi, boy. You remember me, don't you?" She held out her hand, and Bingo left the other barking dogs behind, edging close enough to sniff for a scent he recognized.

When the older dog's tail began to wag slowly, the other two muted their barks to nagging yaps, and Rebecca was allowed to pass. Bingo stayed close to her side all the way to the porch where Reever came out to greet her.

"If I'd known you were coming, I'd have tied 'em up," he said, reaching to shake her hand. "Guess old Bingo still remembers you. That truck been giving you any more problems?"

"Oh, it's running great." Rebecca smiled up at the old man, sorry for what she was going to have to tell him. Reever was tall, like his brother had been, like Cody was, with broad shoulders and the lean frame of a man who had worked hard all his life.

"I been wondering when you were going to get by." His strong hand released hers, and he stepped back to allow her through the door.

"I should have come sooner." She had always liked Reever. He had been her father's friend when they were young and had always stayed close to her family.

And though Reever had never been a match for his harridan of a wife, Rebecca had always admired the way he tried to take the place of the father Cody had lost. Even as a little girl, Rebecca had always thought that the men of the Lockhart family would have been a lot better off without Dora.

"Why are you here?" Dora's viperish voice lashed out as soon as Rebecca stepped through the door.

"I don't think that's any way to talk to a guest, Dora," Reever answered in the same mild way he dealt with everything.

Looking from Reever to Dora, Rebecca wondered if she would ever understand what the two of them were doing together. Reever was at least fifteen years older than Dora, maybe more. She was a spoiled, selfish spitfire who made trouble as easily as she drew breath. He was a decent, hardworking man of great patience and generosity. And in spite of their differences, their marriage had lasted thirty years and, on the surface at least, produced perfect contentment in them both.

Dora looked at Reever and huffed. Then she turned her festering anger back to Rebecca. "If you've come here to apologize, just let me warn you, it may not be enough."

"I didn't come here to apologize, Dora. I came here to get some things straight." Rebecca turned her attention from Dora to the still-handsome man whose gentle eyes held a sadness that tugged at Rebecca's heart. "I'm really sorry about this, Reever. I'm afraid I'm going to have to say some things I never wanted to say."

"If it's the truth, then it needs saying," he answered quietly. "Why don't we come on in here and sit down? Might as well be comfortable while we're about it."

"Oh, good grief, Reever, this isn't a Sunday social. Why don't we just hear what she's got to say and send her on her way?" Dora snapped.

"Because the Carders and the Lockharts have been friends and neighbors for six generations," Reever said sternly. "And you're not going to be the one to put quits to that, Dora." He pointed to Rebecca. "That little girl's granddaddy was one of the finest men I've ever known. And her daddy's been my friend since we were in diapers together. Now, sit down and shut up, woman, while we try to make some sense of this mess you've made."

"Mess *I've* made," Dora gasped. She clasped a hand to her heart and sat down as ordered.

"Yes, mess *you've* made." Reever turned to Rebecca. "She thinks that because she and J.D. go into the next room to talk, I can't hear what they're saying." He swung back to face Dora. "I've been listening to you two whispering and plotting for days now, and I should have said something sooner, but I didn't. And now I'm ashamed of myself because I didn't stop you before it got this far."

Dora bounced up from the chair, quivering. "But you don't understand, Reever. She tried to keep our grandchild from us. She's lied and—"

Reever interrupted, holding up a hand to silence his wife. "Did you ever ask her why?"

As the "her" and "she" being referred to, Rebecca felt a little like a Ping-Pong ball. While they argued, she reached into her purse and pulled out the reports she had brought with her for the purpose of ending the arguments once and for all.

"I didn't need to ask her," Dora said, pacing. "It's obvious. She came here looking for J.D., and when he wasn't here, she went after Cody instead. And now she doesn't want him to know that she was with J.D. first." Dora turned her scathing gaze on Rebecca. "After all, what man's going to want a woman with another man's child, especially when that man is his cousin?"

"But you didn't ask her, did you?" Reever repeated.

"No, I didn't," Dora snapped. "I told you, I didn't have to."

"Excuse me," Rebecca interrupted quietly. Her shaking hand clutched the papers she had pulled from her purse.

Dora glared at Rebecca, then at Reever, who pointed to the couch. With a flip of her head, Dora sat. "Just say what you've come to say and then get out."

"Please," Reever said, indicating a chair across from the sofa. "Make yourself comfortable, Rebecca." He eased his lanky frame into a chair between the two women.

"Thank you." Setting her purse and papers on the coffee table in front of her, Rebecca settled into the chair that faced Dora. "I really don't know how to begin. This isn't easy for me."

Now that Rebecca was here, she wasn't sure that she could go through with it. Her hands trembled and her voice wouldn't seem to rise above a whisper. "I'm truly sorry, Reever. You don't deserve any of this."

"He certainly doesn't," Dora huffed. "Neither do I, and neither does J.D. A person has the right to know about his own flesh and blood. Even Reever could see the resemblance in those pictures I took, and so could any court in the land. You don't even deserve to have that baby. Why, you're nothing but an unmarried floozy carrying on with any man who'll have you."

"Dora!" Reever snapped, abandoning his calm facade.

"That's all right, Reever." Rebecca leaned forward and lifted the papers from the coffee table. "I'm grateful to you, but I should probably thank Dora for making a difficult task a lot easier for me."

Reports in hand, Rebecca took a deep breath as she stood and gazed into Dora's angry, defiant eyes. "You're not going to like what I'm about to say, Dora. But you wanted to know, and so I'm going to tell you."

Before Dora could form a reply, Rebecca turned away and walked to the window that looked out across the front porch to the green and grassy yard beyond, but the images she saw came from inside her own mind. The distant, raucous barking of dogs tugged at her, pulling her back to the present.

"You were right, Dora," Rebecca began softly, "I *did* see J.D. a little over a year ago, in Austin. He knocked on my apartment door one day, without any warning, and asked me to dinner to catch up on old times.''

Too nervous to stay still and too upset to depend on her unsteady legs to hold her up for long, Rebecca left the window and retraced her steps across the room, talking as she went. ''He said he had a job waiting for him in Alaska and didn't expect to be back this way for a long time. He said he was happy about it, but I could tell that he wasn't, not really. He was trying too hard.''

As the quaking in her legs worked its way up through the rest of her body, Rebecca took refuge behind a tall wingback chair at the opposite end of the sofa from Reever. Her back to the kitchen doorway, she took a deep breath and braced herself against the chair while chills crawled along her spine at the thought of what was to come.

She hadn't told the whole story to anyone in a long time, and it wasn't a tale that she enjoyed recounting. But these were J.D.'s parents, and they deserved to hear more than just the facts. While nothing could justify what J.D. had done, if there was a slim possibility that he hadn't been fully aware of his actions, then his parents deserved at least that consolation. It was the one thing Rebecca herself had clung to in the months afterward, when she had asked herself again and again how J.D. could have done what he did to her after she had been like a sister to him for so many years.

''I thought maybe in private he'd be more comfortable,'' she began again in a voice that was steady though soft. ''So I asked him back to my apartment, hoping that he would tell me what was really bothering him.'' Losing courage quickly, Rebecca could feel her legs melting from under her while the pit of her stomach turned ice-cold and queasy. ''But that turned out to be a big mistake. I hadn't realized how drunk he was until I discovered that talking wasn't what he was interested in.''

Her voice cracked, and giving up her struggle to be strong, she felt her way around to the front of the wingback and collapsed into it. "I'm sorry," Rebecca whispered, resting her spinning head against the upraised fingers of one hand while she held out the papers that she still clutched in her other hand. "Here. The rest of it's in here. I just can't—"

Reever's comforting hand rested on Rebecca's shoulder as he gently took the papers from her hand. "Are you going to be all right?"

"I'll be okay in a minute," she answered without looking up. "I'm just a little dizzy. It'll pass."

She didn't know why she had thought it would be any easier just because she was angry with Dora. Since that night of J.D.'s attack, when shock had held the pain at bay through the police and medical examinations, Rebecca hadn't been able to discuss what had happened outside of her therapy groups.

Just remembering that night was almost like reliving it, and she'd done that enough already. She was here today to plead for Matthew, not for herself. What was important now was that he be allowed a normal childhood, or at least as normal a childhood as Matthew's could be with the tag of illegitimacy hanging over his head. He didn't need the additional weight of knowing that he wasn't the product of love, but of violence and hatred.

Someday he would have to know how he was conceived, and when that day came, there was no way Rebecca could keep the truth from hurting him. She could only pray that she would find the wisdom by then to help Matthew see the whole truth, the truth of how much she loved him and how much she wanted him and how little his father's actions so many years ago could change those truths.

"Lies!"

Hearing Dora's angry outcry, Rebecca lifted her head, too emotionally wrung out to want to fight anymore. Across the coffee table, she saw the older woman standing, red faced and shaking, while Reever sat slumped in his chair, his head cradled in his hands.

"You lying little witch!" With a flip of her hand, Dora sent the pages flying toward Rebecca. "There's not a word of truth in this. And if the police had believed your vicious pack of lies, J.D. would be in jail right now."

Bitter resentment and deep, aching pain welled inside Rebecca as she stared back at Dora through a snowstorm of paper. "J.D.'s not in jail because he caught a plane for Alaska as soon as he left my apartment that night," Rebecca said while the sheets of paper floated onto the polished surface of the coffee table and skidded off onto the floor all around it. "And because I decided not to press charges."

"A likely story," Dora jeered.

"Shut up!" Reever shouted, rising half out of his chair. "For God's sake, Dora, just shut up." He clamped his hand around her wrist and tugged her back down onto the sofa.

Twisting free of his grasp, Dora bounded to her feet and cried out to anyone who would listen, "J.D. wouldn't do those things."

"But he did," Rebecca insisted quietly.

"But Matthew—"

"Is my child." The steel in Rebecca's voice cut through Dora's shrill argument. "And if you ever try to prove differently, I'll make you sorry you ever lived. For once in your miserable life, Dora, think about someone else. Think about an innocent baby who already has enough of a stigma to live down. We're adults. We have choices. Matthew doesn't have any choice, and if he finds out the truth before he's old enough to handle it, he could lose any chance he has for a normal, happy life."

"But we're his grandparents. We can give him love."

Rebecca gritted her teeth against the urge to scream. "Dora, think. A baby born out of wedlock from two people in love is one thing. But an illegitimate child conceived from a violent, criminal act of rape is something else entirely. Please," she begged, "if you really love Matthew, give him a chance. Don't brand him with the sins of his father before he can even walk."

With anguished dignity, Reever lifted his head and looked across at Rebecca. "Don't you worry. That little boy isn't going to be hurt."

"Thank you," Rebecca whispered through tears of gratitude while Dora gasped and burst out wailing.

Ignoring his wife, Reever said quietly, "If you don't mind, I'd like to see him sometime. I hear he's a mighty fine little boy."

"You can see him anytime you like, Reever." Her heart twisting for the old man, Rebecca could scarcely contain the flood of sorrow and relief that threatened to overflow. "And so can Dora. I think it would be good for Matthew to have people around who cared about him. Someday I'll even tell him about his father, and if Matthew wants to see J.D. then, I won't try to stop him. But until Matthew is old enough to understand and make the decision for himself, I won't allow J.D. to come near him."

"But J.D.'s his father," Dora cried piteously.

At the same instant came another, deeper voice from behind Rebecca. "You won't have to worry about that."

Recognizing the voice as Cody's, Rebecca caught her breath in a quiet gasp and turned to face him while dread pounded in her heart. The question foremost in her mind— *How much had he heard?*—stuck like a lump in her throat. "Where did you come from?" she asked instead.

"I came in the back way." His voice carried the low, grim rumble of thunder, and the taut muscles of his jaw flinched with the effort of control.

"How long ago?" Rebecca asked quietly as a whisper, knowing the answer before he gave it.

"Long enough."

She was too late. Unable to look at the painful truth etched so clearly on his face, Rebecca turned away. Her strength gone, she curled forward, clasping her arms across her stomach while the hollow ache inside her mushroomed.

Tears she could no longer contain coursed soundlessly down her cheeks at the realization that Cody had heard everything. She had waited too long to tell him, and now there would never be another chance. If she had lost him, she would never forgive herself.

"If you all are through," Cody said into the quiet that had fallen, "I'll take Rebecca home now."

"Where's J.D.?" Dora demanded, sniffling.

"I don't know and I don't care," Cody answered.

The warm, earthy scent of his cologne found its way through the folds of Rebecca's hair as he drew near, and she hastily swiped at the tears on her cheeks with the back of her hand. Through lowered lashes, she watched him bend to retrieve the papers on the floor next to her chair.

"J.D. and I have said all we have to say to each other," Cody continued without looking up.

Startled out of her silence, Rebecca lifted her head. "What?"

"Oh, did I forget to tell you?" Dora cooed with a smile that was closer to a sneer. "J.D. went to find Cody just before you got here. He thought there were still a few things Cody might not know."

Ignoring Dora's barbs, Cody moved around the coffee table, gathering and assembling the police and medical reports, his gaze raking slowly down each page as he straightened and stacked them neatly on the table. When he was through, he turned to Rebecca. "Is this all of it?"

Too heartsick to speak, afraid even to look directly at him, Rebecca nodded. She didn't want to hear what twisted story J.D. might have told Cody, but she knew eventually she would have to ask.

Cody leaned nearer and asked gently. "Can I take you home now?"

"I drove." Her voice sounded like an anemic imitation of her real one. She could feel that Cody's self-control was almost as fragile as her own, and as much as she longed to be near him, she wasn't sure she was brave enough to be alone with him right now.

"I don't think you should be driving. Reever and I can get your truck back to you later." Cody gathered up her things and placed them in her lap. "Are you ready to go?"

Obviously silent for as long as she could stand, Dora sprang to her feet and cried out, "Where is J.D.? I demand to know where my son is."

"He's gone, Dora." Cody didn't bother to turn as he slipped his hand under Rebecca's elbow and guided her to her feet. "J.D.'s gone back to Alaska, and he'll be there for a long, long time."

Cody's eyes found Rebecca's and offered her a promise that chased the cold, dark fear from her soul.

"Gone?" she whispered.

"Gone."

His hands tightened on her arms, and he would have pulled her to him, Rebecca knew, if Dora had not chosen that moment to cry out, "But why?"

"Because—" for the first time, he let his fierce anger flare openly as he released Rebecca and whirled to face Dora's challenge "—we had a long talk, J.D. and I, and we came to an understanding." With effort, Cody forced his harsh tone lower, to a quiet, grating rumble that vibrated with harnessed fury. "I understand that J.D.'s worse than I ever knew, and he's never going to change. And he understands that if we ever meet again, my badge won't stop me a second time."

With a gasp, Dora brought her hand to her heart. "What did you do to him?"

"Not nearly enough." A shudder rippled over the taut muscles of Cody's back as he drew a deep breath. "J.D.'s bruises will heal soon enough, and he seemed more than happy with a one-way plane ticket back to Alaska.'' Cody's voice softened to genuine regret when his gaze shifted from Dora to Reever. "I'm truly sorry, Reever, for your sake. But this is the way it's got to be. For now, and for a long time to come.''

With effort, Reever heaved himself out of his chair. "No,'' he said with a shake of his head, "you're right. God forgive me, but J.D.'s my son, and *I* don't want to see him. I can't believe what he's brought us to.''

Bent by the burden of his sorrow, the older man walked slowly across the room. When he entered the hallway leading to the back of the house, Dora called out for him to come back, but he walked on. As the slow shuffle of Reever's footsteps faded away, Dora threw herself onto the couch with a fresh flood of tears.

His eyes sad, Cody turned finally and took Rebecca's hand. "Can we get out of here now? If Dora says one more thing, I'm going to send her packing to Alaska with that stinking son of hers.''

"I was going to tell you,'' Rebecca said into the silence that had stretched for miles.

"I'm glad to hear it.''

Cody suspended his intent study of the road long enough to glance toward Rebecca, chilling her with the hard frost that had replaced the fire in his eyes. She turned away and rubbed her hands over her arms as a shiver ran over her skin.

"I didn't mean for you to find out this way,'' she said quietly, once more trying to find a way through the wall he had built between them.

"I appreciate that.''

Desperate to reach him, she turned and cupped her hand over the hard muscle of his forearm. "Cody, please, we need to talk.'' The pain of reliving J.D.'s attack had been nothing compared to enduring the agony of Cody's anger. "I'm sorry."

His face twisted in a grimace, and Cody slammed on the brakes, jerking his arm free of her hand as if her touch were a hot poker. Rebecca froze, staring first at Cody and then at the startling vision of a swiveling landscape as the brakes on the truck locked and the rear wheels went into a sideways slide through mud that was inches deep on the unpaved ranch road.

Too startled to cry out, she threw up her hands to brace herself against the dashboard and discovered to her immense relief that she had fastened her seat belt without realizing it when they'd left Reever's house.

When the pickup finally slid to a halt at a forty-five-degree angle in the middle of the road, she exhaled a long, shaky breath and turned her head to watch Cody unpeel his clenched fists from the steering wheel and slowly sag forward, still staring straight ahead.

"Damn it, Rebecca." His hoarse words were loud in the breathless silence. "You have nothing to apologize for. I'm the one who's being a bastard. I'm the one—"

Her heart still pounding from fear, Rebecca turned to stare at him in surprise as his voice grew thick and then faded away to nothing.

"Cody?" she asked with concern when she could speak again.

"It's my fault," he answered in a harsh whisper. "It never would have happened if I hadn't run him out of town."

"What?" She leaned toward him, only to be restrained by her seat belt. "What are you talking about?" Impatiently she felt for the buckle that would release her from her protective prison.

"J.D. He left Eden because of me." Cody's words were little more than a strangled growl. "He went to Austin, and you, because of me."

"Oh, no, Cody." Pushing aside the harness, Rebecca moved closer to him. "You can't think that."

"It's true."

"No." She gripped the curve of his shoulder, only to have Cody flinch away, warding off her touch with a shrug.

"Yes, damn it," he exploded. "It *is* true." He turned his head away, and his voice dropped again to barely more than a whisper. "I had him run out of town without any thought of where he might go or what he might do to someone else."

"Now you listen to me, Cody Lockhart." Rebecca again laid her hand against his powerful shoulder and shoved with all her might, succeeding in turning him back toward her out of surprise more than strength. Smoothing her fingertips over the pain so naked in his face, she slid her fingers into the soft waves of his chestnut brown hair and held him captive.

"Never," she whispered with passion. "Never think that. You saved me. You, and Matthew, are what made me want to live again. And don't you ever forget it."

Cody's arms closed around her, crushing her to him as his lips brushed her cheek and his breath warmed her with the words she longed to hear.

"Oh, God, Rebecca, I love you." His hands, gentle, tender, urgent, traced the contours of her back and pressed her closer still. "I love you so. I've known for so long that something was wrong, but I never dreamed—"

Again his voice faded as he buried his face in the dusky folds of her hair. His breath, so close to her ear, came in harsh, ragged intakes, and the body that held her with such tender strength trembled with emotions too strong to control.

Rebecca tightened her arms around him in a surge of love that carried her beyond doubt or fear. "I should have told you. I wanted to tell you, but I was afraid. Afraid you wouldn't want me if you knew," she finished softly.

Cody slowly lifted his head and stared down at her in wonder. "Wouldn't want you? Why wouldn't I want you? What kind of jerk do you think I am?"

She smiled through tears that turned her voice husky. "A lot of men wouldn't," she said simply, remembering for what she hoped was the last time the suspicious eyes of the elder policeman, the same suspicion that could easily lurk in the heart of any man.

"I'm not a lot of men."

"I know. I've known that for a long time, and I should have trusted you."

His sea blue eyes searched her russet brown ones. "Do you now?"

"Yes." The tears burned in her throat, longing to be set free.

"Good," he said softly, "because we've still got a lot to talk about."

"Oh, Cody." Her heart pounding with a mixture of emotions that left her dizzy, Rebecca curled deeper in his arms, molding her aching breasts to the hard contours of his chest. Feeling wanton to the core, she realized that there was only one thing she wanted from Cody right now, and it wasn't conversation.

A lazy, one-sided grin tugged at the corner of his mouth. "You're distracting me," he warned.

Rebecca tilted her head to the side and parted her lips in an invitation. "Oh, really?"

"Really." He traced the lush outline of her mouth with a longing gaze while his tone dropped to a throaty rumble. "Extremely." The tip of his tongue dipped to taste the sweetness of her lips, then slipped inside, drawing her mouth hard against his while his arms lifted her off the seat and draped her across his body.

"Oh, Cody," she sighed, whispering his name with a mixture of wonder and desire, of thanksgiving and promise.

"Yes," Cody answered, his lips still brushing hers, "oh, yes." Hunger for her consumed him once again as his kiss became a gentle ravagement that grew more impassioned with each second he held her body locked in his embrace until, breathless, they drew apart once more to gasp for air.

"I love you," Rebecca murmured solemnly between intakes of oxygen.

"I had hoped." Cody kissed her lightly, then lifted his head to smile down at her. "I've certainly been working toward that goal."

She drew back as far as his embrace would allow and blinked to bring him into focus. "You have?"

His grin broadened, and his hand cupped the back of her head, guiding her toward him once again. "I sure have. And I must say, you didn't make it very easy on me in the beginning."

"What—"

Rebecca's question died unvoiced as Cody's lips closed over hers in a sweet, succulent kiss that lengthened and deepened into a passionate plundering that in the end left them both breathless yet again, with pulses racing and senses inflamed.

Limp in his arms, she rested her head on his shoulder and sighed, staring blankly at the fogged-over window of the pickup. Her idle gaze roamed upward, to the top of the pane on the driver's side where the glass was unfogged, but all that was visible was a sheet of water coursing down the outside of the closed window.

"Well, would you look at that," she said with passion-clouded puzzlement. "It's raining. I wonder when that happened?"

Cody reached around her and turned on the windshield wipers and the defroster. Within seconds a round patch of the windshield was cleared, revealing a torrent of rain that noisily pounded the outside of the truck. "That's not rain, sweetheart, that's a flood."

Rebecca ducked her head and laughed, a light, tinkling ripple that was nearly drowned out by the onslaught outside.

Drawn by the music of her laughter, Cody leaned his head toward hers and inquired softly, "What?"

"I can't believe we didn't hear that," she whispered back to him. "Talk about being lost in our own world."

"Yeah." He slipped his hand around the back of her neck and dipped his head to the side just enough to find her lips with his in one more slow, sensuous exploration, body against body, soul to soul.

"Oh, Cody," she sighed when the kiss ended, "I could stay here forever." She rested her cheek against his chest and listened to his heart, pounding in her ear like a pagan rhythm, fueling the fires that burned inside her.

"I know, sweetheart." His hand stroked her hair, then hugged her to him in a brief but fierce embrace. "But don't you think we'd be more comfortable at home?" He shifted his weight under her, lifting them both more upright in the seat.

His voice of reason penetrated Rebecca's cocoon of lethargy and brought her back to reality with a jolt. "The bridge!" Hurtling upright as she remembered the rising creek, she grasped Cody's arms with both hands and turned to him in wild-eyed panic. "The bridge, Cody! Matthew—"

"It's okay, honey. Calm down." His voice became a soothing croon while his hands stroked her shoulders and his level gaze assured her that she could trust what he said. "It's all right. Matthew's with Margaret, at my house."

"At your house?"

He nodded. "I got them out before I came looking for you."

"They're safe? You saw them cross the bridge?"

"I swear. Matthew is safe. And Margaret packed some of your things in case the bridge was gone by the time I brought you back."

The fist that had clamped down around her chest loosened, allowing Rebecca to breathe again. "It's not that I don't trust you, but could we go now?" She fought back tears of relief and remorse. *How could she have forgotten Matthew like that?* "I need to see him."

"Sure, sweetheart." Cody caressed her cheek with his palm. "We can go right now."

She moved to the side, still close enough for her thigh to rest against his, but with her body no longer draped against his.

Cody kissed her once more, briefly, then put the truck into gear.

"What about Junior?" Rebecca asked with a second worried glance as she remembered yet another thing she had forgotten.

"The dog?" Cody looked to the side, toward her, while he accelerated slowly.

"Yes. He wasn't home when I left."

"Well, I guess he came home, because I saw Margaret put him in her car. What the hell?" He glared at the road and tromped harder on the accelerator.

Rebecca's heart sank as she heard the loud whine of spinning tires. "Are we stuck?"

"Don't even think it." He shifted into reverse, and the truck rocked back a few inches, then came to an abrupt halt, followed by the high-pitched whir of tires digging a downward trench through soft mud.

With a muttered curse, Cody shifted again, and the truck lurched forward, then stopped as the tires began to spin. Scowling, he put it in reverse, and the pickup barely moved before jerking to a halt and commencing a high-pitched, mud-slinging whine. "Damn, damn, damn." He shifted into

Park and brought an angry fist down on the padded steering wheel.

"We *are* stuck." Rebecca tried hard not to sound as desolate as she felt. She ached to hold her baby in her arms and put the awful events of the day far behind her. Cody had said that he loved her, but did that include Matthew? Was Cody's heart big enough to accept the child of a man he despised?

"I'd better get out and see how bad it looks."

As he reached for the door handle, she caught his arm in her hands and pulled him back. "You can't go out there. It's pouring."

Cody's tight expression relaxed in a lopsided smile. "Sweetheart, I got us stuck here. I've got to see if I can get us out. Here." He quickly unbuttoned and stripped out of his denim shirt and handed it to Rebecca. "At least I'll have a dry shirt to put back on."

She took the shirt with no other sound than a quick intake of breath. In the intimacy of the pickup cab, she could see the rippling of his powerful muscles beneath bare skin so close she could almost count the pores. Without thinking, she laid her hand on his shoulder, gazed into his aquamarine eyes and, in a voice too husky to be her own, uttered the single word, "Stay."

Cody touched her cheek. "Rebecca," he answered softly, "it could be tomorrow before someone comes looking for us. You need to get home to Matthew."

Outside, a jagged shard of lightning lit the sky with a sulfurous, sizzling clap echoed by a boom of thunder that shook the earth.

"No," she said with a shiver. "I don't want you out there. It's too dangerous."

"I've been out in this weather for days now. And at least this afternoon I'm dressed for it." His spreading hands indicated the faded blue jeans and battered cowboy boots that he had changed into before leaving work.

"Okay. But if you go out there, I'm going with you."

Cody grinned and shook his head. "I need you to drive the truck while I push. Now, no more arguments."

He kissed her then, a quick goodbye that grew longer when Rebecca wrapped her arms around his neck and pressed her body to his with a promise of all the days to come.

"Couldn't you wait just a little while?" she whispered against his mouth. "Until the rain slows down?"

"The mud's just getting deeper," he whispered back, making no move to leave. "And it'll be dark soon."

"If anything happened to you, I couldn't stand it."

"Nothing's going to happen to me." With a sigh that was part moan, he broke off the embrace. He took Rebecca's hands in his and looked deeply into her eyes. "Tonight we're all going to be together under one roof. You, me and Matthew. And, if you're willing, it'll be that way for the rest of our lives."

He brought her hand to his lips and kissed first the inside of her wrist and then her palm, slowly and tenderly, before he lifted his gaze to hers. "I love you, Rebecca, and I love your son. If you need more time, I'll wait if I have to, but someday I want you to marry me. I want to be a husband to you and a father to Matthew. I want to give him brothers and sisters, and I want us to grow old together in a house filled with the sound of laughter and the fullness of love. But first—"

Cody released her hands and kissed the tip of her nose. Then he straightened. "We need to get out of here," he said in the same quiet, solemn tone he had maintained throughout his speech.

"Don't you want to know my answer?"

"Think about it while I dig us out."

With that, he was gone, opening the door and slipping out into the darkening, rain-slashed afternoon. Alone, Rebecca couldn't hear the storm for the joyous *yes, yes, yes* chanting over and over in her mind. Cody loved her and he loved Matthew, and nothing else mattered.

Whatever happened in the future, Cody would be there, just as he had been today, to stand as a barrier against disaster. Reever would be true to his word, and in time even Dora would mellow. Matthew would have a real family, with parents and grandparents, and a future more normal and complete than Rebecca could have ever hoped for just two short months earlier.

And for herself, she would have Cody, who had grown to manhood as so much more than the boy of her girlhood dreams had been. Tempered and tested by a heartbreak as great as her own, he was a man who yearned for the kind of love she longed to give.

Unable to stand her solitude another minute, Rebecca flung open the passenger door and stepped out into the maelstrom. Squinting into the stinging rain, she looked to either side and saw nothing but the mud brown road and the tender green of new grass across the pasture, all tinted a silver gray beneath the sodden sky.

"Cody?"

He rose from behind the truck, a shovel in one hand and flat, narrow board in the other. "Rebecca?"

"Yes!"

"What are you doing out here?"

Beaming as the rain poured down on her bare head, she flung open her arms and cried out again. "Yes!"

"Yes?" Cody took a halting step toward her and threw down his shovel and board. "Yes?"

Rebecca smiled, almost whispering. "Yes."

He came around the corner of the pickup in a slow slide, laughing, while his boots dug a trench through the mud. Still laughing and struggling to regain his footing, he called out "be careful" when she started toward him. "This stuff is slick as glass."

Too late, his fingers brushed the side of the truck as his feet went forward and his body tilted backward.

"Cody!" Rebecca rushed toward him, her feet sliding with each step until she reached him and tried to stop. One boot heel dug into the slippery mud while the other foot flew into the air, pitching her backward. One leg under her and the other sprawled, she came down with a thud next to Cody only seconds after he landed.

Laughing, Cody wrapped his arms around her and lifted her into his lap. "When?" he asked, grinning from ear to ear.

"When?" Still trying to catch her breath, she looked at him blankly until she realized he was talking about a wedding date, and the flutter of butterfly wings rustled in her stomach. "Oh, gee. Well, I guess—I don't know, how soon do you want?"

"Tomorrow would be fine. And, Rebecca," he said, growing hesitant, "I'd like to—I mean, if you want— Oh, hell." He took a deep breath and blurted, "I want to adopt Matthew. If it's okay."

"Oh, yes," Rebecca cried as she wrapped her arms around him and tilted back her head to gaze at him through the rain. "That would be wonderful, Cody. I'm so happy, but, darling, don't you think tomorrow's a little too soon for the wedding?"

Cody laughed again and, ignoring the rain that dripped through his hair to roll down his cheeks, he tenderly smoothed the raindrops from Rebecca's face. "Take as long as you want, sweetheart. We might as well do it right, 'cause it's gonna last us a lifetime."

"Oh, Cody, I love you." Rebecca snuggled against his rain-slick torso and rested her head on his shoulder. "I love you so much." Blinking away the rain that gathered on her lashes, she gazed into the distance behind them and saw a hazy gray shape far down the road. "Cody, I think there's something coming toward us."

He twisted around and looked behind them. "Well, I'll be damned. There sure is. Maybe we should get up before it runs over us."

Helping each other, they rose cautiously in the treacherous footing. Rebecca stared down at her mud-coated lower half, then gazed into the distance once again. "Who do you suppose it is?"

"Reever, most likely." Cody held out his hands, turning them over to confirm that both sides were caked with the brown goo. "What a mess."

"Do you suppose Margaret called him?"

"Probably."

Lifting one foot, Rebecca shook it vigorously before she stopped worrying about the mud and brightened. "Then we're rescued?"

Cody wrapped his none-too-clean arms around her and pulled her against him. "That we are, darling. That we are."

"We're going home." She rubbed her cheek against his bare chest and thought of the old farmhouse where her grandparents had reared their family and where she and Cody would do the same.

"Home," Cody echoed, brushing his lips against the top of her head. "That word's never sounded so good."

Rebecca smiled softly as she nestled closer and wrapped her arms tighter around him. "And life's never been so sweet."

* * * * *

Silhouette Special Edition

COMING NEXT MONTH

THAT BOY FROM TRASH TOWN
Billie Green

Ever since a tough fourteen-year-old from the
wrong side of the tracks rescued a lost little girl,
Dean Russell was wealthy Whitney Grant's hero.
But now they were all grown up. . .

LUSCIOUS LADY
Phyllis Halldorson

Brody Monroe was an enigma with a secret-
shrouded past. Victoria Chambers wanted to
convince him that it didn't matter what he had been,
that the present was all that mattered—the present
and, ultimately, the future.

NOBODY'S BRIDE
Judi Edwards

Ariel Johnson had gone to remote Blackfish Bay to
avoid men and civilisation, whereas Scott
MacKenzie had been sent to the bay to stay out of
trouble. But Ariel could see that this very
*un*civilized male was destined to *cause* trouble for
her!

COMING NEXT MONTH

WEDDING EVE
Betsy Johnson

Shelly Barker didn't believe in happy endings for ordinary people like her and men like Dan Sutherland. He belonged in a glamorous, glittering world far removed from responsibilities and broken dreams. Fairy-tales never come true. . .

WORLD'S GREATEST DAD
Marie Ferrarella

Tragedy had struck Flynn O'Roarke twice—he'd been widowed and he now found himself having to raise an orphaned boy. He felt too emotionally raw to do it, but Susanna Troy seemed keen to help. Could he start over?

CAPTIVATED
Nora Roberts

The Donovan Legacy.

What would a horror-film writer do when he meets a real witch? Treat her as research material or become bewitched? And how does a normal man feel when he's in love with an extraordinary woman?

4 SILHOUETTE SPECIAL EDITIONS

AND 2 GIFTS ARE YOURS ABSOLUTELY FREE!

The emotional lives of mature, career-minded heroines blend with believable situations, and prove that there is more to love than mere romance. Please accept a lavish FREE offer of 4 books, a cuddly teddy and a special MYSTERY GIFT...without obligation. Then, if you choose, go on to enjoy 6 more exciting Special Editions, each month at £1.85 each. Send the coupon below at once to:

SILHOUETTE READER SERVICE, FREEPOST, PO BOX 236, CROYDON, SURREY CR9 9EL.

YES! Please rush me my 4 FREE Silhouette Special Editions and 2 FREE gifts! Please also reserve me a Reader Service Subscription. If I decide to subscribe I can look forward to receiving 6 brand new Silhouette Special Editions each month for just £11.10. Post and packing is free. If I choose not to subscribe I shall write to you within 10 days - but I am free to keep the books and gifts. I can cancel or suspend my subscription at any time. I am over 18.

Please write in BLOCK CAPITALS.

Mrs/Miss/Ms/Mr _____   EP42SE

Address _____

_____

_____ Postcode _____

(Please don't forget to include your postcode).

Signature _____

THE DONOVAN LEGACY
from Nora Roberts

Meet the Donovans—Morgana, Sebastian and
Anastasia. They're an unusual threesome. Triple
your fun with double cousins, the only children of
triplet sisters and triplet brothers. Each one is
unique. Each one is. . . special.

In January you will be *Captivated* by Morgana
Donovan. In Special Edition 768, horror-film
writer Nash Kirkland doesn't know what to do
when he meets an actual witch!

Be *Entranced* in February by Sebastian Donovan in
Special Editon 774. Private investigator Mary
Ellen Sutherland doesn't believe in psychic
phenomena. But she discovers Sebastian has
strange powers. . . over her.

In March's Special Edition 780, you'll be *Charmed*
by Anastasia Donovan, along with Boone Sawyer
and his little girl. Anastasia was a healer, but for
her it was Boone's touch that cast a spell.

Enjoy the magic of Nora Roberts. Don't miss
Captivated, *Entranced* or *Charmed*. Only from
Silhouette Special Edition. . . .